WHEN MEN ARE IMPRISONED;
GOOD MEN THINK OF FREEDOM,
BAD MEN THINK OF REVENGE...

GTed Welsh

THE**BEAR**

AN AMAZON BOOK

The story in this book is total fiction and does not depict any real events in the story line. Though the story line is tied to real historical events for contextual relevance. The characters are fictional and are not based on any US citizens or their lives. In some cases, the characters in foreign nations resemble actual persons, but the context in which they are used are completely fictitious and have nothing to do with the lives of any actual persons.

Author: Gary Ted Welsh

Publisher & Editing by GEM Welsh Enterprises LLC

Technical Consultant: T. Connor Gooding, USMC

Cover Design by RaidoDesigns

This book is the first in the "VEGA" series, future editions yet to be imagined. She knew she wanted to be a Spy since she was five years old. Now she is realizing her dream, and the reality of her lifelong dream has come to life in ways she never imagined.

This book is dedicated to my Loving and Supportive Family:

"Without whom, I would not dare to imagine!"

THE**BEAR**

Preface

November 7th 2009, New Mexico, USA

In a top-secret prison deep under the New Mexico desert approximately thirty miles west of Las Cruces, a prisoner was about to be released as part of the conditions for Russia's acceptance of the new 'START II' treaty.

The treaty is an extension of the first 'START' (Strategic Arms Reduction Treaty) signed in 1991 by President George H.W. Bush and Russian President Mikhail Gorbachev. The new START II treaty was negotiated by the governments of President Barack Obama and Russian President Dmitry Medvedev.

In a private meeting of the two world leaders just two days before the highly anticipated signing of the START II treaty, President Medvedev added one private stipulation to the signing of the treaty.

"You have a man held in one of your prisons that I must see released before I can sign this treaty," said the Russian President, leaning forward in his chair. "He has been held in secret for twenty years with no trial. He is Uncle to me."

President Obama could not afford the political fallout that would come if he went home without this treaty. Arms reduction was one of his key campaign promises.

The release happened late, or perhaps early in

1

the morning, insuring that the activity around the prison would not be noticed. In fact, the prison was nothing but a fenced in parking lot and what appears to be four storage sheds on the ground. Underneath the surface there exists the most secure maximum-security prison in the world.

There is no escape from this facility and for most of those incarcerated at the 'hole' there would be no hope of seeing their loved ones or even the light of day again, ever.

"2791 get your stuff, you're going on a trip," the guard said to the prisoner as he approached the cell.

"My stuff! I don't want this shit," Grigori Medvedev said with a cynical sneer.

He didn't know where he was going and he didn't care. Anything was better than this place. Perhaps he was going to be allowed to defend himself at one of those big American trials of his peers. No, not likely.

After twenty years in this hell hole without so much as an explanation of his rights, no trial and no contact except for these bastards that keep him here, he was more likely to be on his way to the executioner. That is how they do it in Soviet Union why would it be any different for him here.

"Where are you taking me?" Grigori said with an indifferent scowl.

"You're going home."

1

April 14th 2017, Flagstaff, Arizona, USA

There comes a time in a man's life when he must look back and ask himself if he made the right choices. This is one of those times. Lou Bennett is a realist though. He knew that whatever the answer to that question, it wouldn't change the place that he was in now. He would still likely be beginning a twenty-five to life sentence for the murder of the man who killed his son. That choice was the right one for him. It was what he had to do and if he had it to do over, he would do it again without hesitation.

When the cops questioned him about the murder of Boyd Johnson he did not volunteer any information but he didn't lie about anything either. So, when the cop nonchalantly asked Lou if he had any idea who did this? Lou said, "Yes I do."

"Who was it Mr. Bennett," the officer said not expecting the answer he would get.

"I did it Officer Warner, He killed my son," Bennett said with no hesitation. Louis Bennett only had one son, Martin. They were close and when the unimaginable happened…Lou took matters into his own hands, an eye for an eye. knowing that the law would not see it his way.

"You can't take the law in your own hands Mr. Bennett. We are a country of laws. Where do you think we'd be if everybody just bypassed the law, we'd fall apart as a nation," the DA said when he questioned Lou during their initial interview.

That's true but everyone won't give up the rest of their life and do what I did, Lou thought. *Most Americans are law abiding citizens; but then most*

Americans won't have to see their 25-year-old son brutally murdered like I did.

Boyd Johnson did it, that everyone knew. It was just one of those times when a killer walked due to a technicality, a screw-up by the arresting officer; he wasn't read his rights properly or something? By taking that low life out Lou simply sent him to his maker without the fanfare of a big trial. No, the matter is settled, God will now judge that man.

Martin Bennett was a very smart kid with a bright future. A very handsome young man, 6-2, broad shouldered and a rock-hard body that's been toned by his passions, football and spelunking.

As captain of the Lumberjacks, NAU's football team, Martin led his team to the brink of the championship of the Big Sky Conference. His popularity at the university, and in the city of Flagstaff, made him recognizable wherever he went.

On Saturdays Martin would volunteer at the Salvation Army feeding the homeless breakfast before heading out into the vast wilderness of Northern Arizona to exercise his true passion, spelunking. His first exposure to the art of cave exploration came at the age of eight when his father first let him go with him to explore a cave in the Superstition Mountains southeast of Phoenix, he was hooked. In the next sixteen years he would explore many of the hundreds of caves in the Southwest. When he started high school, he joined a spelunking club and would explore many of the caves around central Arizona.

When he had the time, Lou would go with the club. The spelunkers respected his experience, much of which he had gained with his Army Ranger buddies when they had some time off. It was the bars or the caves, they were all responsible and mostly married men who worked close together and played just as close, they did choose the bars often enough too, however.

While attending NAU, Martin continued the hobby with a group of spelunking students from all over the world. Lou joined the group on many occasions but these cavers were serious about their passion and would take their time off in some of the most amazing caverns in the world.

As a geologist, Martin was doubly interested in the geologic makeup of the caves he explored. He would write detailed descriptions of the caves which were often picked up by some renowned scientific publications and the local papers. Martin Bennett was a local celebrity, for his sports, for his hobby, and for his ability to connect his passions to the community. His sudden and untimely death shocked the community; but, no one was more affected by his death than his father.

He was a month short of getting his master's degree in Geology from Northern Arizona University. After graduation he was going to work for the Shell Oil Company in their exploration division. He was very excited. All the hard work he had done the past six years was finally about to pay off. Lou was just as excited for him and his pride, that his son had such an optimistic future, showed it.

A tragic loss on that rainy night when Martin was walking to his car from the geology lab. A transient named Boyd Johnson walked up to him holding a knife, "give me your money."

Martin, the son of a cop, just handed him his wallet. "Here you go pal, I don't want any trouble." He thought about fighting him, but, it wasn't worth it. Boyd took the wallet and stabbed Martin in the stomach anyway, and ran. Two witnesses in the parking lot positively identified the assailant, and a surveillance camera in the parking lot that picked up the whole thing.

There was no discussion when Lou found him leaving the Museum Club. Lou just walked up to him, flashed a badge and shouted, "Boyd Johnson you are convicted," and shot him. He then called the Flagstaff police to report that a murder had been committed.

The badge was not real. It was a toy badge that Martin got on the Grand Canyon Railroad when he was deputized by a fake Sheriff just before the fake train robbers tried to rob the train, entertainment for the tourists. He was five years old. Lou found it among Martin's things just hours before tracking Johnson down at the Museum Club.

Lou waited until the punk left the bar. He wouldn't commit such a brutal act in the bar; the owner was a friend of his. Lou was an honest man and meant to own the situation. *Capital punishment is my way out of this life that had been so good until everything went completely wrong,* he thought.

Louis Jerome Bennett sat in a holding cell in the Coconino County courthouse awaiting the jury verdict in his murder trial. Lou had plenty of time to reflect on his life and just where he was right now. State law required a jury trial in any capital murder case. But there was no doubt in any mind on the jury that Lou Bennett killed Boyd Johnson. Lou insisted that he testify on his own behalf. He answered all the questions truthfully, so that his guilt was perfectly clear.

What didn't come out in the trial was that he was still grieving over the loss of his wife, Lynne, of twenty six years when a drunk driver ran her compact car off the road into a power pole; she didn't have a chance. That was two months before he lost his son. Lou was devastated. When Johnson had the charges against him dropped, because he was not read his rights by the arresting officer, Lou promised himself that there would be justice. Hell, the kid was all drugged up, totally incoherent and not able to understand anything. He bought the drugs with the money that he took off Martin's dying body.

Lou certainly wasn't going to watch this guy walk. The DA assured Lou that it was not over yet. He said that he had options and that, "You just be patient, Lou, and we'll get that bastard and make it stick this time." Lou had his doubts and wasn't about to take any chances. So, he did the only thing that he could to ensure that justice would prevail, he executed Boyd Johnson. That night he used his weapon for the first time in his life, as a cop, other than in his military days.

Boyd Johnson, it was said, was a transient who roamed from town to town supporting himself by doing whatever he had to do to survive. He had no conscience. His life was a roller coaster ride between good drugs and his ability to pay for them. That was the only reason for his existence and for him to live when his son was dead…*Martin had his whole future ahead of him; The boy never hurt anyone* …Well, it just wasn't right.

When Lynne was killed his life fell apart. Lou really couldn't see any reason to live except for his son, Martin. It all fell to living so that his son could live his dream. He put all his attention to that task, maybe too much so for when that was over, everything was over. He wished that he would be executed for his actions, a fitting end to a life turned up-side-down. This act of passion would never get that outcome. The whole matter was in the hands of the jury now and then the judge would sentence him to the max sentence for this crime, that was what he wanted.

"Can I get you anything, a magazine or a drink," the deputy said as he sat in the holding room awaiting the verdict.

"No Greg, I don't think I can read right now. I'll take that water, no make it a double Johnny Walker Black and I'll take the water on the side." laughing half-heartedly.

Greg laughed too but it was subdued. He rarely allowed himself to get emotionally connected to a case but this one, he has a son the same age as Martin. The whole town felt sick over this one.

The newspaper had a scathing article about the necessity for law and order. The columnist Randy Jackson had no sympathy for anyone taking the law into his own hands; and when the perp is a retired cop, well that made it even worse. He said that Mr. Bennett should get the maximum sentence as an example to all those right-wing gun toting…well anyone that might have the same idea. It wasn't a pretty article and the paper took a lot of flak over the article. The readers were overwhelmingly supportive of getting people like Boyd Johnson out of the picture for good, as long as they weren't the ones that had to do it.

Flagstaff, Arizona, was a typical college town that seemed to attract his kind of drifter in the summer time. The winters were too cold; but in the summer they seemed to come out of the woodwork, and the crime rate showed it. The people were tired of it all. The paper probably lost some subscribers over that editorial.

"What do you think is taking so long, Greg? It doesn't get any more open and shut than this case," Lou said.

"It's not unusual, Lou, the jury has to go over the evidence and they don't want to make it look too quick. Besides they don't want to miss that good lunch that they get at noon so they put off the call until after lunch, one more free meal on the taxpayers, you know." Greg gave Lou another chuckle.

About 1:30 in the afternoon the call came in, the jury was ready. "Pack your bags, Lou, you ready for that vacation?" Greg asked, referring to an inside joke between the two of them.

The deputy escorted Lou to the courtroom where he took a seat at the defendants table. It took a while for the jury to get seated and Lou was noticing that they were in a somewhat jovial mood. "Well they don't have to be so happy about sending me to prison for the rest of my life," Lou said to his lawyer, Randy Woods.

"All rise," said the bailiff as the judge entered the courtroom and sat at the bench.

Judge Hickman pounded his gavel on the desk,

"This court is in session, be seated… Has the jury reached a verdict," looking at the foreman.

"We have your honor," said the foreman as he handed a slip to the bailiff who in turn took it to the judge to review…

"The Jury finds the defendant, Louis Jerome Bennett, not guilty!"

The courtroom erupted into sudden chaos.

2

"Well, this is quite a turn of events," Lou whispered to himself as he sat on the couch in his fifth wheel at Black Bart's RV Resort. This is not what he expected and now he felt like he was left hanging, *no pun intended,* he thought to himself with a half laugh.

He jumped up and exclaimed, "If God has a damn plan for me I wish he would at least give me a hint or something, this just doesn't make any sense." He put his hands on his head and sighed.

The next thing he knew he was unhooking the RV from its space and preparing to leave…Where to? He didn't know. He just knew that there was no way that he was gonna stick around here another day. In twenty minutes, he was on the I-40 heading east. "OK Jesus, take the wheel."

The rig: a forty-foot Vista fifth wheel Toy hauler pulled by a 2009 dodge 3500 Cummings diesel and Martin's jeep in tow behind all that. It is the dream that he and Lynne put together for their retirement. They planned for years that as soon as Martin graduated from NAU they would hit the road and never look back. The highway is full of baby boomers with the same idea. The accident that killed Lynne put an end to that dream. Now, with nothing left to do, Lou was going to do it alone. Lynne would want him to do it anyway. They worked so hard to get everything in order so they would be debt free. The anticipation acted like an aphrodisiac to their relationship.

Maybe Lynne was a little distracted when she was coming home from shopping that night. She saw the car in her mirror weaving in the lane. She slowed down as he tried to pass her. He swerved suddenly to the right and hit her, hard, pushing her off the side of the road into a power line pole. The coroner said she died instantly.

Three days later they found the car with all the damage to the passenger's side. Not long after they found the driver, he was still drunk…So was Lou when he got the call.

Maybe a long drive is just what Lou needs to get his thoughts in order. He had no real direction but forward. He isn't the kind of guy to just give up, and he still has a few good years in him. Hell, he was only sixty and in good shape. That was part of the plan too. He would run almost every morning and went to the gym three times a week with Lynne. They wanted to have a good quality of life in their golden years. Lou is in good shape anyway, a mentality that he acquired in the Army where he spent ten formative years. When he met Lynne, he got out and they settled down.

"That's where I'll start, Albuquerque I'll look up Juan," he thought. Juan Vega is a real doctor now. Back then he was the medic on his team. *"I haven't seen Doc in two or three years, except on Facebook."* Lou thought to himself as he remembered saving Juan's... Yes, and Juan saved his life a couple of times when they got themselves in some tight spots.

One time they were on loan to the CIA in Honduras. Their mission was the rescue of an American citizen that was being ransomed by militant rebel forces seeking to overthrow the government. These guys were real nasty and thought nothing of massacring an entire village. They saw a profit in holding Dr. Adel Werner hostage for ransom, but there was no telling what horror she had been subjected to in her capture. Today she is head of neurosurgery at UCLA Medical Center; her captors, they are all dead.

In the fracas Lou caught one in the chest. It didn't hit any vitals but it hurt like hell and bled like a motha. Juan stabilized the wound, gave him a shot of go-go, and went back to the primary objective: rescuing Dr. Werner. Being more critical than Lou, Juan had to carry her out to the LZ. Lou managed to walk there under his own power while the rest of the team swept the area and loaded the chopper. Mission accomplished.

"That was the best team I ever worked with in the six years I was a Ranger," Lou talked to himself, "I should look them all up, the ones still alive." It was about time they had another reunion.

It's only about a five-hour drive to Albuquerque from Flagstaff. He called Juan and they agreed to meet at the Casa De Benavidez, in NW Albuquerque, at four.

Juan is about five years younger than Lou. A Doc at the Vega Clinic, drug addiction and rehab. His patients call him Doctor 'No', a play on Nancy Reagan's anti-drug campaign, 'Just Say No'. He is highly respected, especially among veterans, who get hooked on opioid pain meds that are freely prescribed at the VA Hospitals; drug therapy was cheaper than treating the veterans. Dr. No, 'the biker savior'. He shows up at the office looking like a Hell's Angel, leathers, boots, and lots of tattoos. Everybody in Albuquerque knows who he is, from the mayor to the homeless.

On Interstate 40 about 10 miles east of Winslow, Lou stopped to give a ride to an old Indian walking along the Interstate. It was kind of strange to see anyone walking this far from town; but this close to the Navajo Indian reservation, not so rare.

The man is just walking, in the middle of

13

nowhere, Lou thought. An old Indian, probably in his seventies, although age is hard to peg with Indians, they seemed to age different than we do. He wore dingy blue jeans, moccasins, and an off white cotton pullover shirt. A scarf or bandanna was tied around his waist. His gray hair had two long braids that hung below his shoulder blades and he wore a baseball cap. He didn't have any food or water for that matter.

Lou pulled over on the emergency lane just in front of him and waited for him to catch up so he could offer a ride to the next town. The next thing he knew his passenger door opened and the old timer got in. He didn't say a word so Lou pulled onto the interstate, eastbound.

Lou noticed that his cap has the logo of the Northern Arizona Suns, a local basketball team from Prescott, Arizona. "My name is Lou," trying to spark a conversation. The old Indian didn't say a word so Lou kept driving figuring he must be at least going in the right direction.

After a long moment of silence, the old man said, "Louis Jerome Bennett," never turning his head. The long rig passed through Holbrook as the conversation continued.

"How do you know me?" Lou asked, intrigued. "Have we met," knowing that they have never met before.

"No, but I read the papers" he said softly. "You are a hero up here on the Nation. It's about time someone stood up to those thugs that have been invading our cities. Our young boys are buying the drugs and alcohol and its ruining their lives. It has to stop!"

Lou was taken aback by this old Indian dressed in very plain reservation clothes. "Well," Lou said, "I have to admit that I didn't expect you to be that up on the current events. You look like…"

"Like a dumb 'ole Indian," Tim said, "that's typical stereotyping."

"No, no not at all," Lou said embarrassed "I mean…"

"Don't worry about it Louis. I'm just messin with ya." The Old boy said with a smirk on his face. "Take the next exit."

"The Hopi Travel Plaza? Is that where you're going? You want me to drop you off in the front?" Lou asked.

"Follow 77 north," the old Indian said, still looking straight ahead, "Tim"

"What?" Lou asked

"My name is Tim, Tim Masauwu. I am of the Hopi nation and, I am not Indian, They live on the subcontinent of Asia on the other side of the planet."

"Well Mr. Masauwu, I'm very happy to make your acquaintance." Lou said as they continued heading North into the Painted Desert. *This is getting off the plan a little,* he thought*, but I'm not held to a time frame. I'll just give this guy a ride home and get back to the plan soon enough.*

"Just over the next hill take the left on the other side of the bridge." Tim said finally looking at Lou as he spoke.

Lou turned west on the dirt road. It was a well maintained road so Lou kept going as the terrain turned to some of the most amazing country Lou had ever seen. Like Monument Valley in Northern Arizona and Southern Utah, but on a smaller scale. There were monoliths that seemed to stretch to the heavens and cedar juniper trees that contrasted with the multi colored terrain of the Painted Desert. It was natural art, a picture of nature on her best behavior. Lou was mesmerized by the beauty of this land. He never imagined anything like this in this desolate part of the Navajo reservation.

"This is really amazing" he said "I didn't know that there was anything like this on the Navajo reservation, Tim"

"We are in the "Hopi Nation" Tim said stoically, "this is not a reservation. The Hopituh Shi-nu-mu has never been conquered by the blue coats. We have always been free on this, our own land. Your government might think that they allow the Hopi the land as a reservation, but we have always been here. We are in the Hopi Nation."

For the next hour or so they didn't say a word as they traveled over hills and into green valleys with running streams and boulders as big as houses piled on top of each other, like God himself had created his own artwork in this wilderness. Lou was driving his hundred-thousand-dollar rig over two track dirt roads that most would think twice about taking the jeep alone.

He drove the rig in four-wheel drive and never gave it a second thought; only about the beauty of the land that he was traveling through. He also never could imagine that the events of the next two days would change his life forever.

The Sun was beginning to set behind the mountains to the left as Lou and Tim pulled into a very picturesque village, a Hopi pueblo, not in ruins, as one would imagine, but an active community.

"I didn't know there were any pueblos still around, Tim. I mean occupied and working. Is this a tourist trap?" Lou asked.

"This is an ancient pueblo and my people have been living here for centuries," Tim said. "This city is called Orayvi. Few white men have ever seen the Hopi as they truly live. You can park your house over there next to that wall, you are self-contained?"

"Yes…yes," Lou said, still a little stunned by the events that seem to be unfolding around him. Tim walked over to talk to an old woman who was getting water out of a common well in the middle of a large courtyard.

Lou went about the business of parking his rig out of the way of traffic, then went inside to fix himself a bite to eat. He wouldn't see another soul for the rest of the night. It was the quietest night he had ever spent in his life. He slept like a log.

3

The Sun was barely sneaking up behind the top of the wall when Lou stepped out of his rig for his morning run. He would get an early start to Albuquerque when he got back, but first he needed to release some of the frustration that has built up over the past months. He needed to get over it all and get on with his life.

It felt good to run again. It had been months since he was locked up with only a little exercise area to walk, alone. He had been quarantined from the rest of the jail population. Lou had refused to post bail, and The warden didn't think a retired, decorated, investigative officer of the Department of Public Safety would last too long among the hardened criminals in the Coconino County jail. Some of whom he had personally been involved in their arrest.

Orayvi Pueblo was coming alive with the new day's morning Sun. Lou started his run on a well-worn path that snaked up and down between huge granite boulders. *This is just what I need* Lou thought as he rounded a boulder and headed down a tortuous path of short switchbacks that would take him down to a wide flat that looked like a farming area.

About two turns below he caught a glimpse of another runner as she passed between trees and boulders. *It's a woman,* he thought. *Rather tall for a Hopi.* About 5-7, slender with very long hair that was braided into three ponytails that reached below the small of her back. She wore a running outfit like you might see worn by any student running around the campus of NAU. The thing about this woman is that she seemed totally out of place in this Hopi Village; and that she is no young student. *She's a mature woman, perhaps, 50ish,* Lou thought, which is indicated by the fact that her beautiful hair is pure white.

"Good morning!" Lou shouted as he picked up his speed to catch up to her. As fast as he picked up his speed she matched him and kept the distance between him. "Don't be afraid, I'm not going to hurt you," Lou shouted. It seemed that she didn't wish to be caught, so Lou slowed down to his normal pace to continue his run. He figured he would run around the field and head up the path back to the pueblo.

His illusive running companion slowed her pace down to match his pace; maintaining the same distance that had been separating them all along, about fifty feet. As she rounded the field Lou could more clearly feet make out her face. *She's certainly a mature woman, in her late forties or fifties, and very pale. Still, she has the indigenous features of the Hopi.* Lou became more intrigued as he once again attempted to catch her. However, she still didn't seem to want to be caught. She ran the switchbacks with the agility of the pronghorn antelope that was native to these parts.

She's beautiful, Lou thought as he now wanted to catch up to her more than ever. For the first time in years all his thoughts were on another woman, other than Lynne, and he didn't even realize it. He felt that he needed to meet this woman. He has to know who she is.

When Lou finally ran into the pueblo common she was sitting on the edge of the well drinking from a gourd. Lou ran up to her, breathing heavily. She offered him her cup and he gladly took it. "Who are you?" Lou blurted out rather rudely instantly regretting his mannerism.

"I am Soyala, My grandfather asked me to see to you." She said with a confident smile. For a few minutes they just looked at each other, as Lou sipped from the gourd, taking in the morning and a sort of magic in the moment. "Did you sleep well?"

"Oh, yes, better than in months," Lou replied. Forgetting that he was planning to pack up and hit the road by 9 a.m.

"Grandfather asked me to be your guide today," she said as she took his hand and led him toward the buildings. "He has breakfast waiting for us in his kiva."

Lou followed her like a child might follow his mother. He seemed to be totally receptive to her will, mesmerized by her very presence. She could probably lead him off a cliff right now if she wanted too. Lou would soon come to his senses, but he was a changed man from the moment he first set eyes on her.

"Good morning," Tim greeted them as they entered his apartment. A small but spacious place, probably due to the Spartan furnishings in the single room. About twelve feet square with a single bed along the right wall. A table made of rough cedar wood with four cedar stools sat along the far wall. In the corner a small cooking area that is also used for heat. Next to the fire pit, on the left side, a wooden counter and pantry, Lou noticed there was no faucet at the basin, and no bathroom. Lou turned to take in the room. There was only one window, next to the door, with no glass, only an Indian blanket draped over a pole that spanned the top of the window. The walls had paintings of Hopi petroglyphs, very interesting.

"I have prepared a small meal for us to share. Please sit." Tim handed each of them a rolled plain bluish looking corn tortilla, "This is Piki," Tim said, "traditional flat bread made of blue corn and burnt ash of juniper berries." Then he gave each of them a drink in a wild gourd cup. The drink was bitter, not water, but more like a raw agave nectar. It was good. "There is much to do today." Tim said.

After eating, Soyala took Lou by the hand and led him out the door. Lou looked back as if to want to help clean up the dishes but Soyala tugged on his hand and quietly told him that Tim will take care of it. They walked to the door of his fifth wheel. "Get dressed, we will be riding today. I'll meet you at the corral in five minutes." She turned and headed to the pueblo.

Lou, dressed in blue jeans, tee shirt, boots, and a baseball cap, with the logo of the NAU football team, the 'Lumberjacks'. He left the fifth wheel and walked down to the corral where there was a boy holding the reigns of a bare-back horse. "Oh, yeah, ah, no saddle?" Lou looked like he forgot to put pants on.

"Put a saddle on the Mustang for this half-breed, Georgie," Soyala said as she walked up to the two. The boy walked over to the corral to get an American Western saddle.

Soyala mounted a beautiful black and white Mustang that whirled around in anticipation of the ride to come. She wore blue jeans and a long sleeve cotton smock. She had a wide brimmed hat on her head and dear skin boots with fringe along the top.

Soyala's Mustang had no saddle, only a hackamore, a bit-less bridle. She sat the horse as natural as she wore her blue jeans. Lou looked at her for an extended moment, "Wow," he thought out loud.

The Mustang is shorter than the horses that Lou had ridden in the past. Mustangs are bred from the wild horses that escaped or were left abandoned by their conquistador masters. They are smaller and thus easier to transport by ship from their Spanish origins. The Mustang easily adapted to the harsh climate and terrain in the Americas. The natives, who traveled on foot before the Spaniards appeared, easily adapted to the Mustang.

The Mustang that Lou was to ride was not quite as beautiful as Soyala's. Lou suspected that just the fact that Soyala was on top of the mare made her seem brighter. In no way, Lou would discover, is his stallion any less than Soyala's mare. He swayed his left arm outward into a wide gesture, "Shall we ride."

They headed down the same path that they were running on just a few hours ago, Soyala in the front. When they got to the bottom they worked their way down the valley where the farming, for the pueblo, was done. The valley widened as they traversed the rough terrain, crossing the dry creek a number of times before they came to the first of several earthen dams that formed the irrigation ponds for the community farms. There wasn't much water in them due to the extreme drought conditions in the southwestern states. Still the trees looked healthy and the contrast of the green of the juniper and pinion pine trees made against the reds and tans of the rounding cliffs and the stark blue of the cloudless sky was stunning.

There was no conversation for the first hour or so of their ride until they were well onto the plain that gradually turned to the dry and colorful Painted Desert. Lou didn't want to ask Soyala where she is taking him or how long they would be out, probably a macho thing; but the desert didn't seem to have any place to go. There were a number of rounded mounds of striped blue gray, red, and almost white colored dirt. In the distance there were some cliffs that didn't seem to get any closer as they rode on.

Finally, Lou couldn't keep quiet any longer and had to ask, "Do you have someplace that you are going? He spoke in jest.

"I was wondering how long it would take you to say something," she said laughing. "We are heading over to those cliffs right there." pointing, "I want to show you something that should interest you."

It seemed that the outcrop of cliffs suddenly were right there. Soyala led them around to the south side where there were some flat, sheer cliffs. "Notice the petroglyphs on these rock faces. They are hundreds of years old." Soyala was serious now.

"Yeah I can see 'GW loves MF' that must be ancient." Lou said smiling at Soyala. They both laughed and she explained that someday even the graffiti will be ancient.

"Here, this one is very vivid. You can see the concentric circles. They represent various times of the sun. Here the winter solstice, my name sake. And this one is the time of the days of wandering." She pointed at a squiggly line that stretched between the suns. "Our people were forced to seek a place with better water. It is when we first came to the Third Mesa. It is when the first Hopi pueblos were built. Orayvi is where my clan settled, we are the clan of the corn. We came from the south." She was totally into the history of the glyphs. "Look at that one. Notice that there are animals and people, some with their arms up, some with their arms down. The ones with their arms up are the deities. The others are the people. Look some have big round bubbles around their heads. Scientists think they are aliens, looks like it huh? Over here this was done by the wolf clan, which is the clan of your grandmother."

"My grandmother? Is that what you said?" Lou asked now curious.

"Yes, your grandmother was Zuni, the clan of the wolf," She said softly. "The Zuni are cousins of the Hopi. We have the same ancient blood."

"Yes, how did you know that? My grandmother was Zuni. My grandfather married her when he came to the west in the 1870's, he was a gold miner. They had ten children, my father was born in 1900; he was the baby. I never knew either of my grandparents on my father's side. I never knew much about my grandmother; the family didn't talk about her" Lou related.

"The Zuni are a proud nation, like the Hopi." Soyala said "Your grandmother was LaQuata, the granddaughter of a great Hopi chief. Her mother, Kaya, was married, by arrangement, to the son of the Zuni chief. You have many cousins on the reservation in New Mexico and in the Hopi. "Our pueblo traded with the Zuni and our people share blood ties. It is important that you know who you are, your ancestry and your destiny."

Lou was quiet, taking in all the information that was coming at him. He knew some of it but couldn't imagine how Soyala knew his family history. "Why are you telling me this Soyala?" he asked.

"Tonight, you will be included in the ancient ceremonies of our clan," she replied, "you could not be there if you were not Hopi, you are, from your grandmother. Grandfather has prepared this ceremony in honor of your visit. It is very important, grandfather said."

The day grew longer as Soyala explained some of the glyphs in detail. She was especially passionate about one that she said was called the prophecy rock. It showed Man's journey from the creation event. The two paths that man could take and how the one path of evil would have three very evil periods. "Some say they prophesied the three world wars," She said. "See how the paths come together into a time of great peace and prosperity? Kind of like the bible prophesies." She got up, brushed the dust off her jeans, "We should be getting back, it's getting late and we have a long ride. I'll race you to the blue mesa!" She shouted as they ran to the horses.

Lou jumped up and let his competitive side take over. It was a dead heat, they decided, when they rounded the outcrop that had a blue hue to it in the afternoon Sun. The rest of the ride was slow and full of conversation. It was like they had known each other their whole lives. There was a connection between them that was surreal but wonderful.

It was late afternoon before they got back to Old Orayvi. The full moon rising over the pueblo was the biggest Lou had ever seen, and blood red. They were both tired and, after Soyala handed her Mustang to the same young brave that was there in the morning, she rose onto her toes and gave Lou a peck on the cheek. "Get some rest and clean up for the dance tonight," she left.

Lou went into his fifth wheel and made himself a drink; Johnnie Black, neat, that's how he liked it, straight and to the point. After a quick shower he laid down on the bed for a short nap. There was a gentle rap on the door. Lou put on his robe and opened it to find Soyala standing there with folded clothing in her arms. "Come in," Lou said. She walked up the four steps into his RV. Lou took the clothes from her. "I guess you want me to wear these." He laid the clothes on the arm of the chair and turned to thank her.

Soyala was so beautiful in the low light. Lou was compelled to take her hand. "Thank you," he whispered as he leaned over and gave her a gentle kiss on the lips. Soyala did not try to back away and returned the kiss with gentle acceptance. The moment was there and they both were drawn by a mysterious attraction. Lou reached behind her beautiful head and pulled on an end of the red ribbon that held her hair. It quietly fell to the floor. They both felt an attraction as their eyes melted into each other's. They made love.

The next thing Lou knew, someone was banging on his door. "Mr. Bennett, they're waiting." a young man's voice.

It had been two hours and he was late. Soyala was no longer there and he wondered whether she was ever there at all. "Okay, I'll be there in a minute."

In five minutes, Lou stepped out of his fifth wheel dressed like a native Hopi Prince. He walked toward the sounds of native drums in the village common. Soyala got up from her seat next to Tim and walked over to Lou, took him by the hand and led him to a seat on the other side of Tim. "Hello Tim, I'm honored to sit next to the chief." Lou said, smiling.

"Oh no," Tim replied, "I'm just an 'Indian'. Soyala is the head of this clan."

The moonlit dance featured four male Hopi dressed up like Kachina dolls. Their ceremonial costumes were made of deer skin, beads, and feathers arranged in a very colorful way that made them appear to resemble a bird. They danced in swooping circles like a bird in flight. The dance told the story of the ancient prophecies. "Of the time of the origins and the people of long ago, the Hisatsinom."

All this was related to Lou by Tim as the dances moved through the story of the "Hopituh Shi-nu-mu." As Tim explained the prophecy Lou was amazed how the Hopi prophecy was similar to the biblical accounts and prophecies. There was a flood, and the people and animals were saved by sealing themselves in hollow reeds.

The most amazing thing was of prophecies yet to come. It foretold a tribulation or purification, as they put it, and Finally a time of peace as all the evil spirits are driven from the world.

As the night grew late a bon fire was lit and the dance moved to the more religious purpose. Each of the people in the circle drank a special tea that made Lou feel relaxed and sedated. The music, which included drums and flutes, took on a more serene and meaningful tone.

"Now we must move into the sweat lodge and purify our bodies and our spirit. Only the men will go into the lodge tonight," Tim said to Lou. The sweat lodge was hot and smoky due to the coals that were kept in amber throughout the night. If not for the tea that was readily imbibed, and the serenity that it gave, the sweat lodge might have been unbearable.

After a few hours of meditation and purification the men chewed on peyote, which is a wild mushroom that the elders use to induce a hallucinogenic experience. Lou started his first experience with peyote by puking his guts out into a bag that Tim gave him when they entered the lodge, "Keep this bag close," is all he said. Each time he threw up he moved to a higher level of hallucination; which, in The Hopi religion, was the purpose, a connection to the Gods.

Lou found himself running through a forest. He ran with ease even though the ground wasn't flat. It felt to him like he was made to run. When he looked at his legs he saw that he had the body of a dog, or rather a wolf. That's it he was a wolf. He remembered what Soyala told him while they were riding, "Each of us have an animal spirit within us. It is part of our being and will influence our lives." Apparently, Lou was a wolf in his animal spirit. Then he was joined by five other wolves to form a pack. They ran through the forest as if they were seeking something that eluded them at the moment.

Finally, the pack came onto a cave and Lou knew that it was the home of a bear; a bear that was their nemesis. The bear suddenly blasted from the cave and attacked the pack with a ferocity that was full of hate and vindictiveness. He tossed the wolves around like nothing.

The wolves were persistent and regrouped to form a coordinated attack; but the bear was powerful and not easily taken. The wolves spread out and came at the bear from different directions at the same time. The bear took a position at the entrance to his cave, making it difficult for the wolves to flank him. Two of the wolves, Lou on the right and another on the left climbed up the hill with the intention to jump on the bear from the top of the cave but the dirt and rocks above the cave were loose and slipped as the wolves gained their position. The rocks began to slide causing an avalanche which built in its intensity picking up bigger rocks as the whole earth above the cave gave way to topple the bear and collapse the opening to the cave.

The bear was buried alive and the wolves took off through the woods in a dead run. Suddenly Lou found himself jumping onto the back of a giant eagle. They soared high into the clouds. Lou was fascinated as the eagle flew above the clouds as if to reach the heavens. There appeared a clearing in the clouds where there was a green meadow next to a swift flowing stream. He could see a person sitting on a blanket next to the stream, there was a picnic basket. It was Lynne!

As the eagle got near the ground the wolf jumped off its back and immediately Lou found himself a man again. "What took you so long" Lynne said as he jogged up to her.

Lou felt elated and he reached down and picked Lynne up into his arms and they kissed with a passion that he missed so desperately. "I have missed you so," Lou whispered as he hugged her tightly.

They sat and talked about everything for seemingly hours. She told him that everything was going to be alright. He will find love again. She said that he has "things that he must do in life so not to be reluctant to follow his instinct. All things will work out in time and he will be happy again."

Lou asked her if Martin was with her and she said "Martin has already gone back. He has things to do and his life will be renewed."

Suddenly there was a deafening roar and crashing trees. Then the giant bear with gleaming claws on his raised forelegs exploded from the forest, pouncing onto their picnic trampling Lynne as he tore at Lou in a revengeful tirade.

4

Flagstaff Medical Center

Lou's eyes fluttered sending the nurse out of the door to get the doctor. He was not alone, Juan Vega was standing at the side of the bed when Lou finally opened his eyes after being out for a day at the hospital.

"Doc? Where am I, is this a hospital? Am I in Albuquerque?" Lou asked groggily.

"No, bud, you're not in Albuquerque. You're back in Flagstaff," Juan Vega belted out, "you are a lucky man Lou, what do you remember... anything?"

Just then Lou's doctor, a friendly faced Iranian with a bedside manner to match, came into the room with a big smile on his face. "Well, well, well, it's alive," Doctor Addari said almost laughing. "You must have a guardian angel on your shoulder, Lou. Another day and I don't think you would have made it out alive."

"I don't get it," Lou said, "I don't know what happened. One minute I'm on the Hopi reservation watching a Hopi ceremonial dance. There was a very beautiful Hopi woman, Soyala. The next thing you know I'm waking up in the hospital back in Flagstaff?"

"Well," Juan said, "I don't know what kind of dreams you were having while you were out, but you were knocked out in the wreck of your rig for at least two days. We found you in a gully off a really bad road on the Navajo reservation. What the hell were you doing way out in the middle of nowhere in that rig anyway?"

31

"No! Doc, I really was on the Hopi nation," Lou retorted "I was there two days. I don't know how I wrecked. I don't remember anything about that."

"I hate to tell you Lou, but the Navajo police told me that your rig had to be in that gully at least two days," Juan said impatiently. "There's no way any of that other stuff happened, you were dreaming that partner. When you didn't show up in Albuquerque I got concerned so I called Black Bart's. They said you left alright, but you were nowhere to be found. So, I figured you had a problem and I called your buddy, Jim Ortega, at the State Police. He put out an APB on your RV. A Statie on the I-40 reported seeing a rig like yours alongside of the interstate just past Winslow."

"Yeah, that's where I pulled over to give Tim a ride," Lou said excitedly. "We got off the interstate at the Hopi Travel center and headed into the reservation."

"The search helicopter spotted your wrecked rig north of I-40, about eight miles west of Highway 77 on the Navaho reservation." Juan said, not conceding to the obvious inference that he had been on the Hopi for the two days. "Only you were turned the other way and on your side in the gully. You must have turned around. The whole rig was totaled except for your jeep. It somehow survived with little damage. It was all towed to the All City Towing impound yard. We can check it out when you get released if you're up to it."

There was a knock on the door and a tall lean, blond haired man entered. "I have to say you don't look to bad for a dead man," he said with a hearty grin.

"Boom is that you, ya old goat," Lou said elated. Charles Woolsey was the sapper, combat engineer and explosives expert, on Lou's Ranger team. The team called him 'Boom' for obvious reasons. There was no one better than Charlie at the art of making things disappear suddenly. "What the hell are you doing here? What's it been three years?"

"I've been keeping up with your story these past few months and when you got off I thought I'd better get out here and make sure you didn't get yourself into any more trouble," Charlie joked. Charlie was always the joker on the team. It seemed that no matter how bad things seemed he could crack a joke to lighten things up; an asset in his line of work.

He and Juan sat and talked with Lou over old times, and new, for hours until the nurse finally came in and ran them all out of the room, except Lou that is. She said the doctor will release Lou tomorrow morning and they can come back then, "right now he needs his rest." They wanted to observe him for twenty-four hours to see if the concussion was going to give him any issues.

The next morning by eight o'clock, Charlie was back in the room with his jovial spirit brightening up the place. Soon after that Juan showed up with donuts and they were right back reminiscing.

About ten o'clock Special Agent Randy Withers of the FBI came into the room to give Lou an update on the background check that they were conducting on Boyd Johnson.

"We couldn't find anything about him anywhere," he reported. "We tried everything. For all practical purposes he didn't exist. Finally, one of our researchers in DC tried a different approach. He sent a photo and his prints to Interpol to see if maybe he wasn't who he said he was. We got a hit.

"It seems our Mr. Johnson is really a Russian named Vladimir Medvedev. He came to the states on a student visa but soon after he got here he disappeared into the Brighton Beach Russian mafia.

He was twenty-eight years old and our New York office found out that he got himself into trouble with the boss when he was caught skimming heroin for his own personal use. That usually would have been enough to get him killed but, as it turns out he is the nephew of one of the big bosses in Russia; a Grigori Medvedev. Our man on the inside is making some inquiries to see if there is a connection but you know how that goes, he can't blow his cover over it."

Juan spoke up "Grigori Medvedev? Where have I heard that name before?" looking at Lou, then Charlie, "Wasn't he…" his facial expression was contorted in thought but it just didn't come to him. He knew the name but couldn't place it. "I guess I must have read it in the papers someplace. Wait, I know…that was the name of the package in the Yazy mission back in '89."

5

The Yazy Mission: 'Operation Silent Night'

The 'Yazy' mission, as the team referred to it, officially dubbed 'Operation Silent Night' was part of a CIA Delta mission to five Soviet top secret listening sites at various locations surrounding the Soviet Union. The Soviets used the sights to monitor classified NATO and American communications around the world. The mission was to silence all five of the Soviet listening stations on the same night effectively cutting off the Soviet Union's ability to monitor the West's satellite communications, as well as some traditional radio transmissions.

It was believed the Soviets also had the ability to input dummy transmissions that could, potentially, create confusion in Western defenses; but that would be risky and could result in raising some red flags over the source of the transmissions. In fact, it was during a very short test of this ability that enabled NATO intelligence to detect the existence of the stations in the first place. Some very diligent CIA espionage over the next six months resulted in the determination that there were five stations strategically located around the USSR. The signature for the short test of the original hacking effort was detected and traced to locations in Croatia, Hungary, The Russian coast in the Gulf of Finland, On the Siberian coast of the Bering Strait and a location just north of the Soviet Union's border with North Korea.

The 'Yazy', or Zyazy, mission was given to Lou's Rangers. Zyazy was actually the name of a small village just a few kilometers south of the location. The

'Resort' where the station was hidden was actually a KGB retreat. The location was important as it could monitor all normal and classified NATO, Northern European, communications.

There were seven operatives assigned to the mission, six rangers and one Navy Seal who was specially trained to locate and identify the equipment needed at the station. Chief Petty Officer First Class Paul J R Wells was a specialist in controlled demolition and had worked with Lou before on a mission in Granada. He also spoke fluent Russian, as did all of the rest of the handpicked team; that could prove to be vital to their extraction. Paul had been working with the CIA over the course of the investigation and was familiar with the location and the target equipment to be destroyed.

Recount of The Yazy Mission, January 9, 1989
Fort Greely, Alaska

The briefing was held in a conference room on one of the coldest military bases in the US defense system, Fort Greely, Alaska. Colonel Bert Spencer, the chisel chinned head of the Delta Force detail, didn't waste any time on the formalities.

"Gentleman, the project for today will, perhaps, be the most complicated mission you've been on to date. The location is a small compound, designated the 'resort', on the coast of Russia in the Gulf of Finland. It is cold and desolate, which is why we are conducting our trials in this God forsaken ice box. It is known that the 'resort' has an array of high tech antennas and other secret listening devices with which the KGB use to monitor the classified communications and computer activity between

NATO members in Northern Europe. Also, and most important, they have developed the capability to corrupt the data that is transmitted through the US Air Force spy satellite that has been in low stationary orbit over the Northern NATO region.

"We discovered these capabilities in April of last year (1988) and by September our Intel found that there are five known locations of these Top secret Russian spy stations. The Russians as of yet do not know that we know about them, to our advantage.

"Gentlemen, you have been chosen because each member of your team is fluent in the Russian language and your experience in past missions has proven your abilities to work in unison. This will be the most challenging mission you have been on yet. If all goes according to plan you will be in and out in less than an hour but if the contingencies are needed you may need to find your way home using your native skills. The CIA contact will brief you on these contingencies.

"For now, we will be drilling the details into your brains like the alphabet, only you will need to know it front and backwards. The model will have as much detail as we know and we will change the scenario often to cover the possibilities. The CIA has assets within the maintenance crew of the resort so we are confident of a high degree of accuracy. We will train until we get the go from the front desk."

The Colonel took a breath and had a sip of water, or something stronger, and continued. "It has been decided that due to the civil unrest that has been affecting the USSR the time is ripe for taking out these spy stations which will further stress the vulnerable

Soviet government. We intend to coordinate the simultaneous attacks on all five of the known similar stations on the same night, within a very tight time frame, which will be somewhat of a challenge due to the time zone differences. Your mission will be late night, the eastern locations will be early a.m.

"The other locations are not your concern. This team will focus on the compound along the Russian coast in the Gulf of Finland. It will be the dead of winter, so we will need to be on your best behavior. Any slip-ups and they will be digging your body out of a glacier a hundred thousand years from now and calling you Crow Eatus man." That got a little chuckle from the team, point well made.

The colonel picked up his pointer and referred to a satellite map of the compound on the wall, "The compound, located on the coast, includes multiple buildings, a twenty meter pier in the channel, an inlet that is used for protected boat docking, four private lakes or ponds, and a private access road. The property is surrounded by a fence and multiple remote camera surveillance. The sign at the main gate says that it is called the Novgorod Resort. The locals say that it is an exclusive resort for high party members. Intelligence had determined that it is a retreat for KGB operatives, or a training center.

"There are two targets in this mission, dubbed 'Operation Silent Night.' The primary mission is the demolition of the listening station and its corresponding data analysis databases. We will attempt to procure as many hard drives as time will allow. But, as fate would have it another opportunity may be developing that cannot be ignored.

"Intelligence has reported that the KGB arms dealer and war criminal Grigori Medvedev will be arriving at the compound on February 5th thru the 9th. The nature of the visit is apparently R&R so there should be only a minimal occupancy in the compound because of the time of the year.

"You will procure this package and transport it to Ramstein Air Base to be debriefed before he is taken to The Hague for trial. This is a secondary target, taking Medvedev, who has been indicted by the international court for war crimes and human rights atrocities, is the cherry. In no way should his taking jeopardize the success of the primary objective, do you understand?" Everyone nodded. The colonel cleared his throat and continued, "The plan was originally to approach the resort by boat to a location just north of the resort, About two kilometers north of Zyazy, Russia, on the Gulf of Finland. The winter, though, has been particularly harsh and that part of the gulf is iced over.

"Plan B is to approach, from Finland, in three small, two-man hover crafts that could easily and quietly traverse the open water and the ice.

"Plan C is a HAHO (high altitude high opening drop). In either plan the team will enter the compound about two hundred yards north of the main buildings. Intel indicates that there is only ten staff attached to the compound at this time of year, housekeeping, maintenance and a six-man regular army guard detail.

"They won't be expecting us but we're not going to be taking any chances. Medvedev will be arriving the morning of the 5th, unless his plans change, and will be settled in for the night. He will be accompanied by two body guards and his personal assistant. That makes the total number at the resort fourteen, ten armed.

"Grigori Medvedev, a notorious KGB operative and arms dealer is wanted by the international courts in The Hague for war crimes related to his activities in Croatia. He is at the top of Interpol's version of the top ten most wanted list. He is a ruthless sociopath who will sell arms to anyone, for any reason. In Croatia he had his operatives bomb a café full of Christian Serbs, and then claimed responsibility in the name the pro-Muslim separatists. They both bought their arms from that bastard. Bringing him to justice would be a very good thing. The primary mission comes first. Capturing Medvedev is just the icing on the cake."

Colonel Spencer looked over his team for a moment. "Any questions you will have will be answered over the course of your training; which will be intensive." He turned and left the room.

Over the next two weeks the team, the Wolf Pack as they called themselves, trained in a scaled mock-up of the Novgorod Resort. The mission had the added challenges of operating in the Russian Republic of the Communist Soviet Union. A nation in a state of undeclared war, or 'Cold War', with the United States of America.

If anything went wrong with this highly sensitive operation that would indicate a United States involvement, the consequences could be World War III. For that reason, all equipment and personal items that were used had to originate from the Soviet Bloc or be in use in the bloc.

The presence of even a Tic-Tac could throw suspicion to the US. This team had been working together for more than four years and six major missions. They worked together, they played together and they risked their lives together.

The mechanics of a mission certainly cannot be taken lightly, the slightest miscalculation could have fatal consequences, to the team or the country. Every member of a Ranger team understood this. Any mission was about the protection of the country. Every Army Ranger, or any of the elite US Special Forces, knows that their lives are as disposable as the ammunition in their weapons, if it comes to that. That comes to life every day in the Ranger Creed:

"ENERGETICALLY WILL I MEET THE ENEMIES OF MY COUNTRY. I SHALL DEFEAT THEM ON THE FIELD OF BATTLE FOR I AM BETTER TRAINED AND WILL FIGHT WITH ALL MY MIGHT. SURRENDER IS NOT A RANGER WORD. I WILL NEVER LEAVE A FALLEN COMRADE TO FALL INTO THE HANDS OF THE ENEMY AND UNDER NO CIRCUMSTANCES WILL I EVER EMBARRASS MY COUNTRY."

An Army Ranger is an elite fighting machine, eyes wide open. After three weeks of training in the target resort they had covered about every contingency imaginable, except for those ruled by Murphy's Law: 'If anything can possibly go wrong, it will.' This team had a couple of glitches though. The eight-man Wolf Pack was trimmed to six, with the other two designated as support. Two were reassigned due to their ethnic appearance, one is Asian and the other is Black. They simply wouldn't fit into the Russian countryside incognito. Master

Sergeant Tommy Hu Sung and Staff Sergeant Tyler Perry would be on the critical extraction team. Even Juan Vega came under strict scrutiny. His fluency in Russian and his Eastern Bloc like appearance got him through, not Russian but Soviet.

The plan put the blame toward a group of Chechen Rebels, the Chechyan Islamic Liberation League, 'CHILL'. The Chechnyan's have been fighting their Russian occupiers for 200 years.

The other glitch was the addition of a Navy Seal to the team. Chief Petty Officer Paul J R Wells, not entirely unknown to the Wolves, had fought alongside them in the invasion of Granada. Wells was a top-notch weapons expert. As a Seal there was a natural competitiveness with the Rangers; well, the special forces of either service didn't give an inch to the other and believed their teams were the best. Though the invasion of Granada didn't show them the action that they hoped for, the Wolves developed a respect for this Seal; Wells was compadre.

They were ready. You can train all day every day until the mission begins but, in the end, it is up to the unforeseen circumstances that determine the outcome. These men worked like one. They knew that the slightest misstep could be the failure of the mission.

Every United States Army Ranger is cross trained in multiple skills. As a Special Ops team member there is additional honing of these skills plus additional training in intelligence gathering and population assimilation. As a Delta operative, a candidate must satisfactorily complete an additional eight-week course in high skills proficiency. 75% of

Delta operatives are recruited from the Rangers. Delta operatives are the highest skilled fighters in the world along with the Navy Seals. The planning and execution is as good as it gets. When the Delta's are called, there is no limit to the cost of the mission; success is the only option.

The success of 'Operation Silent Night' required a higher level of professionalism because of the dire consequences of a failure. The rewards, though, have been weighed against the possibility of failure and the rewards won. The key determining factor was, without question, the record that the Delta Force program has established for itself. A record of almost perfect success since their most famous failed attempt to rescue the Iranian Hostages in 1979. That debacle was studied over and over until a clear policy of action was instituted that would successfully guide future Delta operations for decades.

It was a perfect night, dark, overcast, and cold, very cold. The Gulf of Finland was frozen over for more than fifty miles from the Soviet Coast. For that reason, and that there was a sustained east wind, it was decided that the team would do a variation of the HAHO drop from 28,000 ft. They could jump outside of the Soviet airspace and quietly glide the thirty kilometers to the resort undetected by radar. The intelligence service was able to commandeer six heated Russian made high altitude winged drop suits.

The weapons that the team were using were also those that could be available to a group of Russian dissidents. The AS"Val" (Avtomat Special'nyj Val) Assault rifle used by the Soviet Spetsnaz of the GRU and KGB would be carried by all of the team except Anderson, who would be carrying a VSS Vintorez sniper rifle, similar to the AS"Val" but more effective at long range. The side arm each of the team carried was a Russian made Makarov PM. It was the standard pistol used by most of the Russian police and military agencies. Its light weight was beneficial to the light armor needed for the mission, but the magazine did not have the capacity of their American made counterparts.

The other armaments included Russian made F1 grenades and Russian made C4 explosives. It was essential that every element of their equipment had been manufactured in the Soviet Bloc. Will Anderson had to leave his lucky St. Christopher medallion behind because it was not something you would normally find in the USSR.

The flight in the German C-160 takes one hour twenty-two minutes from the Flughafen Hamburg, Germany, the Hamburg Airport. The C-160 Transall Twin Turboprop transporter is similar to the US C-130 Hercules. First built in 1959 by the company's MBB (now Daimler Aerospace), Nord Aviation and VFW. It became the workhorse of the German, French and Turkish air forces. Like the US C-130 it has a rear cargo ramp through which it can load a cargo of 16,000 kg including tanks and 68 fully equipped paratroopers.

On this mission it will be carrying a load of watermelons to Helsinki, and six paratroopers; who will not be listed on the manifest, nor will they be on the plane when it lands.

The Pilot flew the C-160 in an arc that takes them close to where the Finnish and Russian airspace meet. After the jump the C-160 would turn northwest toward their destination.

The jump, from 28,000 ft, is particularly difficult in the harsh winter conditions. The temperatures at the jump altitude was about the same as it would be at the surface, about -30F, but the night was ideal for the jump, save for the distance that they would have to fly.

And Fly they would, covering twenty kilometers at terminal velocity before they could open their chutes at 12,000 feet, then glide to within 200 meters of the resort. If all goes well, if the heating units work properly; if not the chutist would be dead. In their training at Greeley, all went well on three trial jumps.

Once the C-160 reached an altitude just below 10,000 ft the PT (Physiology Technicians) would have them breathe 100% oxygen for thirty minutes while the pilot holds the altitude. This will purge nitrogen from the bloodstream, eliminating 90 percent of the cases of decompression sickness.

The technicians, all experts in the field of human performance and the effects of flight on the body, monitor the aircrew and parachutists looking for signs of impairment caused by altitude. No one will make the jump without the OK from the PT.

The minutes before the jump were critical as the warriors checked then double checked their equipment; there was no room for error, then triple checked. "Five minutes" came the warning from Staff Sergeant Kiel Butler. That was when they put on their oxygen cylinders which had been checked and rechecked previously.

The red light on the panel turned to yellow

indicating one minute to jump. Fifty seconds later the rear deck began to open and the yellow light turned to green and they were out.

The plane banked to the left and headed toward the airport in Helsinki, Finland where it would unload its cargo of watermelons.

There aren't many things in life that could be as exhilarating as a parachute jump from twenty-eight thousand feet and then flying as horizontal as possible for twenty Kilometers in four and a half minutes at 126 mph only to be violently jerked to a near stop for a slow glide of another twelve kilometers; all at thirty below zero. If not for the high-tech heating elements in their Russian made jumpsuits they could not have pulled this off. An error was averted when the batteries being used in the suits were Duracell. They were very quickly replaced with Russian alkaline batteries.

The Wolf Pack was not new to this kind of superhuman acts of valor. Within twenty minutes the team landed on the ice about two kilometers from the mainland. After a few minutes to regroup and do a health check they headed toward the lights to the east. The ice was fairly level and easy to traverse. Heading northeasterly in their approach they entered the compound near the satellite barn. Here they all got out of their jump suits and gave them to Boom.

The plan had Wells and Woolsey peeling off to secure and set the charges in the barn. There they put the jumpsuits to be blown up with the satellite dishes, antenna, and other equipment to be destroyed. They then moved to the control room where the computer hard-drives were taken before setting C-4 charges destroyed that building as well. The charges were set on a thirty-minute delay, leaving no room for Murphy.

Now that they were dressed down to their Russian tactical fatigues they had to get the job done and get out before the cold got to them. Each man had the latest in Soviet night vision and communication ear plugs. They had this whole compound drilled in their head at Greely so the only unknown was the location of the armed guards. If all goes well they will be out in thirty minutes.

Wells and Woolsey entered the barn and the remaining five continued on toward the main buildings. First Sergeant Eric Christopherson (Buzz), the team communications specialist, along with Sergeant First Class Derrick Yablonski (Gunner), were charged with gaining entry to the control room and removing the hard drives before the sappers arrived to blow it. "Gunner you're on, we got the perimeter" Lou directed Buzz and Gunner; each clicked twice on their com units to acknowledge. That left Anderson (Snapshot), Vega (Doc) and Bennett the team leader. They would secure the compound as needed and locate the package.

There was a light on in the main building. Lou used hand motions to send Snapshot to the left and Doc to the right. He walked up onto the deck at the front door and to the window with the light. "We have him," Lou whispered into his com. "Snap, take the back," double click. Lou and Doc slowly opened the front door, it was unlocked, there was a slight squeak to the hinges but not loud enough to be heard, they hoped. It didn't matter, they were in now. On the left there was a door that led to the room in which Medvedev and another man were sitting.

Doc grabbed the door handle and swung it open and Lou went in loaded for bear. The room was a library, warm and comfortable with its cherry wood paneling and a crackling fire in the hearth.

The two men inside were startled by the sudden appearance of these apparent Soviet Spetsnaz troopers. It was soon obvious that they were not going to be friendly. The Assistant pulled out his Makarov PM out of his jacket but Lou fired first dropping him instantly to the floor. Doc had a hypodermic needle ready for Medvedev as Lou jumped to subdue him. In thirty seconds, Medvedev was out.

Just then all hell broke out as gunshots were fired in the hallway. Doc tended to the package getting him ready for transport while Lou headed toward the shots; Snapshot was in trouble.

Lou burst out of the door just as Snap passed between him and the three soldiers. He was unloading his magazine on the men when he suddenly hit the floor. He was down.

Two of the soldiers looked up from Snapshot just as Lou fired two short bursts hitting one in the chest, the other in the head. Lou knelt down next to Anderson "Where ya hit," he said as he prepared to take him up into a rescue carry and get out of there. "Doc, you got the package?"

"I got him," Juan Vega said as he rolled him on a body sling preparing to drag him out to the LZ (landing Zone). "I hear a chopper, I hope it's our ride!"

Outside there was the distinct sound of a Soviet MI 8 'Hip C' transport chopper that would extract the team and their package, right on time. Five Hip-C's were bought from the government of India for use in the five 'Operation Silent Night' missions. If the plan worked out they could fly through Soviet Union's airspace without suspicion. They were made to look like standard KGB choppers that no one would question and the pilots were Russian CIA operatives who knew the S.O.P. (standard operational procedure) for Soviet air space. It was hoped that they would be well out of the area before there was any reason to suspect anything.

The four Saboteurs were finished on time, as planned, and they all met at the LZ just as the chopper came in for a pickup and go. Yablonski helped Doc load the package as Lou came down from the main house carrying Anderson.

"He is losing a lot of blood, I packed it tight but he's gonna need your best work, Doc." Doc worked on him all the way back to Hamburg. He had been shot twice in the abdomen and the hip, shattering his right hip. His Ranger days were over. After he recovered he was retired with honor and distinction, and disability.

The co-pilot had a digital video camera and as they left the compound the pilot banked south so that he could film the explosion. Thirty seconds out the whole thing erupted into a ball of fire.

Nothing in those buildings could have survived that blast. Later the eggheads would go over the videos from each source to determine the success of 'Operation Silent Night' at all five locations.

When they got back to Germany they found out that the package would not be turned over to the Hague; it was feared that he would get off too lightly. They were not told what happened to Grigori Medvedev, his fate was classified.

6

Flagstaff, AZ

About two p.m. Doctor Addari came into Lou's room to give him a final look over before he could be released. He told Lou again how lucky he was before making him get into a wheelchair for the ride out the front door. "We can't have you tripping on the way out the door and suing us now, can we?" He said. They all laughed. Charlie had his pickup at the door and graciously helped Lou into the passenger seat, patting him on the ass and calling him 'old man'. Juan had his Harley, so they agreed to meet at the Museum Club in five.

As they walked into the Museum Club the bartender Gary, a tall, lanky, good hearted cowboy with a handlebar mustache that coiled around his cheeks, rushed over to them giving Lou a strong handshake. "The boss told me that you don't pay for a thing in this bar again, ever," he said. "It's crazy how many strangers come in just to see where the vigilante administered the western justice." Gary didn't take any money from any of them; they could have drank there all night. "Stick around boys, we got a good band tonight. There's gonna be women all over the place it's Ladies Night."

They just had one and then went to the tow yard to check out the wrecked RV. The RV was in the back lot of the All City impound yard. It was pretty banged up, totaled, the insurance agent told Lou earlier when he talked to her. "Except for the Jeep, that just needs some touch up paint and a new front bumper and it'll be ok," she said. "Take about a week and I can cut you a check for 87 Grand, or do you want it deposited directly into your account? Lou told her to deposit it; he won't be in town that long.

He couldn't believe the damage. The pickup was crushed on the right side and the roof. The fifth wheel had obviously rolled over on its side and was twisted and the nose where the bedroom was crushed in. He grabbed the handle to the door but he had to put his foot on the side and pull hard to get it open. He climbed in, took in the depressing condition of the interior. He and Lynne had put everything they made for four years to buy this fifth wheel and a diesel pickup to pull it. The jeep he bought new in '84. He didn't want to get rid of it because he had given it to Martin for his sixteenth birthday. "I'll just get the stuff I need," he said to Charlie; but Charlie was nowhere to be found.

Charlie and Juan were outside checking out the damage. Lou needed time to work this out they figured. Beside he was thinking that it was a little too strange that Lou lost control so he thought he would check out some concerns he had about this freak accident; *Lou wasn't about this kinda crap*, he was thinking.

Lou got his clothes together in a bag and then opened a door to a closet where he had a hidden gun safe built into the back wall. He opened it and took out his Glock-19 and a 12-gauge shotgun, his Remington 30.06 and an M-16 that he had in the service. There was more that he had to get but he decided that he would ask Tommy, the owner of All City to clean it out for him later. He grabbed his gun bag and duffel and headed for the door when he saw something red sticking out under the couch. He put down the bags and reached down to grab a red ribbon, "Soyala," he said to himself.

As he stumbled awkwardly out the door with

the two bags Juan called to him, "Lou come on over here we got something to show you."

Charlie was on his back under the pickup. "It looks like this wreck may not have been any accident. You know why anybody might want to sabotage your brake lines?" Charlie said looking at Lou.

Lou got under the truck to see for himself. "I guess I've made a few enemies over the years working in the DPS."

"Look here," Charlie said, as he took a number of pictures with his cell phone. He pointed out a section on the break line that was missing. The ends were mangled on both sides of the break line and there were signs of powder burns on the frame of the truck in the immediate area around the missing brake line. "I've seen this before," he said "this is a favorite of the mob in LA, the Russian mob in particular. They have a device that they attach to the break line with just enough C-4 explosive to blow the line but not enough to do much more damage. It's an ingenious device, really. Radio controlled from a cell phone or with a timer, it's not much bigger than a bottle cap and attaches in a second around the brake line." He Put his fingers around the break line.

"Russians like to send messages and don't care much about collateral damage. The first time I saw the results of one of these it caused three unrelated deaths and an eight hour back up on the San Diego freeway. The message was understood by the councilman who had a change of heart and a vote for a shipyard construction project at the LA harbor. We couldn't prove a thing, of course, the case is still open."

As an explosives investigator with the LAPD bomb squad, Charlie had seen some interesting things. He started with the LAPD right after leaving the Rangers, where his particular skills as a Sapper had made him a valuable addition to the police force. It was an active career that should have ended abruptly on many occasions if not for the steady hand of this decorated professional.

Charlie was from a long line of sappers, as the Army called their demolitions experts. His great grandfather was a sapper with Grant in the Civil War. During the siege of Vicksburg, the sappers dug tunnels hundreds of yards across 'no man's land' until they reached the ramparts of the city defenses, stuffed it with dynamite and blew several gaping holes in the walls that eventually led to the surrender of the city to the north. Charlie would send the pics to the State Police when they got back to the hotel.

That night they sat in the hotel lounge and contemplated the bazaar facts of the last few years in Lou's life. The one thing they could conclude was that there are no such thing as coincidences. Lou slept in the extra bed in Charlie's room, Juan had his own room.

About 2 a.m. Charlie got up to take a leak. Lou sat up in his bed and began a line of thought that only two professional investigators could confront, only for Lou it was personal. They talked about the facts, particularly the name of the killer of Martin and his connection to the Russian mob.

Then, was there a Russian connection to Lou's wreck? They wondered what Lou did to cause the Russians to have a vendetta against him. Lou told Charlie about Lynne's death. "It was just a drunk driver," Lou said getting a little emotional. "That was when it all started to fall apart, my life I mean."

"But, didn't the driver insist that he was home that night; drinking, but not driving?" Charlie asked, moving the conversation back to their investigation mode. Lou told Charlie about the evidence; how the prints were wiped from the door handles, the steering wheel, and the shifter knob. There was one thumb print on the button on the side of the shifter, but it didn't match the driver, or any records for that matter. But the paint on the left side of the driver's car had paint from Lynne's car on it and vice-versa. That was definitely the car that ran Lynne off the Road, and it was parked in the owner's garage.

The next morning the three of them had breakfast at the hotel. After they ate Juan jumped on his Motorcycle, said his goodbyes, fired up the Hog, and headed back to Albuquerque. Lou will get there as soon as he took care of some business.

"Let's go to Belmont," Lou said, "It's about ten miles west on the interstate."

He and Charlie headed to the Camperworld in Belmont, Arizona. Camperworld is where Lou had bought his fifth wheel, so he knew he could get a replacement there.

The salesman was Pete Wilson. He saw Lou come through the door and walked up to him, took his hand and shook it enthusiastically.

"Lou, how you doing buddy is everything alright," he said immediately regretting his obvious misstatement. "I mean, what brings you in today Lou."

"Pete, I beat up my fifth wheel and I need a replacement. I have $87,000 to spend and I have my eye on that Winnebago out there. I need a tow bar for the jeep and I need a loan until the insurance money comes in next week or so."

About an hour later Lou drove out of the Camperworld with a gray and gold 35-foot Winnebago diesel pusher. The price on the sticker was $91,000 plus tax but Pete talked to the manager and worked out a deal. The store didn't make much on the deal but that didn't matter; they didn't lose anything either. Lou was well respected in Flagstaff. Everyone was on his side, almost everyone that is.

While Lou was negotiating the deal, Charlie made a call to the Flagstaff police department. He talked to the investigator who handled Lynne's accident. Mary Lucerne listened to Charlie's thoughts about the case and promised to run the thumb print again, this time sending it to Interpol. She said she would get back to him. Then he made another call to a friend in LA who might shed some light on the Medvedev twist. He knew the name figured prominently in the Russian mob.

7

Lou drove away in his new ride and went straight to Black Bart's RV Park on Butler Street in Flagstaff. Charlie followed him in his pickup. After taking about 30 minutes to hook up the RV, they walked over to Black Bart's Saloon to have a beer. Charlie would be heading back to LA in the morning, about a seven-hour drive. They still had some big questions on their minds. Both professional investigators had a sense of trouble that was stuck in the back of their minds. Each being somewhat disinclined to speak out for fear of raising undo alarm.

After a couple of pints, they began to loosen up and finally Lou broke the ice. "You know, Boom, I have a bad feeling about this whole thing, it just has an awkward momentum to it. You know, like, too many coincidences; and you know what I think about coincidences."

"Yeah, Coincidences are just a little too convenient. Someone is after you, that's for sure. First Lynne then Martin and now the traces of an explosive on your brakes, does the Flagstaff PD have the knowledge to analyze the forensics?" Charlie wondered out loud.

"They are a good police department and besides they have called the State police to assist; and with Boyd being Vladimir, the FBI is on it too. Something, though, is pulling at me that I can't make out. I have some questions that I want answered, or at least asked." Lou said as he ordered another round. "You can sleep in the RV tonight and get your stuff on your way out."

Black Bart's Saloon is a popular restaurant in Flagstaff. During the dinner hour the staff, presumably drama and music majors from NAU, or, least kids of talent, perform for the patrons singing show tunes and other entertainment skits in between waiting on tables, it's fun. The parking lot usually has a tour bus parked in it on the weekends to insure a packed crowd of happy diners.

Lou and Charlie sat in the bar area which was seldom crowded. They could see the entertainment through a large opening through which the bartender passed drinks for the dinner crowd. He was very busy but still managed to keep up on some of the conversation of the two only patrons in the bar. When he heard the name Vladimir he perked up. It wasn't a name you often hear in Flagstaff, Arizona.

"He was in here a few times, a strange man," Bill, the bartender, said.

"Vladimir, Vladimir Medvedev?" Lou asked.

"That's the name," Bill continued as one of the waiters started singing 'Yankee Doodle Dandy'. "He had been in here a couple of times, Lou. Said he had a friend staying here and he was waiting for him to show up. Drank the good vodka. One time he got a phone call, they asked for Vladimir Medvedev, I asked if his name was Vladimir and he took the call. He mostly listened, looked a little peekish as he hung up and left, just like that. Left his drink on the bar, haven't seen him since; that was months ago."

Lou looked at Charlie and they both said, "He was stalking me/you."

Just then Charlie's cell rang. He reached in his jacket to pull it out and with it came a business card which fell to the floor. Rather than pick it up Charlie answered the call, it was Mary Lucerne. He talked to her for a minute or two mostly nodding his head and acknowledging her monologue. Lou got off his stool and picked up the business card that apparently

Boom had not noticed. The card read "Paul Wells construction and maintenance, Alexandria, VA."

When Charlie got off the phone Lou had a question for him: "You dropped this, Paul Wells? Wasn't he the Seal that went with us on the Yazy?"

"You got me," Charlie decided to fill Lou in on the real reason he is here. "Paul contacted me last week when you were acquitted and asked me to come over to see what's going on. He got word from the FBI that one of their undercover agents within the Russian mob in New York recognized the name Boyd Johnson."

He took a sip of his beer, "I was about to tell you about it but I wanted to be sure that our concerns weren't, well, just coincidental." He said with a contorted smirk. "Paul is with the CIA in DC, this is confidential of course, he had been following your case and, he too, has his suspicions about some of the circumstances. When the FBI contacted him about the name Boyd Johnson and a possible Russian connection. Paul asked me to check out the facts on this end, to see if there were anything to them. That call pretty much confirmed his, our suspicions."

"Was that him on the phone? Lou asked.

"No that was Mary from the FPD." Charlie continued, "She ran the thumb print on the shifter of the vehicle that ran Lynne off the road, the one that didn't have a match. I asked her to run it on Interpol, she did but also ran it on the FBI database again. That one got a hit this time that was confirmed with an Interpol match. Lou it was Vlad."

"Boyd…Johnson…is…Vladimir…Medvedev?"

…Taking it all in, "His print was in that car?

…He - killed - Lynne - too?"

Charlie put his hand on Lou's shoulder…

"We believe he stole the car out of Mr. Siever's garage while Siever was drunk, followed Lynne when she went to the store, and used it to run her off the road into that utility pole. After which he drove the car back to Siever's garage and parked it. Siever didn't even know it was gone, like he said, but was naturally charged with the act, but he is innocent. When Bill said Vlad had been in here I knew he was stalking you. He must have been planning it for some time."

"How does that get the CIA involved in the case?" Lou questioned.

"I called Paul yesterday because I knew he had been attached to the surveillance of Grigori Medvedev, The package from the Yazy mission. Well in 2009 Greggy was released from the prison where he had been incarcerated since we helped to put him there in '89. Apparently, his nephew, Dmitry Medvedev, now the Prime Minister of the Russian Federation, then the President, put his release as a non-negotiable stipulation before his government would ratify the START II treaty. Our president caved and released him with no attempt to contest it. What's one prisoner when it comes to his landmark campaign promise?"

"Nobody cared about an Old Russian, even if he was the biggest world criminal of his time," Lou interrupted.

Charlie continued, "Vladimir, AKA Boyd Johnson, is another nephew from another brother. Paul had a tap on Greggie's phone. He called his nephew Vlad. That call was traced to a phone in Flagstaff, Arizona; but it wasn't immediately tied to the name Boyd Johnson; not until his fingerprints were identified by Interpol. Now that is of great interest to the CIA, considering the subsequent events related to

Vlad and, well, your misfortunes. I mean, Lou, this is just a little too circumstantial to not have a connection; don't you think?"

There was a long moment of silence while they both just stared blankly at the entertainment. A Young lady started tap dancing and broke into a rendition of 'Singing in the Rain'.

"What connection, Boom, does this have something to do with the Yazy mission? How does that figure?" Lou had a look of dark confusion. They both had a brief moment of thought...

"I don't know."

8

St. Petersburg, Russia

The Russian Federation in 2017 is a bustling mix of royal extravagance and capitalist modernism. Well at least that's what they say in the tourist brochures. Underneath it all are the remnants of the old Soviet establishment in a new suit of clothes. That suit fit the lifestyles of an elite group of billionaires. Some would more accurately refer to it as a fascist state; where the government is run by the big business oligarchs' self-interests. The people must serve that interest; like a giant corporation, with muscle.

Learning from the failed attempt at fascism by the Nazis of Germany, the Russians allow their people the belief that they are an important part of this 'capitalist' paradise. Considering the history of the Russian people I am sure it must seem that way. Freedom has never been in the Russian vocabulary except in Soviet propaganda.

The city of St. Petersburg has been through many transitions over the centuries. Its origins date back to the 9th century as the capital of the principality of Novgorod. The city of Novgorod was a center of domestic and international trade. The Gulf of Finland, as it is known today, gave Novgorod access to Northern and Western Europe and the towns of the Hanseatic League. The Neva River and Lake Ladoga gave the merchants of Novgorod access to the many inland towns.

In the Northern War (1700–1721) 'Peter the Great' finally gained control of the region from the Swedes, built the 'Fortress of Peter and Paul', and the

'Cabin of Peter the Great'. Czar Peter moved his capital from Moscow, and the city of St. Petersburg was established, officially in 1703.

After the Russian Revolution (1917) and the communists takeover of the Soviet Union the city was renamed Petrograd. The city was renamed again to Leningrad after the death of their leader, Vladimir Lenin. The communists built communal apartments as they transformed the Soviet Union into their version of a communist utopia. The 'party' members received more benefits in their 'Utopia', but long lines and food shortages were the rule in the general population which was reduced in great numbers throughout the country by starvation.

When Hitler broke the Molotov-Ribbentrop Pact, commonly known as the German-Russian non-aggression pact, by invading Russia on its Eastern Front, the Russian people came together to halt the takeover of their homeland by their historic German enemies. Millions of Russians died but the Germans did not succeed. Leningrad, St. Petersburg, endured a siege of 900 days until the Germans were forced to withdraw due to harsh winter conditions and an overextended army, battling on too many fronts. The human cost to the heroic people of Leningrad was horrendous. Death tolls range from six to eight hundred thousand souls.

During the 'Cold War' there was relative peace for the people even though they had no freedom and the food lines were still a fact of life. Certain party members, though, did very well. Grigori Medvedev was one of those; quickly advancing through the ranks of the Soviet intelligence service. His brother, Anatoly, took to the academics and became professor of chemical technology at the University of Leningrad.

Grigori's total loyalty to Soviet cause soon caught the attention of some very powerful Soviet officials. His manipulative prowess and ability to establish valuable links to the outside world put him into the enviable position of self-determination in his activities. He only needed to bring in the capital to the Soviet coffers. It is said that he kept a file on his adversaries as well as his 'friends', at least that was the rumor. Sometimes a rumor is enough to instill the fear he needed to maintain his status; but in this case it was true, and Grigori used his knowledge to get his ways.

By the mid-eighties he was the most successful arms dealer in the service. He utilized the most extreme methods to make a sale; often selling to both sides of a disagreement. He would manipulate the passions of both sides until they were begging him for his product. The leaders of the party loved, and feared him, for the arms that he sold brought millions into their overextended budget. He was a money maker. The Croatia massacre and others put him on the most wanted list for Interpol, as well as the western spy agencies making him a marked man with little time before fate would intervene. All they needed was the opportunity.

That came in 1989 in Zyazy when he mysteriously disappeared at the same time the North West communications complex was destroyed. The acts of sabotage were credited to a revolutionary group that called themselves the Chechnyan Islamic liberation league. The same group also claimed responsibility for the attacks on several other secret communication complexes in other parts of the nation. The loss of these facilities essentially blinded the KGB's ability to monitor the intentions of the United States and its NATO allies. Whether it added to the downfall of the Soviet Union in 1991 is the subject of debate in certain circles.

With the collapse of the Soviet Union in 1991, Leningrad was dropped and the city was renamed St. Petersburg. Today it is the second largest city in the Russian Federation. It's beautiful blend of old world and modern architecture make it the number one tourist destination in Russia. Grigori Medvedev was born there in 1954. This is his City.

Grigori Medvedev opened the door to his plush office in a modern a high rise on Galemyy PR-d, a waterfront boulevard near the harbor district of St. Petersburg. He walked over to his eighty thousand ruble desk, tapped the button on his intercom and summoned his personal assistant, Timur Balaban, "Timur clear my calendar for the next two weeks, we must go to Prague to check on the progress of the weapon they are making for us. I don't trust them with this so I want to see for myself if they are following my instructions. These people are corruptible and will sell us out at the right price."

"No, I don't think so," Timur said with a reassuring tone, "they know what you do to those that betray you. You are well known to these people and they wouldn't have agreed to take on this project if they weren't going to complete it. They remember what you did to the families of the Syrians that thought they could betray you. Assad was lucky you didn't kill him too, but we need his power and money, and his loyalty, even if it is built on fear. Besides our friend Artem will protect your interests. You also have other reasons to go, you must miss her, it's been weeks."

"You are right Timur," Grigori replied, "but I still don't trust them. You are the only one that I trust, Timur, ever since we were children, you saved my life when I fell through the ice on Lake Ladoga, we have been together and through so many things. I could not have done any of this without you at my side. Even while those pig Americans had me locked up you were there upon my release. It was you who taught me how the new Russia works. They tried to tell me to retire to my villa on the Black Sea but you knew that I would never sit around without my revenge. You are a true friend, Timur," Grigori smiled at Timur and took the coffee that he brought in for him. He took a sip, winced, and said, "Shit! Timur are you trying to poison me, put some Vodka in this so I can get this day going right."

Timur pulled a flask out of his jacket pocket and poured a healthy bit of U'luvka Vodka into the cup, "I was ready, here you go. Maybe tomorrow you will listen to your doctor." Timur walked over to an oversized chair, sat down and began giving his morning report on the activities of their enterprises. "We have made delivery of the RPG's to the Chechen rebels, they are planning to use them on Russian soldiers occupying the Northern Province, it will be messy."

Grigori winced a puff of breath and said "Yes, for them it will be messy. The Russian Prime Minister has received an anonymous text telling him of the details that we know. There will be no mercy for those traitors and we will use the money to build my new weapon."

"The Iranians have requested that we provide them with spare parts for the MIG-29 fighters. They really want the new fighters that you have promised would be available soon. I told them to be patient, they are being built. The more anxious they get the more they will pay," Timur laughed.

"Yes, that is right, oh business is good." Grigori chuckled with this.

"Grigori," Timur got serious, "do you not think it

is over with the American Rangers? We have so many profitable things going on. This obsession of yours over those pitiful soldiers is not good for business."

The anger flushed into Grigori's face, but then he controlled himself. "You are the only one that can talk to me like that, Timur, but be wary, I am doing this, and I won't take any insubordination on it, even from you. Now this Lou Bennett has killed my nephew Vladimir, the Son of my brother. I will have my revenge on that too. These Americans will suffer as I have NEVER MADE ANYONE SUFFER BEFORE," raising his voice to a hysterical rage.

This Timur had seen many times before and it concerned him of his friend. Grigori continued, "I spent twenty years of my best years in that prison with not so much as a hearing before their judges. They just LOCKED ME UP AND TOOK AWAY MY LIFE. I WILL KILL THEM ALL. I WILL KILL THEIR LOVED ONES AND THEIR FAMILY AND CAUSE THEM THEIR AMERICAN GRIEF. THEN I WILL LOOK THEM IN THE EYE AND KILL 'THEM' TOO!" Grigori was yelling and his blood pressure was exploding. "THEN I WILL RELEASE MY WEAPON ON THEIR COUNTRY AND KILL THEIR,"…coughing… "COUNTRYMAN TOO." More coughing, "they will know that I have done this to them. they will fear my revenge!"

Timur gave Grigori a bottle of water and told him to sit and relax. "It will be done my friend, we will make them suffer. I will be with you." Timur continued his report detailing the many business dealings of their company, The 'Liberty Arms Company'; The name designed to offend America.

Finally, Timur came to the last item to report. "I have received word from our friends in America, they have looked up your Ranger, Juan Vega in New Mexico. It seems that Doctor Vega will be having a most happy occasion in his family very soon. Our people have made plans for his daughter's bachelorette party in Las Vegas."

THE BEAR

9

Lou texted Juan, in Albuquerque, that he would be there for supper tomorrow. Juan returned that he would be ready and that he was going to be alone. His four daughters were going to Las Vegas for a long weekend before Gina, his oldest, will be getting married in two weeks. He could use the company and Lou could use the reprieve from the events of late.

Las Vegas? – Jilani, Lou thought, *I haven't talked to him since his dad died, what, three years now.* Then he had another thought. He picked up his cell phone and looked up Jilani's number and touched the call icon.

The phone rang and a young man answered, "Hello,"

"Jilani, Uncle Lou, how you doing kid?" Jilani is the only son of Bill Anderson, the sniper on the team. When Bill died of respiratory illness, Lou gave the eulogy at the funeral. He was closer to Bill, perhaps, than anyone else on the team. Bill took a bullet for him on the Yazy mission. Lou carried him out on his back. That was the Ranger code, no one left behind, especially if they took a bullet aimed at you. They owed each other for that one and their friendship held up to the end.

Bill married a Pakistani woman while he was stationed the Punjab Province of Pakistan, before he joined the Wolf Pack. Zahira was a good woman. They had a son, Jilani Louis Anderson. Louis in honor of Lou; well, that might be obvious. They talked for a while, about Jilani's mom and dad. His mom had passed away when he was ten. His dad was military retired with a disability from that bullet he took for Lou. Bill just happened to be moving in front of Lou to gain

71

the next position as all hell broke out. The bullets may have hit Lou but they hit Bill instead. Bill was never the same and was forced to retire shortly after they got home from the mission.

Jilani joined the Airforce after he graduated from UNLV, with honors. Because of his Pakistani roots, and his ability to speak multiple languages, other than English, he was recruited into the intelligence service and eventually the CIA. He could speak Punjabi and Urdu (the languages of Pakistan), Persian (Iran), and was pretty good in Russian, which he learned from his father. Russian was one of the requirements of the Wolf Pack. "Pop taught me Russian since I was old enough to understand. It was his connection to his glorious past."

Lou wondered if Medvedev had anything to do with Bill's death too; that was freaky. "Jilani, I need you to do me a favor. There are four beautiful girls on their way to Vegas and I need you to look them up." Lou told Jilani that he would explain when he got there, a snap decision. He told Jilani where they would be staying. Jilani told Lou that he would be more than happy to visit the daughters of Uncle Juan.

When Lou left Black Bart's early the next morning he didn't head east, to Albuquerque. instead he headed west, to Las Vegas.

He couldn't get the thought out of his head that Grigori Medvedev was connected to more than the deaths of his family. There was also Anderson who died three years ago; but that wasn't all, at least four members of the Wolf Pack were now dead.

Derrick Yablonski and Eric Christopherson had both died in the last three years; and of causes that were very questionable. Derrick's entire family died when an apparent natural gas leak poisoned them with carbon monoxide. It was determined that a faulty gas line caused the deaths. They had a smoke alarm but no Carbon Monoxide detector. It was a real tragedy, five people gone just like that. The night after they found Derricks body at the house, apparently of a self-inflicted gunshot wound. He couldn't handle the loss, who could?

Eric was killed in a motorcycle accident in Sturgis, South Dakota, when a pickup truck pulled out in front of him, he didn't stand a chance. It was ruled suspicious only because the driver of the truck fled. The truck was found in a wooded area about five miles from the scene of the accident but the driver was never located. The owner had an air tight alibi. He didn't even know the truck was missing until the police tracked him down at the Easy Rider Saloon on Junction Ave. The story was too similar to Lynne's accident.

The fourth Ranger that died, last November, Weapons Specialist Tyler Perry (Freebird). He was in the chopper during the extraction. A big burly Black man with the best personality in the Forces. He lived in LA, had a wife and three kids, all grown up and doing well. Ty and his wife both were killed in what was determined to be a gang related shooting in Compton. They were in the line of fire. They didn't live there but were visiting Tina's parents who had lived in Compton all their lives.

Lou attended the funeral, as did Tommy, Juan, and Charlie, Tyler's partner in the LAPD. Charlie gave the eulogy, "Never a finer soldier had ever been given the privilege of protecting the citizens of his city and country." Tears were flowing.

Too many coincidences, Lou thought, "And I don't believe in coincidences. I just hope I get there in time," he said out loud. He has a bad feeling and now he's convinced himself that the girls are in danger too.

It only makes sense, there is a pattern emerging in his mind. *First Greggy kills the family to take everything from the team members then he kills the team. Is Juan next in line?*

He hopes he's wrong, that this is a wild goose chase. In any event he knows what he has to do, and, as soon as he gets Jilani he is going to look those girls up. He'll be discreet; he doesn't want to ruin their fun. Best case scenario they will not even know he is looking after them; Nothing will happen.

No sooner than he got cruising he put on his Bluetooth and called Joe Capilano at the Nevada bureau of investigation, gaming division. Lou thought that he could use the help of an old friend. After a few courtesies, Joe was doing well, Joanne is as beautiful as ever, the kids were straight A students, they got down to business.

Joe and Lou have similar resumes, they both became cops after doing a stint in the Special Forces, Joe was a Force Recon Marine. His particular skills landed him an invitation to join Delta and work for the CIA. He is twelve years younger than Lou, but he racked up some very impressive creds during 'operation Iraqi Freedom'. Not long after Iraq fell he took a job with Blackwater Security, for the money, he made ten times his pay in Special Ops. After four years of that he had had enough and signed on with the Nevada SP in their anti-terrorist unit; for which he was immensely qualified.

That was eight years ago and now he oversees a special unit dedicated to all threats to the hotels and casinos throughout the state. A cake assignment to date, so when Lou called he was more than attentive. They talked for a while and Lou filled him in on the facts and his suspicions concerning Medvedev. Joe told Lou to ask for Sal Benedetto,

Head of security at the Tropicana, "he will set you up in a special suite," Joe was very helpful.

Lou made the four-and-a-half-hour trip from Flagstaff to Las Vegas in four hours. His new motorhome screamed down I-40 at 90 mph; not a cop in sight. When he pulled into the parking lot of Las Paloma's Apartments on boulder highway. Jilani was waiting for him at the clubhouse, but he was not alone. With him were two of his coworkers from the base, Nellis Air force Base. They were not in the Air force, technically speaking. They worked for the CIA drone program. Jilani was an analyst. The other two, Rebecca and Amanda, flew the drones that were so famous for taking out the Taliban in Afghanistan.

"Park that monster in the back next to the wall, nobody will bother it there, I told the security guard to take real good care of it," Jilani told Lou.

Lou filled them in on his suspicions and what he wanted them to do on their way to the Tropicana Hotel on the strip. He was thinking that they would just watch and observe from a distance; be there if anything happens. Jilani had a better idea for his two co-workers. These girls will work themselves into the sister's inner circle. As locals they knew where to go to have fun. What better way to conduct a close surveillance then to make friends and hang out with them.

"OK", Lou told the three, "Let's consider this a field operation. You game boys know what that is, don't you?" 'Game boys' is a reference to the fact that they sat at a console all day long flying their drones and targeting the enemy with their Hellfire missiles whenever they got the go-a-head. It wasn't real to them, not much more than a game of "Call of Duty" on their Xbox. The only difference is that they were seven thousand miles from their targets and lives were really lost whenever they pulled the trigger. Most of the time they were just gathering video that would be analyzed by Jilani's team.

Lou sent a text to Juan to let him know that he was delayed, again. He didn't tell Juan that he was in Vegas trying to save his little girls from the wrath of Grigori Medvedev's henchmen. Maybe he should, he thought, after all this is Juan's family we are talking about; but Lou thought he and his 'team' could handle anything that came along.

10

Las Vegas Nevada:

Joe Capilano was as good as his word; but Lou never doubted him. Lou walked up to the information desk at the Trop and asked for Sal Benedetto. A few minutes later Sal came out of the elevator and took Lou's hand. "I've been expecting you Mr. Bennett," Sal said, all business like. He got a brief synopsis from Joe but not the possible implications to the hotel. All he knew was that there could be a problem and he had to be in on it from the beginning, Lou had no problem with that.

"Very glad to meet you Sal, this is Jilani Anderson and these two pretty gals are Rebecca DiMartino and Amanda Parcelli." He got straight to business, "You have four Albuquerque sisters staying in your hotel that may or may not be in danger from the Russian syndicate." Lou filled Sal in on their plan to keep an eye on the girls without getting in the way of their fun. They were all professionals and would be discrete.

Sal took the four of them up the elevator to room 538, the fifth-floor suite that the hotel reserved for official agencies that might need to use it for whatever reason that might be deemed necessary. All Sal needed to know was the general reason for the surveillance and be filled in on the plan, every security issue at the Trop was his responsibility. Lou didn't have a problem filling Sal in on his concerns, minus some of the distant details.

Sal showed the team some of the amenities of the room. He gave them a temporary password that would allow them access to the short circuit cameras in most of the locations that the girls might be in, the hallways outside their room as well as the other floors in case they, "well, what happens in Vegas, you know."

The room was really for one purpose, to maintain a surveillance within most of the Tropicana property. There were four separate thirty-two inch monitors connected to a computer that would allow the user to scan multiple areas. Other than that, the room was like any other room in the hotel. It had twin beds and a small sitting area. There was also a mini refrigerator and a coffee pot, which looked like it was well used. The one thing that it did not have was the mini-bar that you would find in the other rooms; probably a good idea considering most of the guests were cops.

Sal had done his homework. The girls had checked in to a high dollar penthouse suite with two bedrooms a Jacuzzi on the balcony and a private entrance with limited access elevator service, a gift from their father, Lou presumed. The cameras would view the hallways, but the rooms were private. There were also camera shots around the hotel, and the pool, also the window view was of the pool. Because of hotel security they were not allowed the close in shots in the casino, only the general scans.

Lou thanked Sal wholeheartedly and sent him on his way. Sal left on the note that his staff will be available to intervene on Lou's behalf if needed. Lou noted to himself that the determination of what would be needed probably will be made before Lou knew it himself. Sal's staff would most assuredly be keeping tabs on the girls too, as well as on Lou and his 'team'.

When Sal got back to his office he summoned his supervisors to a special meeting. Sal Benedetto was no fool. He was a professional from the word go.

His formative years were with the NYPD, where he spent twenty-two years. He started, like most cops in New York, as a beat cop. He was a good cop, but when it came to the streets, he understood the reality. The neighborhood where he grew up, in the Bronx, was Italian right out of the Godfather movies. Every kid that grew up in the neighborhood had some kind of connection. Some of Sal's friends took to it like it was natural, some of them got out, Sal became a cop. After paying his dues on the streets, he got accepted to the SWAT (Special Weapons and Tactics) team where he received the best training and experience of any municipal PD in the world.

Sal's last six years with the NYPD was spent on a special detail assigned to the security for celebrities, dignitaries and even the President when he was in town. He was well known by many people in the federal agencies as well as his very close ties with the secret service, the agency with which he often worked in connection with not only the President of the United States, but also all the foreign Presidents and dignitaries coming to the United Nations. Sal Benedetto was top notch and good at his job.

First things first, Lou made a pot of coffee. Jilani fired up the computer and accessed the cameras on the penthouse floor outside the girl's suite, it was quiet. He gave the controls over to Amanda and Rebecca with the instructions to find the girls.

They were as good as it gets. Rebecca pinned a series of pictures with various portraits and profiles of each of the girls on a pegboard above the monitors for identification. When they were located they would print out and post some more up-to-date photos. The girls could be anywhere, and they might not be together. This would be like finding a terrorist dressed like every native in an Afghan village that looked like every other village; or, to put it another way, 'a needle in a haystack'.

Rebecca picked up the phone and called Sal. If anybody could give them a clue as to where to start, he could. "I was just about to call you," Sal said, "my crew anticipated that you might need to know this so they made some inquiries at the concierge and the front desk to see if the girls had made any queries or made any appointments. At ten they had room service bring up their breakfast." Sal paused for a moment, "About an hour later the concierge made reservations, for Gina, Christina and Esperanza to have a makeover, the 'Glo' special at the Spa at 2:00. The other one, Jessica, was not mentioned but the concierge overheard her saying she wasn't going to waste her day in a Spa, she went to the pool."

Rebecca listened for a few minutes and hung up. She turned to Amanda, "Get your stuff girl, we're going to the Spa." She Told Lou and Jilani what Sal had said. They all agreed that now would be a good time to get these girls introduced into the sister's weekend. Lou couldn't argue with the logic. Rebecca and Amanda would go to the Spa and the staff would put them on the same cycle as the girls. Sal arranged the whole thing, on the house.

The sisters were already there, it was 2:20 p.m. They would be put together when the girls were being detoxed in the steam room. Perfect for the conversation that would allow for bonding with new friends. The best thing is that they didn't have to get all gussied up. The whole purpose of going to the Spa was to do away with the old and create a brand-new look for the night. They would have plenty of time to build on this new relationship. In the end Rebecca and Amanda hoped to be close enough to invite the girls to the Marquee Club at the Cosmopolitan; the most exclusive club on the strip. Tickets compliments of Sal. "I think I'm in love with Sal," Rebecca said. They left the room giggling like a couple of school girls.

Lou turned to Jilani, "I think I'll go for a run. I want to check out the area around the hotel and I haven't run for a week or so." Then Lou changed into his running shorts, a tee shirt and his shoes. "I have my phone if you need me." Lou said as he left, "I should be back in an hour."

He took the elevator in the South Tower down to the pool level. Here he could have taken a direct exit that was used by security. It led out the back of the South tower to the rear parking lot. Instead he decided to walk through the pool area to see if he could see Jessica. She was nowhere to be found, at the pool anyway, she could be anywhere. When he got to the casino he hung a right U-turn and exited the east door onto Tropicana Boulevard.

He thought he would run up the street that accessed the back of the hotels, where there was less pedestrian traffic. Everybody tended to walk the strip, Las Vegas Boulevard. The MGM Grand Hotel was the first hotel he had to get around. It is a Huge complex of casino, Sports complex, Shops, and perhaps the most rooms of any hotel on the strip at about 2200 including a number of suites that tiered down the wings of the hotel taking up two floors each.

Lou had the pleasure of staying in one of those suites one night when he, Lynne, and Martin were driving home from San Francisco to Phoenix. They thought a one-nighter in Vegas would be fun. Lynne had booked them a $69 room special at the MGM. They arrived late and were told that the $69 rooms were gone but they would put them up for the night in one of their town house suites. What a spectacular room with three Jacuzzis, a kitchenette and two balconies overlooking the Strip. The concierge even arranged to have a roll-a-way bed brought up for Martin. They never left the room.

Lou made it around the MGM and jogged along the sidewalk under the monorail. He started out tight but as soon as he gained his rhythm he felt good. Running was a passion for him. He was able to release his frustrations and think about his options. Some of his best ideas came to him while running. A five-mile run was typical but many times he would lose count while running the whole morning.

This was not one of those runs, though. He had a mission to get to know his surroundings. He would run about two miles on this side of the strip. When he passed the Venetian, he would cross the strip and head back behind Caesar's Palace, Bellagio, and particularly the Metropolitan; where the Marquee Nightclub is located.

He needed to know what the area around the club was like in case something happened tonight when the girls would be there. As he rounded the corner behind Caesar's Palace he caught a glimpse of another runner. Probably not unusual except at three in the afternoon you might not see too many runners; it is usually a morning thing.

There was something familiar about this runner. Tall for a woman, maybe about 5ft-7inches, nicely proportioned with long braided hair that reached down the small of her back. "Soyala," he said to himself. "She looks like a young Soyala." She was definitely young, mid 20's. Lou felt like a pervert just noticing her but there was something so familiar about her.

She made a sharp left turn around a wall behind the Met so Lou picked up his pace to catch up to her for no good reason except his curiosity. She suddenly made a sharp left-hand turn into the parking garage of the Metropolitan Hotel.

As Lou made the turn around the concrete wall a palm came shooting up at his nose and he barely had enough time to block the blow. He acted on instinct more than anything as he grabbed her arm and swung her around with her arm behind her back. "Jessica, I thought all those years of Kempo Karate would have taught you to land that blow."

"Uncle Lou, What the hell are you doing following me, I could have hurt you," she said in both surprise and happiness to see her long-lost adopted Uncle.

"Yeah, like you almost got me kiddo," he hugged her then pushed her back with his arms and said, "Look at you, all grow'd up and still the fighter I use to train when you was just a sprout."

"What are you doing in Vegas, Uncle Lou, and on this weekend of all the times?" She surmised by the look on his face more than he would have wanted her to know. "That's what I thought, you are keeping an eye on us girls, aren't you?"

"I never could get anything past you Jessica. You're as sharp as a bowie knife." Just then he decided to tell Jessica what's going on. She was on to something anyway, or soon would be. In any event, of all the girls she was the one to get on the team. She was the smartest and most capable to take care of herself. "Let's get a cup of coffee."

11

The Dassault Falcon 900LX is, perhaps, the best private jet on the market, and that's why Grigori Medvedev owned it. After spending twenty of what should be his best years locked up in a secret American prison he promised himself that he would not settle for anything but the best. The fifty million price tag was well worth it for an aircraft that could get him anywhere in the world by tomorrow. After another ten million, he had the Falcon set up the way he wanted it.

The flight plan that his pilot registered at the Pulkovo airport, St. Petersburg, was for a quick flight to Prague; but, in this fast-changing Russian capitalist state it was no big deal to change the flight plan without notifying the authorities. "I love this Falcon 900," he said to Lyev, his pilot and body guard. "It can make this 6000-kilometer flight in eight hours non-stop. We'll be in Prague before they realized we diverted from our original plan."

The seatbelt light lit up as they made their final approach to an obscure landing strip near the Eastern Russian town of Khasan in the Primorski Maritime Krai. It would be a short chopper ride across the Tumen River to a small laboratory in a secure compound just on the southern end of the 'Railway Bridge of Freedom', Josan Ri, North Korea.

The chopper was a MD-500 Defender, an American made light combat helicopter that was acquired from the Hughes Aircraft Corporation in 1984. A shady third-party deal that circumvented the American ban on sales of military supplies to North Korea. The broker of that deal was a young KGB upstart named Grigori Medvedev, it was the deal that propelled 'The Bear', as he came to be known, to the top of his subversive profession. By the time he was captured in 'Operation Silent Night' he was the first one called when the enemies of America needed fire power.

The CIA first noticed him when he brokered the mobile labs necessary to produce mustard gas for Saddam Hussein's Iraqi defense ministry in 1987. The deal included the scientists and military advisors. Toward the end of the Iraqi war with Iran in 1988 the Iraqi army used the mustard gas on the Iranian army in the battle of Halabja. At the same time the Iranians returned the volley with the use of a blood gas, a cyanide-based gas. The subsequent condition of the thousands of Kurdish bodies that were caught in the middle of the battle indicated that many were killed by the cyanide-based agent, the Iranians. The Iranians happened to get the technology to produce their chemical weaponry from a brokered deal by 'The Bear'.

The short jaunt across the border took about fifteen minutes door to door. This isolated nation has the most secure borders of any nation in the world, yet the passage of this helicopter did not raise an eyebrow. As soon as the chopper landed, Colonel General Hyon Yong-Chol emerged from the building, one hand on his oversized cap and ducking under the spinning rotary blades of the machine, his other hand extended in a welcoming greeting to his good friend Grigori. His Russian was good.

"I have everything prepared for our project Grigori, all we need is the shipment and we will have your concentrate in two weeks' time."

Grigori and the Colonel General had a long history of dealings. He and Yong moved through the ranks of their prospective organizations with the successes of their secret partnership. Grigori for the KGB and now his own interests and the Colonel General within the ranks of the Peoples Armed Forces becoming its Minister in 2014, the highest rank he can achieve. Their first deal was for this very MD 500 helicopter that brought him across the border, and many others. They have been good friends as well as business associates ever since that deal in 1984. It was not beneath Yong to personally supervise this delicate project with his good friend; with the knowledge of the supreme leader, of course.

"That is good, my friend." Grigori put his hand on Yong's shoulder, "I have a gift for your glorious leader, a case of U'luvka Vodka; and a case for you, of course." He indicated to Yong's body guard to get the two cases from the helicopter while the two of them walked to the lab building. "This will be my greatest project ever. We will hurt our mutual enemy. It will take years for America to recover, and they will never trace the source. I have it all planned out." Grigori was in a good mood.

"Come, My longtime friend, I will show you the facilities, you will be impressed." Colonel General was likewise in good spirits.

12

Las Vegas, Nevada, 3:30 p.m. PST

Jilani was on the computer diligently researching everyone registered at the Tropicana for any connection to Mother Russia by name, location, specifically Russian concentrated neighborhoods in the US, or by any connection to the Russians by their business or diplomatic professions. To get the hotel info he was tapped into the hotel registry using a special password supplied to him by Sal. For the other searches, however, he used a special access on his secure agency lap top.

With access to all but the most classified CIA and FBI files. Identifying the Russians here and around the world, he could cross reference any of the names that might pop up on one search and determine the risk factor of the hit on the other data banks.

His research gave him five guests that were both of Russian connection and registered guests. Of course, the people he was looking for did not have to be staying at the Trop, but it was a good bet. They would want to have the access to the facilities that the girls would have, like the pool and the health center, that are for guests only.

He heard the buzz of the key slider activating on the door lock to the room followed by the click of the door handle, then the door opened. Jilani knew that Lou was due back about now but to his astonishment Jessica, the very girl that he had been searching for the past two hours walked in.

Lou followed her in but the look on Jilani's face was of bewilderment and wonder. Jilani had a range of mixed feelings when he saw Jessica enter the room. First, he was simply surprised to see one of the girls that he was supposed to be discretely protecting right in front of him, and in the room that served as the headquarters of their clandestine endeavors. This is highly unusual and contrary to all his training at the Farm, the CIA training camp.

That look must have really been apparent because when Lou followed her into the room he couldn't help saying "Jilani, you look like you've seen a ghost, that's unbecoming to your profession." Lou laughed all the while knowing what a surprise Jessica's appearance must be.

"Jilani? This is the little scrawny kid that I use to have a crush on when I was twelve?" Jessica said with a big smile. She walked up to him and gave him a big hug, noticing the pictures of her and her sisters pinned to the pegboard on the wall. "You have aged well, I think I could still have a crush on you, Jil," her pet name for him from ten years back.

Jilani was still stunned, though he was not going to let Lou, or Jessica, know that he always had a crush on her too. He was fifteen back then and he always looked forward to the periodic reunions with the 'Wolf Pack'. Jessica was the cutest girl he had ever seen. As his father got more disabled they stopped attending the reunions.

At his dad's funeral all the 'Pack' were there, as color guard and pall bearers but Jessica was not there, much to his disappointment. Now, here she is standing right in front of him, a grown woman. A grown beautiful woman. He couldn't help blurting out awkwardly "Jessica, you, ya, you're here?"

"Alright" Lou interjected "you two love birds can get reacquainted later, right now we have to revise our plan. Jessica is on board with us and we need to fill her in on all the concerns that we have for this weekend. She will be our access to getting Rebecca and Amanda inside the circle. I have a better feeling developing about this." Lou looked at Jilani, then at Jessica "You two need a minute? Maybe I should leave you alone for a bit…Naw, you'll have plenty of time to catch up later. We have work to do!"

Jilani flushed with color, but soon came to his senses. "Oh…well, I've been doing some research on the guests and have come up with some that might have a connection with the Russian mob," he was all business now, "Two of them are husband and wife, Mr. and Mrs. Kovalevsky, in town for their thirtieth anniversary. They are from a little village on the east shore of Lake Lagoda, near St. Petersburg; but they are in their fifties and don't exactly fit the profile. Still we should keep an eye on them anyway, because of their origins, near St. Pete. There is a young man, Peter Chaban, a twenty-three-year-old accountant from Albuquerque, highly suspic…"

"That's the boy I told you about, Uncle Lou," Jessica said, "he must have followed us here."

"Jessica and I stopped at the Starbucks at the Cosmo where I grilled her on what was happening in the girl's life," Lou explained, "of course, she thought I was just curious since it's been awhile. Anyway, she told me about this kid. He is Esperanza's boyfriend. They met about two months ago. Esperanza says she is in love. The timing is about right for our scenario, I think he is a plant. We need to find this kid, Jilani."

"I got-em, he is at the pool. He's reading a book." Jilani walked over to the window and pointed, "right there in the lounger next to the jacuzzi, there! With the flowered bathing suit on."

"That's him! what a geek, I don't know what Esperanza sees in him. He's been nice enough but a little weird. Now I know why, the little prick." Jessica had fire in her eyes.

Lou turned back to Jilani, "He looks harmless, perfect disguise, I guess. Tell me about the other two guests."

"Girls, in the same room, 1248 in the west tower. I don't think they look too suspicious. They look like lesbos to me. I think they are just here, not connected." Jilani was tapping on the keyboard, "They are from New York City, uh, Brighton Beach, probably just on vacation."

"We can't rule anybody out so let's keep an eye on all of them." Lou walked over to the coffee pot, poured a little into a Styrofoam cup, took a sip. His expression was instant and contorted. Still he swallowed, "That's terrible, who taught you how to make coffee, Jilani?"

"You made that coffee about three hours ago."

"Yeah, that's right."

At the Spa, Rebecca and Amanda were getting to know Gina and Christina. Esperanza remained aloof, she was thinking about Peter. They were all laying on their respective massage tables getting run over by the most misogynistic male missuses ever. Gina shouted, "Take it easy, are you trying to dig out my liver!"

"Pardon me ma'am, I…"

Ma'am! Did you call me Ma'am! I'm only 28 and I'm not married yet!" Gina was a bit testy.

"Pre-marital breakdown," said Amanda. "Take it easy on that poor girl, she is about to take the plunge and needs a little TLC."

"Yeah," said Christina, "Soon enough she'll be an old lady with ten kids keeping her busy 24/7. Don't rush her misery." everybody laughed, including Gina.

Shortly afterward, each in their own showers

they joked about getting a massage from the best-looking guys in Vegas.

"Gays, you mean," said Gina.

"No, do you think…no, they're not… What a waste." Esperanza grimaced.

After their showers they moved to the salon to get their mani-pedis. They were all in the same room so they could laugh and joke with each other as the pampering continued on their fingernails and toes.

"This feels wonderful, I haven't had my nails done in months," said Amanda. They got their hair cut and styled while their nails dried. By the time they were done with the air brushed makeup, Esperanza was into the moment and they all acted as if they knew each other all their lives.

Amanda suggested that she could get them into the Marquee that night and the girls should join them. "It's the best club on the strip. It has three pools and aquarium and like six bars and lit up dance floors. My friend Billy is the bouncer at the door. He will get us the tickets and let us get in ahead of the line, like the VIP'S!"

"No," Gina started.

"Gina! This is the most exclusive club in Vegas, the movie stars have trouble getting in there. It costs, like a hundred just to get in," Esperanza shouted. "This is why we are here, your last dash girl."

"Ok, okay!" Gina gave in, this is what we came here for, is it not! Let's meet at the penthouse at seven, this is going to be fun."

"Seven will be fine but the Marquee doesn't even open 'till Ten. We can get warmed up at your place then let's go to the Rio for the 8 p.m. show. That will really warm us up for the Marquee." Amanda failed to mention the show at the RIO was the Chippendales.

"Great, it's a date." said Christina. "We'll meet at the Tropicana Bar at Seven, I want one of those Wavy Margaritas, that'll warm me up!"

Jessica was shocked when Lou and Jilani got finished with the details of their reasons for being in Las Vegas. They didn't tell her about all the suspicious deaths that seem to be connected to one psychopath in Russia. She had to be filled in on the Russian connection, though, that was out already. But the true intentions of the Russians were not necessary for her to know.

She will be very helpful on the inside with Amanda and Rebecca, and Billy Butler, the bouncer at the Marquee. Jessica was a very levelheaded young lady, very mature for her age. In her conversation with Lou at the Starbucks that afternoon she confided to Lou that she had applied to the CIA and was doing an internship in Langley while waiting for her review.

Although Lou wasn't sure how he felt about that, he knew that she would be good at the job. Jessica always said that she wanted to be a spy when she grew up. That's why she took Karate and that was the direction in her college degree. She spoke fluent Russian, learning it from her father as well as in school. She also spoke fluent Spanish, her heritage language, and recently had been taking classes in Farsi, or Persian, the language of Iran. Her Latin complexion would enable her to fit into many of the cultures in Latin America as well as the Middle East and Eastern European countries.

She will be a good spy, Lou thought, but still he wished she had chosen a safer profession, like a dental hygienist. "Ok, it's almost five o'clock, Jessica you better get to your room and get yourself ready for the nightclub. You'll meet Rebecca and Amanda tonight. We'll tell them about you and you'll have to become fast friends. It's important that you don't let your sisters know what is going on."

"Got it, Uncle Lou. Don't worry about me, I'll be there if needed, otherwise I'm going to have some fun...with my eyes wide open."

"Good, Jilani, give her a transceiver and earpiece so we can communicate tonight; how's our boy at the pool?"

"He's up and moving, and he is on his cell phone, he could be talking to his handler."

13

"Come on Esperanza, what's the hold-up?" Gina looked back and saw Esperanza on her phone. "Oh, talking to Peeeter."

Esperanza flipped her hair to the side and hung up her phone. She had a big smile on her face. "You go ahead, I'll catch up in a bit."

Amanda and Rebeca had already left the girls and were on their way to control central. When they walked into the room Lou and Jilani were on the monitors. Jessica was about to leave. "Girls, we have Gina and Christina in the penthouse, but Esperanza isn't with them, What happened to Hope!?" Lou shouted.

"We left them all by the elevator. They were on their way up. We saw the VIP elevator open and thought..."

"I have her!" Jilani shouted. "You'll never guess where she is." The monitor that was following Peter Chaban showed Esperanza diving into the arms of her lover."

Jessica ran for the door, quickly commenting, "He's going to hurt her," as she disappeared through the door.

"He doesn't look like he wants to hurt her to me." Lou smirked. "Jilani, go with her. Make sure they are okay. Find out what's going on!" Lou shouted as Jilani also disappeared through the door.

"You two girls better do whatever you have to do to get ready for tonight." Lou didn't even notice that they both were ravishing beauties after a day at the Spa. All they had to do was put on their designer dresses that they 'borrowed' from Allsaints-Spitalfields, their favorite dress shop located at the

Cosmopolitan Hotel. They would return them tomorrow, unless they could charge them to some expense account.

Jessica got to the location on the monitor first; she was fast but Jilani was not far behind her. "They're not here, Jil, where are they?"

A voice came through Jilani's ear piece, "They went to the Tropicana Lounge, the booth in the corner, they want to be alone," Lou informed them.

"Jessica, they are at the bar, put your ear piece in your ear, we'll get to them." Jilani took her hand and led her in the direction of the bar.

"What are you doing here Peter?" Jessica said obviously annoyed that he would come to Vegas on this Girl's Weekend.

"I asked him to come. Jessica, don't tell Gina," Esperanza pleaded, "Who is that with you, you're no better than me." Esperanza tried to turn the table against Jessica.

"This is Jilani Anderson, you remember him, don't you? Maybe not, it's been ten years. He lives here and he is going to be at the Marquee tonight."

"Well then Peter can go too, if he is going. What's the difference?"

Jilani interrupted the argument between the two siblings. "Good to see you, Hope, you have certainly grown up to be a beautiful woman."

This comment eased the tension as Esperanza smiled. "Now I remember you, Jilani, you used to call me Hope, the English for Esperanza. Peter is the only other person to call me Hope, I like it."

"Yes, you liked it and of course Peter can come to the Marquee tonight, I'd like to get to know him a little," Jilani smiled. Jessica threw Jilani a fierce look.

"Keep your friends close, but your enemies

closer," Lou's voice came into her ear piece.

Jilani suggested that the girls go to the penthouse to get ready. They were to meet at the bar in an hour and Jessica didn't spend the day getting dolled up. She would need to get ready. He turned to Peter. He was actually a good-looking boy, or man, about Jilani's size and build. It was the glasses that made him look like a geek. "Do you have a suit, Peter, the Marquee has a strict dress code."

"No, I don't own one."

"No worries, I have one that will fit you. We'll need to go to my place. I have to get changed too, come on." Jilani didn't plan to go to the Marquee tonight but it seems that he is going now. Lou will have to work the stakeout. Maybe he can get some help from Sal, or Paul, he will call Paul Wells, He can send some people.

A half hour later Jessica came out of the bathroom looking as beautiful as anybody. She kind of looks like… J-Lo. She will turn some heads tonight. Gina took one look at her and couldn't help it, "We spend the whole day at the Spa getting all primped and primed so we can look beautiful tonight and you look better than any of us in thirty minutes in the bathroom…It's just not fair Jessica." Every one of them broke out in a hysterical laugh. "Let's go have some fun!" They left ready for La Vegas.

When they got to the Tropicana Bar Amanda and Rebecca were already there. Christina walked up to the bar and ordered a margarita for herself and one for everyone else. That was six at thirty dollars each, she charged them to the room. And gave Phil, the bartender a twenty for a tip. Then she led the girls to the front door where there was a stretch limo waiting to take them across the interstate to the RIO.

When they got there and stepped out of the limo,

Christina pointed to the giant sign on the side of the building. "Chippendales! Girls, that's the show tonight?"

"WooHoo" came the reply from the other girls in unison. "We'll be partying tonight!" Said Rebecca.

14

Albuquerque, NM

Something was wrong, thought Juan Vega. One-minute Lou Bennett was on his way to Albuquerque for the third time and the next minute, for the third time, he canceled just like that. This time, however, Lou left a text on his phone saying he would be delayed but didn't answer the reply and did not answer the call either. Shit was happening these days that was too strange to take anything lightly.

So, with no one to temper his concerns, his survival instinct kicked in, his thoughts were of his four daughters in Las Vegas. Normally they were old enough and have good enough sense that a trip to sin city doesn't concern him; but, with everything that's happened over the last few months he now has reason to worry. Is there really a pattern to the madness? Will he be the next target of a madman? He's about the only one left.

He has a plan developing. He's going to personally insure that his girls have a great time in Vegas and that their weekend is not molested for any reason, including the worst. He wanted Lou there, but understood that Lou probably has some other business that had to be taken care of. Their friendship worked that way, no judgement, no limits.

Flight 454, from Albuquerque to Las Vegas, glided on to runway 3 north into the wind. The roar of the engines as they reversed forced the passengers into their seatbelts. "Ladies and gentlemen, this is Captain Ballard. Welcome to McCarran International Airport and Las Vegas, the most entertaining city in the world. As we taxi to our gate please remain in your seat until your flight crew gives the go-a-head. We will disembark the plane from the front to the back. Please be patient, wait your turn, there will still be plenty of money for you to win in Las Vegas. Thank you for flying United."

Juan's seat was just in front of the wing so he had to wait a bit for his turn to disembark the plane. He only had a carryon, so he did not have to mess with the baggage claim. Once he was off the plane he would catch a cab and get over to the Tropicana.

He could see the Trop as they landed, it is the closest hotel to the airport, but the cab ride still took about fifteen minutes to get there. The girls were not answering their phones, none of them!

This only added to his paranoia. What if he could not find them? It was already 7 p.m. They could be anywhere, and this is a big city. He'll start at the Trop. All he knew is that he had to do something. He wanted to talk the girls out of the trip but they had planned it for so long; he didn't want to disappoint them. He was in denial. He knew that there was a risk that his family could be in danger. "What an idiot!"

When he got to the hotel he had to wait in line at the check-in for a few minutes. He was very impatient, but the line surprisingly moved fast. When he asked if he could get into the pent house the clerk said that hotel policy forbid her to give him access. It didn't matter that he was the one that paid for the suite. A man came out of the office door and introduced himself as Sal Benedetto, head of security.

"Is something wrong," Juan said with a hint of exasperation.

"No, we just take the privacy of our guests very

seriously."

"That's all fine and dandy," Juan rebuffed "but these are my daughters and I paid for the room and I want to see them!"

"Okay, Mr. Vega," Sal said very calmly, "come with me, I'll take you there." They got on the south tower elevator and got off on the fifth floor.

"I know the penthouse is not on the fifth floor, what's going on here."

"Just a quick stop, there is someone you should meet."

Sal knocked on a door, a second later Lou opened it, a smile busted out on his face. "What the hell. Juan, have you come to visit me?" Sal left the two of them staring at each other for a while.

"What's going on Lou? I thought you…"

"Juan, I didn't want to worry you." He led Juan into the room. "This is 'command central." Lou explained the whole setup to Juan. "I don't really have any proof that something is going on here, Doc, just a hunch. There are too many coincidences to be a coincidence, you know what I mean? Anyway, we are…"

"We! Who else is in on this!"

"Jilani and some of his co-workers and…"

"The CIA!" Juan smirked. "You have the CIA doing a steak-out on my daughter's weekend in Vegas?"

"Well, yeah, I guess that just about covers the whole thing," Lou said with a little humor in his tone. "I would rath…"

"Okay! I get it," Juan cut him off, "I was thinking along that line too. These girls are all I've got in the world and if there is even a possibility of danger I'm in."

"Good," Lou got serious now. "Come over here.

This room has special surveillance capabilities." Lou went over the amenities of 'Command Central' and the plan for the Marquee that night and how tight the security around the girls is going to be without their even knowing that they are being watched over. "I'm sure that all this is for naught, it's going to be a great weekend for the girls, a weekend that they will never forget."

Lou didn't mention that Jessica was in on the plans, he didn't need to know everything. Juan Vega was the consummate professional but when it came to his daughters everything else was tossed out the window. Now that he was here Lou had to tread lightly when Juan was in the room.

"Who are they?" Juan asked, looking at the monitor screen that showed the hallway outside the penthouse. Lou turned and looked.

"The maid and, looks like room service." Lou said as he studied the monitor. "Only there is nobody in the suite that would call for room service." They looked as the maid opened the room, and, with the man from room service entered the room, leaving their carts outside. The maid carried a black case into the room.

"They are not with the hotel! Come on!" and they both bolted out of the room and headed to the elevators. The fifth floor was the only other floor that the penthouse elevators stopped at but you needed a special key to get it to stop there. That was because of this very situation, the agencies that might be using room 538 might need to use that special elevator. Lou had the key card. No sooner had the elevator door close when Lou's phone buzzed, "That's Sal, I put that ringer on his number. Sal…"

Sal was aware that they accessed the penthouse elevator but didn't see the maid and room service enter the penthouse. His people had 473 cameras within the hotel complex to monitor every part of the hotel. In his security center there was a whole wall dedicated to thirty monitors that scanned the various regional camera settings. Also, at the control panel his crew could view any area of the hotel that they wanted.

There should have been no activity on the penthouse floor since all the guests were currently out of their rooms. Not that the security routinely spied on their guests but considering the circumstances they would have a monitor fixed on that floor if the girls were in the room. Since the girls were all out they switched the monitor to a camera at the craps tables where a young lady was making large, risky bets; and it was paying off at the moment.

Lou hung up and told Juan that Sal would meet them at the penthouse. If Sal didn't call Lou, Lou was just about to call him. Lou didn't have a key to the room and they might be legitimate employees of the hotel. It was only right to call Sal with his suspicions, though he was sure they were up to no good.

When the elevator door opened at the penthouse floor Lou was surprised to see that both carts were gone, along with the employees that brought them. Not long after they got there another elevator door opened at the far end of the corridor, Sal got out with two of his security personnel. "Where are they?" Sal asked excitedly. "You came up that elevator and I came up this one, there are only these two elevators, and the emergency stair well."

One of the two guards that came up with Sal rushed over to the stair well, pulled out his Glock and slowly opened the door. There was no sign that they had left that way. Besides the carts would be too troublesome to get down the stairs. They would be inside the corridor but likely left at the top of the stairs; no sign of them, Carl, the guard, reported.

Sal pulled out his master key card and swiped the reader on the door. The green light lit up with a click and they all entered the room, guns at the ready, those that had guns. No carts in the suite either. They started searching the room for the black bag that the maid carried into the room. It was next to the couch. Doug, the other guard, was an explosives expert. He slowly and carefully took stock of the bag as it lay on the floor.

They moved the couch and Doug made his assessment. "It could be a bomb, or a listening device. We'll have to get the equipment up here so I can secure the package before I can open it up." Sal called the office.

While they waited for the bomb gear, Sal suggested they figure out where the couple went to and who they were. "Oh, I know who they are,' Lou said. "They are a Russian husband and wife. A Mr. and Mrs. Alexi Kovalevsky, guests of your hotel. Can we look in the other penthouses suites to see if they hid in one of them? There are six penthouse suites on this tower. Sal started with the closest one.

"This one is currently unoccupied." He said as he swiped the key card. When he opened the door, it was apparent that no one had been in the room. "Carl, you look in the other rooms and on the balcony. If you see anything suspicious, I mean anything, call me. We'll go on to the next suite."

They opened the next door, another unoccupied room, "Bingo!" the two carts were in the living room of the suite. Sal checked the other rooms, pistol at the ready. The rooms were vacant.

"They must have slipped out when we were in the girl's suite looking for the bag. Now they know we are on to them."

Sal picked up the room phone and dialed a four-digit number. He told the person on the other end to check the tape of the camera at the PH elevators for a middle-aged couple going in or out within the last hour. Check the registration for a Mr. and Mrs. Kovalevsky and get someone up to their room pronto. They are still in the hotel, find them. And consider them armed and dangerous."

Yuri and Anna Anatoli, AKA Alexi and Nadiya Kovalevsky have been married for thirty years, as they stated when they registered into the hotel. "What a wonderful Anniversary we will have in Las Vegas," Alexi, Yuri, told Margarete as she handed the couple their room keys. His English had a heavy Russian accent.

They met in Moscow at 'Spy' school in 1987 and were immediately attracted to each other. Anna Uvarova was a smart student who could blend into the background and was a good actor. She believed in the Soviet world view and felt that it was her purpose on earth to further the interests of Mother Russia. It was that seriousness encased in an outward appearance of innocence that attracted Yuri to her.

They had an immediate connection which bloomed into one of the most competent, and deadly, assets in the post-Soviet Russian Federation's clandestine network. Over the years they played a part in the take down of Boris Yeltsin. Anna, a very pretty young Russian caught the eye of Boris Yeltsin and worked her way into the Russian leader's bedroom. When the affair was discovered, part of the plan of rival Vladimir Putin, the Russian President was forced to resign in disgrace.

That historic event essentially ended the

potential of Russia's entering the world as a Democratic Republic. Consequently, under the leadership of Vladimir Putin, the Russian Federation has become an image of the former Soviet Union with intentions of re-establishing its former territories and regaining its status as a superpower in the world.

A good spy can truly affect the destiny of a nation. Over the years the team of Yuri and Anna had their hand in many quiet secret missions but their most notable was their role in the poisoning of Alexander Litvinenko in London, 2006. The couple had spiked the sushi in his meal, at a posh restaurant that he frequented in London, with polonium-210; a tasteless, odorless and deadly poison that killed the Ex KGB spy turned MI6 British informant and double agent.

The murder created quite a controversy around the free world. Imagine the implications of the ease with which this modus operandi could be used to assassinate world leaders and, has it been used previously? The murder was charged to Andrei Lugovoi, who vehemently denies involvement. Of course, he was innocent, Anna and Yuri handled that job.

Yuri and Anna did not go back to their room in the hotel. They knew they were discovered and their concern, now, was to escape without a trace. Like any good operative they had plan A, B, and C, if needed. They entered the Service elevator and took it down to the pool floor where they exited the hotel through the security exit that Lou had passed up that afternoon. Once outside they simply disappeared.

Lou and Juan let Sal handle the details of tracking down the Russian spies. They went back to the girl's penthouse suite and searched the room with a fine-toothed comb. The bomb technicians had determined that the black bag did not contain a bomb.

When Lou inquired of the contents, detective Jack Smith of the LVPD pulled out a small black 'Teddy Bear'. "What the heck is that, what does that mean?" Juan said.

"I don't know, some kind of message I assume," the detective said. He had bio-gloves on and put it back into the bag. "We'll take this Teddy back to the lab and check it over really good," almost laughing. The detective put the black bag containing the Teddy Bear into an evidence bag. Then he picked up an apple from the fruit basket that had been placed on the table by the hotel staff. Something that every VIP guest found in their room when they checked in.

"I wouldn't eat that," too late, "before you have that checked out too!" Lou almost shouted to the detective.

Detective Rick put the rest of the apple back in the basket and spit out the bite he took onto the plate too. "Yeah, right," then he put the entire basket into another evidence bag. He also put the complimentary box of chocolates into another bag, marked them as evidence and walked out of the room.

"What is this!" Juan said puzzled, "and who's is this!" he added as he came out of one of the bed rooms carrying a slinky black, almost nothing. "Why would any of my daughters need something like this on a 'girl's weekend'!

"A girl's weekend in Vegas" Lou added, "I don't know, What'ja think."

15

When you're among the young 'in' crowd in a city like Las Vegas, Nevada, one must be very versatile. This desert wonderland avails the outdoorsman in you and the glamour of the entertainment capital of the world feeds the sophisticated side. Jilani is in that crowd. He drives a souped-up F250 4x4 yet dresses very comfortably in a black Armani tux. He is both handsome and rugged, sensitive and confident. Vegas was his for the taking, and he took all that it would give him. He was on the phone with Paul Wells when Peter came out of the bedroom looking like he had just wrapped up his latest movie. Peter was amazingly handsome when he cleaned up.

"You look good, Pete. That's one of my best tuxedos. Hope is gonna get a look at a whole different side of you tonight." Jilani reached for the glasses and took them off Peter's face, "These will have to go though. Can you see without them?

"Yeah, I can see pretty good, let's get going." Peter put his glasses on and said, "I'll take them off when we get there."

Jilani needed to see Lou before the night started cranking up but he didn't want to let Peter know what was going on. There was still a chance that Peter was not what he appeared to be. They were waiting for the profiles of Peter and the other four Russian guests at the hotel. The Kovalevsky's had tipped their hand already but that doesn't mean that the others are in the clear. When they got to the hotel Jilani told Pete to go to his room and get whatever he needed, money or a nap or whatever, and he will meet him at the Tropicana lounge at nine, about an hour from now.

Jilani went to command central. He entered room 538 to find Lou and Juan looking at a dispatch from the FBI. It was the profile on the Russian girls.

"They are not lesbians but twin sisters. That explains their closeness," Lou said and read on. Their father is a diplomat at the UN. A, Vladimir Roskinov. He is the Russian consultant on international commerce and trade. The girls are on holiday from their studies at NYU, where they are majoring in international relations. They must want to be diplomats like their father. Doesn't seem like the assassin types, no record, honor students, quite exemplary."

"Do we know what they are planning for the weekend?" Jilani questioned. Maybe I'll call Sal and see if he knows anything. He picked up the phone and asked the operator for Security.

There was a ding indicating a notification of an email, It was from an Interpol search. Lou clicked on the new email, "The FBI didn't have anything on the Kovalevsky's, so I expanded the search to Interpol. They ran a face ident program on the pic's I sent them. Their real names are Yuri and Anna Anatoli." Lou read on, "These are some bad hombres. Suspected in a whole array of badness from blackmail to assassination, their specialty. When the Soviet collapsed they went private, while still maintaining their connections in the FSB." The Russian Federations version of the KGB.

He looked at the report, which was a summary really but enough to raise some flags. "Holy shit," he said. "One of their MO's seems to be poisoning food. We'd better give the LVPD a heads-up so they can go over that fruit basket for poison." He picked up his cell and dialed the number on the card that detective Smith had given him.

"I'm Sorry, Mr. Bennett, but Detective Smith has gone home sick for the day." (silence). After some further inquiry it was suggested that Smith may have been poisoned and that an emergency team should be sent to his house, to ensure that he would be okay. Also, they needed to expedite the testing of the fruit basket, "and the box of chocolates," Lou insisted.

"Uh-Oh," came the reply over the phone. "We didn't think there was anything wrong with the chocolates, being still in the plastic wrapper and all," she said.

"I'll bet my life that there will be a shortage of police protection this evening." Juan said. "This could be a long night. I'm going to get my girls out of here, it's not safe for them here."

"Now, you don't have to jump the gun, Uncle John." Jilani put his hand on Juan's shoulder. "We have the best people in the agency with those girls tonight. Nobody is getting anything past them; and, your good friend Paul Wells is sending us five more agents to fill in the background of our security. The girls won't know it but the only people to get within five feet of your princesses will be on our side."

"Thanks, but no thanks for the assurance. I don't think that this is going in a positive direction. We need to pull the plug on this scenario before all the shit hits the fan and my girls take the hit."

Lou listened as Jilani and Juan spared over the pros and cons of the likelihood that the girls were safe or not! When he heard enough he broke in, "Doc! you are right. We need to find those girls and get 'em out! There is too much at risk here. If the Anatoli's can get in the penthouse without Sal knowing and poison the whole PD then we are in trouble. I know it is important to get these bastards but not when it comes to the risk to my girls. Yes! I am as close to your daughters, Doc, as anybody aside from you. They are part of my family!"

Jilani had to concede to that argument. The truth be known they were his family too. The men of the Wolf Pack were closer to each other than any natural family can be and for some very good reasons, they all saved the lives of each other every time they stepped into a mission. They were brothers as sure as anything. A 'Band of Brothers' as the saying goes. "I'll call Pete and we'll go get the girls."

"Pete," Juan said. "That little Russian bastard that Esperanza has been sneaking to see behind my back?"

"That would be Pete." Jilani said, "But I spent a little time with him earlier, I think he is okay."

"Good, you get Peter and we'll meet you at your pickup," Lou cut in. They all left the room. Then there was that ding, another e-mail.

It was 9:00 and Peter was supposed to meet Jilani at the Trop Lounge, he wasn't there. Jilani was just about to dial Peter's number when his cell rang. It was Amanda, "Jil, Esperanza is missing." There was now no time to wait for Peter. He left the bar and headed for his pickup truck. If Peter showed up, oh well, right now there was a more important matter to attend to.

They all left in Jilani's f-250 heading for the Cosmopolitan and the Marquee. Amanda said they were supposed to meet there at nine and that Esperanza did not show; no matter that they should never have let Esperanza out of their site. She could be in real danger.

"I think she went to meet Peter, she has been acting kinda funny today. I think they are up to something." Amanda said. "Peter is okay, isn't he? He seemed like a good kid, a Marine I think."

"Hope and Peter are together I figure. We'd better get over to the Marquee. They'll show up there soon enough," Lou said. Nobody said what they all thought; that Peter may be the secret weapon of the psychopath Medvedev. Lou now felt that the table has turned, once again, against them but that was how he worked best. *Prepare for the worst, but hope for the best, Benjamin Disraeli*, Lou thought.

"They will go to the Marquee, get the girls out of there then find Hope and get back to Albuquerque." That will prove to be easier said than done. Lou and Juan had no idea what to expect at the Marquee. When they entered the lobby of the Cosmopolitan Hotel they followed the signs that led to the special escalators for the Marquee.

"There must be something big going on," Lou noticed out loud as they walked past a long line of nicely dressed kids.

"That's the line to get into the Marquee," Jilani said. The line stretched forever and ended at the base of the Marquee escalator.

"Did you notice that the Roskinov sisters are waiting in the line about two thirds back? They won't be getting in until midnight. You get to a point when someone has to leave before you can get in, fire regulations." They walked right up to the VIP bouncer. "Hi Billy, are they in there yet?"

"Yeah, they went up about fifteen minutes ago…Who these guys?"

"Billy Butler," Jilani put his hand on Lou's shoulder, "Lou Bennett and this here's Juan Vega the girl's father."

"Go on up."

"Billy", Jilani pulled the arm of the big bouncer so that he leaned into him to hear, "there are two Russian girls, name Roskinov, blonds, one in a slinky red dress and the other in a black dress. As hot as they get. Find an excuse not to let them in.

"Gotya Boss."

The opulent décor of the Marquee has something for everybody. The cover charge insures the guests are of a unique class of people; not necessarily rich, but definitely seeking a good time and willing to spend whatever it takes to make that happen. The first thing you will notice at the top of the escalator is the size of the place. There is an outside patio, facing Las Vegas Boulevard, taking up the whole front of the third floor of the Cosmopolitan Hotel. The 'Day Club' is in this area with its pools and never-ending Las Vegas sunshine. A well-known band plays their hits while bikini clad models roam the decks; well everybody looked like they are models anyway.

This is the place to be if you're not in the casino, heck it will cost you just as much. When the Night falls upon the city another world emerges with an energy that could power a starship. As the lights of Las Vegas power up this city becomes the center of the universe, and the Marquee Night Club becomes the center of Las Vegas nightlife. Everybody who is anybody gathers here and all the wannabees come to party with them.

The first and largest part of the club is the main dance floor, a huge multi-dimensional room of hard wood and leather seating. Differently lighted areas set the mood for the partiers. The mere size of the place is mind boggling. While the club doesn't open until ten o'clock, the VIP's are let in at nine. That way they can get the best seating. The more famous guests prefer seating that will give them some air of anonymity.

As the guests arrived they are presented with

a sense of attainment, VIP treatment. The bar is near impossible to get to, so every seating arrangement has its own tables with ice buckets for bottle service, and a drink list that doesn't show the price; no sense scaring anybody away.

"Where do we start?" Juan said, with a shrug of his shoulders.

Jilani looked at Juan. "Well, we should check out this room but I have to tell you that this room is not all there is."

"First thing first," Lou broke in, "we better introduce our selves to the security staff. They're waiting for us. Oh, and put in your com units, let's see if they work up here with all the electronics." They didn't.

At the top of the escalators to the right, a hall way led to the security office. There, they met Roger Stelmach, head of security for the Marquee. Roger had been expecting Lou, a heads-up from Sal. He showed them the security systems. It would be very hard to get something past this team. There were metal detectors hidden in the doorway before the escalator. If tripped, the person was quietly taken aside and questioned. If someone had a weapon, or potential weapon, they were not allowed to enter, bye-bye, rules were not meant to be broken.

Roger didn't fool around. He hired professionals from the base, Special Ops who were on their home rotation and some from the 'agency', like Billy. Jilani gave Roger an overview of his security. There's Lou, Juan, himself, Rebecca and Amanda who Roger knew; and then there were four undercover agents, sent by Paul Wells, just be there. They were fully briefed on the circumstances of the 'mission'; though Jilani didn't tell Lou, or Juan for that matter, that they were just off the farm and this was as much a training mission as anything else. No sense wasting an opportunity to get some field experience. There is another agent manning command central, but that should be pretty quiet considering all the action should be at the Marquee. Of course, there is the usual staff of the Marquee all of whom were aware of the situation; but it would be expected that they would have their hands full just doing their regular job.

When you have three hundred partying youths there are bound to be incidents. It is a very impressive system. When Roger was finished with his tour, Juan had changed his mind about getting the girl's out. "It certainly looks safe to me, I don't want to ruin their fun, I'd never live it down."

It didn't take too long to locate the girls on the monitors. They were camped out in a booth next to the dance floor. What a sight, five very attractive women laughing and definitely in the partying mood. The DJ was playing "Can't Feel My Face" and the men in the security office watched as all the girls leaped onto the dance floor and began to gyrate. Obviously they had a few drinks in them already. They looked at the other guests that were near them. Two couples in a booth not too far from them watched the girls, nothing suspicious about that, they probably needed to have a few drinks before they could loosen up. Jilani knew, though, that they were on duty. It was almost ten, soon the place would be a madhouse. The flood gates were about to be opened.

"OK," said Juan, "now we better concentrate on finding Hope and Peter."

Jilani pulled out his phone and tapped on an app. A map appeared with an arrow on it. "Peter is on Las Vegas Boulevard about four blocks from here. I put a tracker in the tux I lent him." Then he tapped on another app and "Yep, Hope is with him. This app is called phone locator. I got her password from Jessica this afternoon."

Juan was very interested in this technology. "Fix my phone so I can track Esperanza, can ya?" When that was done he abruptly excused himself and went off to find Hope and Peter, leaving his other girls in good hands. Lou went with him also confident that the other three girls were well cared for.

16

"I DO!" said an elated Esperanza.

"I now pronounce you husband and wife, Peter, you may kiss the bride." The paid witnesses threw confetti on them as they left the little white chapel. When Peter showed up to meet Hope in a tux, she thought that he was so handsome that she suggested that they get married right then. "Daddy will get over it sooner or later. Once he gets to know you he will love you like I do," she said.

"I hope not like you love me," he said blushing. They left the chapel and headed toward the Cosmopolitan. They had taken a taxi to the chapel but decided to walk the strip to get back to the Cosmo.

Esperanza looked at the ring on her finger, she turned abruptly toward Peter, lifted onto her toes and kissed him. "I can't believe we did it. I'm so happy. Mrs. Peter Chaban." She hugged Peter and kissed him again. She was really beautiful in the aura of the Las Vegas Lights. Not like her sisters who favored their father's Mexican looks, Esperanza was the spitting image of her mother; Red hair, freckles and very light completion, she looked as Irish as someone just off the plane from Dublin. She swung around again with a big smile on her face, her arms swinging, "Peter let's take our time getting back. I want to savor this moment with you. Look there's one of those photo booths let's take a picture." They danced over to the photo booth. Hope sat on the bench while Peter put money in the receiver then sat down beside her and pulled the curtain.

Juan was looking at his phone as they got out of the cab at the corner of Flamingo and Las Vegas Boulevard. "This way," he said turning left. Jilani told him that the arrow is the approximate location but it could be off by as much as a city block. They walked down the crowded streets. Every two feet, it seemed, someone tried to hand them a card showing them where to go to see naked girls.

They ignored everyone. They were on a mission and were not about to be side tracked. Lou and Juan looked into every nook and cranny. They were in the general area but the streets were busy and there were little booths selling knockoff merchandise in every possible free space. They walked past a booth selling Coach Bags for 75% off the regular price. A photo booth emitted flashes of light through the cracks in the curtain as someone, or couple, was having their pictures taken. Lou was about to pull on the curtain.

"There!" Juan caught sight of a red head disappearing into the door way of a casino. He said to Lou, "Come on!" as he ran toward the casino door. When they got into the casino there was no sign of Hope and Peter. Their com units seemed to be working so they split up to expand the search. They were close. Esperanza must be within thirty yards or so.

Peter slid the curtain aside and they stepped out of the booth to wait as their photos were being printed. "You look so beautiful, I just want to take you back to my room and ravish you," Peter said as he pulled her to him and kissed her on the nap of her neck, growling like a bear, sending goose bumps down her arms. She pulled away playfully and then put her lips on his in a long sensuous kiss. The bell rang as the four photos slid out of the slot of the photo booth. They looked at the photos laughing at the crazy looks that they made at each other.

There was a Taxi pulled over at the curb letting

out some inebriated partyers so Peter grabbed Hope's arm and they ran to catch the cab before it pulled away. "The Tropicana Hotel," they said in unison.

"I got her!" Juan's voice came into Lou's ear through the com unit. Juan reached out and pulled on the arm of the red head, spinning her around.

"Hey!" Said the girl, who looked very much like Esperanza from the back but now, face to face, looked nothing like her.

Juan didn't say a word to her as he turned away and headed back to the door. "Not her!" he yelled into the com. "Where is she?" They headed back toward the street.

The Trop was only a couple of miles away, but Las Vegas Boulevard was crowded with people and traffic that moved slower than the people walking. As soon as he could the cab driver took a left turn through the Harrah's entrance and out the back on to Koval Ln behind the casinos. From there they could bee line straight to the Trop.

Peter couldn't keep his hands off Hope as they kissed. "Wait, I'd better text Jessica to let her know that I am okay," she said as she pulled away from Peter and took her cell phone out of her purse. Peter took the phone out of her hand and tossed it on the seat. "Hey!" Hope protested then sunk into his embrace. When the taxi pulled into the Tropicana Peter tossed the driver a twenty and they leaped out of the cab and ran into the Hotel.

They ran up the stairs, Peter pulling Hope by her hand as she giggled trying to keep up. "Slowdown!" she pulled clear and stopped next to a Flintstone penny slot machine. As Peter looked at her curiously, she took a dollar out of her purse and put it into the machine and hit the max bet button.

"That penny machine takes $2.40 for a max bet my young wife," Peter reached over and put two more dollars in the receiver then said, "Now hit that button." She did and the wheels spun rapidly. Peter yelled "A WINNER!" Taking her hand once again, he led her, willingly through the casino.

"Wait, maybe we won!"

"We'll win when we get to the room," Peter said as they ran across the causeway over the pool to the elevators. In the elevator he pushed the button for the 8th floor. room 861 was not a suite, just an ordinary room, but Hope didn't notice as Peter picked her up and wisped her across the threshold to the bed.

When Juan and Lou came out of the casino they were at a loss. "Esperanza should be in here."

They walked back in the direction they came. As they walked past the photo booth Lou turned his head in time to see a hand emerge from the darkness and pull the curtain back. Then a middle-aged couple came out smiling like a couple of teenagers. Lou thought that you'd have to be middle aged to use one of those booths, everybody uses their phone to take selfies these days.

"Check your phone, Doc, maybe they are on the move," Juan booted up the iPhone locator app. "Shit, they are in Henderson, What the hell, are they doing in Henderson?"

Lou ran over to a taxi, put his hand on the door handle as he turned to Juan. "Doc, let's go!" They told the driver to head to Henderson, "FAST!" Lou handed the driver a twenty. "Can you tell what street they are on, Doc?" That was the beginning of their wild goose chase.

"They stopped on the Boulder Highway near... No, now they are moving again, what the...?" The teardrop on the app moved down the Boulder

Highway toward Las Vegas. "Driver, can you cut them off?" The cab turned north to intersect the Boulder Highway. "We'll get them just about at Flamingo. They must be in a cab. I wonder If she dropped her phone in the cab?" Juan said.

Lou pulled his phone out of his jacket pocket and dialed Jilani. The phone rang several times then went to voice mail. Lou didn't waste time leaving a message. He hit the redial. The phone rang again and after four or five rings it was picked up. "Lou, all is quiet here the gir" he was cut off.

"Good, Jilani I need you to check the tracker in Peter's suit, I need to know where he is right now."

Jilani told Lou to give him a minute. He took out his cell and checked his tracker app. It didn't take long since he had it running continuous. "According to the tracker they are at the Tropicana."

"Thanks… Driver take us to the Tropicana!"

The Marquee was starting to rumble. It was past ten and the general public was in and the tempo was kicking up. Amanda, Gina, and Christina were at the main Dance floor camped out in a booth that will accommodate all eight of the group. That group included Jilani who hasn't made an appearance yet. Jessica and Rebecca were at the Library.

The Library is the more laid back of the four distinct venues in the Marquee. It looked like it could be the plush library in the Wrigley mansion with its plush leather sofas and lounges. There's a regulation size pool table on one end of the moderate sized room and a six-foot gas fireplace on the other.

This is where you come to develop a relationship and need the quiet that is absent everywhere else. This is also where two very hot girls will come to play pool with a bunch of macho types who thought they could get lucky. They will not get lucky tonight with these girls, not at nine ball, not at love. Jessica could handle a stick. After a while the guys quit 'letting the hottie win' and got serious about the game.

Jessica took no prisoners. The drinks were lining up as fast as the guys thinned out. Finally, the contest was down to one daring contender. A young, very good-looking Adonis with close cut wavy blond hair and a slight accent that Rebecca took for eastern European or maybe Russian; she was on the alert.

"Maybe we can play partners, is your friend as good as you?" He said as he put his marker on the table.

"I don't know. Amanda, are you ready for a game of partners?"

"Hell yeah! Where is your partner good looking?"

The Adonis smiled, almost melting both the girls in their shoes. He called to his friend at the bar, "Nikolai, come-on lets beat up these girls at their own game." That is when the unbelievable happened. A man, older than the first, who was so good looking that both of the girls could feel all their blood flush into their feet, turned and started toward the trio.

All the girls could see is a man that could be Brad Pitt's good looking brother coming toward them in slow motion, like Indiana Jones making his appearance in the opening scene of his latest movie. He wore a cream-colored silk shirt, long sleeved, untucked over a pair of dark brown Dockers. His rugged looks gave him the appeal of the quintessential 'most interesting man in the world'.

Jessica Slapped Amanda on the arm and said "Ok girl, don't let the wrapper spoil the prize. Let's beat these boys."

"What do we play for, ladies, to make this

126

game more interesting? Nikolai said, smiling widely. "That is if you ladies think you can beat us."

Lou called Sal during the short ride to the Trop. Jilani texted him that they were probably going to Pete's room, 861 in the West tower. By the time they got to the hotel Sal called to tell them the room was empty. "Where are they?" Lou said looking at Juan. "Let's go Doc." And off they were. "Change of plans, driver. They must be going to the Marquee."

Peter put his arm up to hail a cab. "Taxi" he shouted. The cab pulled up to the curb and they got in the back seat. Hope grabbed Peter by the lapels and pulled him close. He didn't even have time to tell the cabbie to take them to the Marquee. The cab took off down Flamingo toward Las Vegas Boulevard. When it got to the intersection the cab turned to the left onto Las Vegas Boulevard, past the Excalibur and the Luxor. Suddenly the cab pulled over to the curb, the door opened and a woman got in the front passenger seat. The door Slammed shut and the Taxi took off down the strip.

Peter looked up and said, "Hey this isn't the way to the…"

"SHUT UP!" The woman said, with a heavy Russian accent. She pulled a pistol out of her bag and pointed it toward the couple in the back seat. Then she said something to the driver, in Russian. "We will take care of these two before we finish this job, Yuri."

The Anatoli's did not know that both of their passengers could understand every word they spoke. Hope put her hand on Peter's leg and looked at him. Peter gave her a half smile and told her not to worry.

Peter was the son of immigrants from Russia who managed to escape from The Soviet Union by hiding in a storage container headed for Canada.

Peter's Papa, Albert, worked at the Leningrad Shipping Yard and planned his escape for months. He did not realize that the trip would take so long and did not pack enough food, what little there was. Albert and his wife, Alyona, barely survived the trip. When the container was opened in Montreal, Canada they were unconscious. They were rushed to the hospital. When they were well enough to be released they went to the American consulate to apply for political asylum, they were free!

One thing for sure, Peter is no Russian spy. His parents taught him their native language but made it very clear that they are Americans now. When Pete was eighteen he joined the Marines, served two tours in Afghanistan and another tour in Iraq before his chopper got hit by a S.A.M. on their way to the airport, they were heading stateside. He spent five months in Walter Reed Medical Center where he was given a new knee and an honorable discharge.

Months later he was called to the White House where President Obama gave him the Navy Cross. It seems he was the main reason why six others on that chopper hop survived the crash before the wreckage exploded, killing the pilot and three of the crew. He used the GI Bill to get his degree in accounting at University of New Mexico.

Esperanza and Peter met in their economics class three months before graduation, they were inseparable; except when Esperanza had to go home. They wanted to marry but Hope told Peter that she had to wait until Gina was married first, she is the oldest and in the Mexican family that was the way, Peter agreed.

The taxi drove south until the strip dwindled into a two-lane road, then they turned off onto a dirt road and headed into the desert. When the cab came to a stop the woman, Anna Anatoli, got out and pointed the gun at the two in the back seat said, "Get out!" Yuri stayed in the cab knowing that Anna could handle this job by herself. He stayed in the cab with the engine running for a quick get-a-way. Anna pointed the gun at Hope and blurted "Move...that way!" and moved the barrel of the gun in the direction off the road.

When the gun was moving away from Hope, Peter swung into action. He stepped toward Anna and grabbed the gun where she held it, twisting her hand back and away from Hope. It all happened so fast that Hope didn't even know it was happening. Anna, a well-trained agent tried to counter Peter's action, pulling back, but was too weak to overpower his move. In the course of the take down the gun went off. The bullet entered below Anna's chin and into her brain, killing her instantly. Yuri didn't wait a second to see if Anna was alright, he saw Anna's brain blow out of the back of her head. He put the cab in gear and was gone before Peter finished gaining his footing.

Just like that Hope and Peter were alone in the desert, with a dead Russian woman laying at their feet. Hope ran to Peter and put her arms around him, "What was that all about! They wanted to kill us!"

I don't know; but we better get walking, that bitch told the cabbie they had a job to finish. If they wanted us dead...He might be out to hurt someone else, come-on Hope." He pulled out his cell and dialed Jilani.

The Marquee

When Lou and Juan got to the Marquee everyone was there except Peter and Esperanza. They were all having a ball. *Las Vegas is a big town, Pete and Hope are probably okay. Hell, so far nothing seems to be happening at the Marquee*, Lou thought, walking up to Jilani, "Where's Peter now, Jil?"

Jilani picked up his phone to check his GPS when it started playing the theme to Star Trek. He looked at the screen, "It's Pete." He put the phone to his ear and listened. "Get back to the Marquee and keep your eyes open for trouble," he said into the phone, He turned to Lou, then Juan, "They were accosted by a cabbie and an old woman, Russian, Pete said. They're alright, a little shook up but surprisingly calm, considering. Peter took the gun away from the woman, she's dead but the cabbie got away. The woman said they had to kill them, then get the job done."

Juan looked at Lou, "That's it, I'm getting these girls out of here and back to Albuquerque where they are safe!"

"Hold on pal, these girls are in the safest place in the world right here. We'd be crazy to take them out of here, now! We need to find that cabbie." Lou pulled out his cell and called Roger Stelmach. After filling Roger in on everything he told Juan to stay here and protect his family. Then he left.

The cabbie, Yuri Anatoli, has a job to finish; and now, after losing Anna, it's personal. He's going to kill all four of those American girls; then, he'll kill Juan Vega, Lou Bennett, and that little puke boyfriend that killed his beautiful Anna. Unlike any time in his dark career Yuri was letting his personal feelings interfere with his professionalism; and that would be his downfall. Yuri was not alone in this hateful endeavor, however. There were always contingencies. Yuri's revenge could not equal the revenge that fed this sinister mission of pure evil.

Jessica and Amanda made mincemeat of those two pretty boys at the Library. "See ya boys," Amanda said as they left those losers to cry in their martinis. "Imagine these guys thinking they can play with the big girls," They both giggled as they left the room.

"Wait ladies, where you going so fast?" said Nikolai, the older of the two, "Michael and I want to show you a good time tonight."

Jessica stopped, turned and poked her finger into the man's chest. "You want to show 'us' a good time? What makes you think that you! can show us! a good time! You typical…"

"Jessica! Stop playing with these two, they just appreciate beautiful women." She turned, "Down boys, we have to get back to our group, sorry." They left them standing in the doorway. Amanda leaned over to Jessica and whispered in her ear, "That was fun, wasn't it." They giggled some more.

When they got to the dance floor Jilani was there, and "Dad?" Jessica said, "What are you doing here?

"I just couldn't stand it alone in Albuquerque, Jumped on the first plane this afternoon."

Jessica pulled her father to the side, the noise was deafening but she pulled him closer and said, "Don't try to fool me Pop, you know exactly what's going on here." Juan pulled back and gave Jessica a stare. There was a commotion on the dance floor. The two pretty boys from the Library were stumbling across the dance floor. They could hardly walk. Jessica called to Amanda, "Hey Mandy, how many of those drinks did we switch with those two creeps?

They must have been spiked!" They were coming straight toward the girls but they didn't quite make it. Two bouncers grabbed them and escorted them toward a side door. They were gone. Nobody ever suspected that these two were 'Plan B'. They were supposed to give those spiked drinks to the girls then help them over the rail to the sidewalk on the boulevard below. They just didn't see the girls switch some of the drinks. The rest they dumped into the planter at the end of the bar. That foresight probably saved more than themselves. These guys were after all of them and didn't care if there was any collateral damage.

Lou stepped outside onto Las Vegas Boulevard and stopped. He didn't know where to start. The street was packed with partiers from one end of the strip to the other.

He got lucky. Peter and Hope were pushing their way through the crowd toward the Cosmo. Lou rushed over and grabbed Esperanza, "Come on! Let's get inside."

"Uncle Lou, what are you doing here? You wouldn't believe what just happened." Just then Peter grabbed her and pushed her aside. A shot rang out. Peter was hit!

Yuri Anatoli came at them with an insane gleam in his eyes. He was shouting something in

Russian. "You murdering pig," was the translation in Lou's mind; along with some unintelligible ramblings.

Lou stepped forward instinctively, pushed a woman out of the way as he hurled himself at the deranged Russian. Still in midair, Lou grabbed the weapon with his right hand twisting the pistol down toward the ground. His left arm wrapped around Anatoli's neck as the weight of Lou's body twisted the Russian's body taking the him to the ground with a crack in his neck. His body lay lifeless where it fell. It all happened so fast that no one in the crowd knew what had happened.

A beat cop was standing on the corner not too far from them. He heard the shot and arrived on the scene just in time to see Lou come up with the gun; the body of a man lying on the ground.

"Drop the gun," the cop yelled at Lou, gun in hand. Lou laid the gun on the ground and put his hands up.

The woman that Lou had pushed out of the way to get at the shooter yelled, "NO! That man stopped the shooting." She pointed at the body on the ground," THAT MAN HAD THE GUN!"

"Officer! That man shot my husband!" yelled Esperanza, pointing to the unconscious body of Yuri Anatoli. "My Uncle Lou knocked him out and took the gun from him! He tried to kill us earlier!" She was crying by now, holding Peter, who was bleeding from a gunshot wound in the shoulder.

"Husband?" That was what stuck in Lou's mind. The crowd was gathering around the scene and two cop cars were pulling up, sirens blazing. Another night on the Las Vegas Strip. The people got their monies worth tonight.

The next morning Peter's hospital room was crowded with his new in-laws and family friends, ten all together; Hope, Jessica, Gina, Christina, their father Juan, Uncle Lou, Jilani, Amanda, and Rebecca; Oh, and Peter, of course, in bed with his left shoulder all wrapped up. The nurse came in to tell them that there were too many people in the room, Jilani flashed his ID at her and sent her on her way, talking to herself.

Billy came stumbling into the room with a big smile on his face, looking like crap, that makes eleven.

Everybody looked at him. "You look like you did an all-nighter" Jilani said smiling ear to ear.

"I spent the whole night interrogating those Roskinov twins, they're not lesbians, at least not last night," Billy said to the roar of laughter.

When the laughter died down Gina broke in, "Tonight we celebrate a wedding, and a new member of the family."

Juan put up his hands, "Not in Vegas, I'm getting you girls back to Albuquerque where I can keep an eye on yous."

"Aww…Party-pooper. Your no fun." Many groans, then more laughter.

17

Phoenix Arizona, Sky Harbor Airport

The pretty little blond personality machine at the United Airline ticket counter at Sky Harbor Airport handed Lou his credit card, "Here you go Mr. Bennett, Your flight 368 will be departing in 53 minutes out of gate 6 to the right. You'll be flying first class. There is one layover at Reagan in DC of about an hour. At Reagan you'll fly first class on flight 1172, departing at four p.m. eastern time, nonstop, arriving in St. Petersburg at one in the afternoon local time. Are you sure you don't want to book your return flight now, Mr. Bennett, you'll save a bundle. Vacation? I've heard St. Petersburg is a beautiful city." She bubbled, making conversation as she handed him his ticket.

"No, uh...Dominika," looking at her nametag. *She could be Russian,* he thought. Russian women are very beautiful, especially in America speaking English. It seemed that the Russian language gave them a coldness in their mannerism; or maybe it was just a slight prejudice he had acquired in the cold war. "Thank you, just business, my schedule is up in the air, no pun intended."

He had a little time to kill so he went to the bar to get a drink. The bartender brought him his double scotch and happily took the twenty and the change as a tip. There was a flat screen TV behind the bar airing CNN. The announcer was talking about the threat of nuclear war if we allowed Iran to continue their enrichment of uranium. The Russians were on Iran's side because of the billions of dollars they were making from of the contracts that they signed for the supply and construction of their nuclear related industry, it was in their financial interest.

The United States is imposing more sanctions on Iran and businesses dealing with the Iranian government, unless they ended their enrichment of nuclear material. That made it all the more lucrative for Russia; and as it turns out North Korea.

North Korea, the most reclusive nation on the planet, is a nuclear power that needs the money that Iran, or anyone else for that matter, was willing to pay for their technology. Russia was willing to let North Korea have a share of the business. They used North Korea as a conduit for some of the more sensitive deals. It was a win-win for all three nations.

The thought of the Russians creating havoc in this world, for profit, left a bad taste in Lou's mouth. It doesn't seem that anything has changed since the days of the USSR. The Russians are just disguising their evil in a new version of capitalism. This version has an old name, fascism, pure and simple. Of Course, this is just Lou's opinion; though he shared it with most of his colleagues.

The whole business of the Russian Federation was a bit touchy these days due to the intricate financial network that exists in this very complicated world. Vladimir Putin knows his adversaries and is not afraid to push his position in an effort to boost the standing of his nation in the world; and his power. It should be obvious to anyone who has an understanding of the Russian mindset, at least those of the former communist party, that there is an effort to restore the super power status of the former USSR.

The screen on the TV suddenly changed, catching Lou's attention as well as the others, mostly businessmen, in the bar. "Breaking News...This just in." It appears that ISIS has beheaded five more journalists including two Americans."

The story continues with a depressing tone rightly due to their fallen colleagues. One of the toughest, and deadly, jobs is a journalist in a war zone. The effort to get both sides of a story puts brave, and ambitious, reporters directly into the fray. Far too many of them are killed or injured; but the survivors whom had made their mark with the most important stories will surely get on the fast track to the best network positions.

It is the stories that don't seem to get reported, Lou thought that could change the face of the conflict. For instance, where do these backward warriors get all their weapons?   Many of the war machinery used now is American made, supplied or left to the Iraqi government for their own security. They were either captured from the defeated Iraqi army or left as the Iraqi soldiers simply deserted. The main supply of munitions comes mostly from Iran, the regions chief supporter of terrorism. Iran has the industry to build the weapons; or they get them from the Russian Federation.

One of the top arms dealers associated with these shady dealings is Grigori Medvedev. Lou has made his mind up that Medvedev must be stopped. He has done enough damage to his team and to the world. Grigori Medvedev is a terrorist in no uncertain terms and Lou is going to stop him; he intends to kill him if it is the last thing he does on this earth, and it probably will be the end of both of them. That is most certain; hence the one-way ticket, and also first class.

"Now boarding at gate 6, United Airlines flight 368, destination Reagan International Airport in Washington, DC." announced a feminine voice over the PA system. With that Lou grabbed his carry-on bag, his only luggage, and headed to the gate. After exiting the lounge, turning left toward gate six, he casually noticed a man reading a newspaper across from the bar. He had seen enough detective movies to make him very suspicious, not to mention his twenty years as a state cop.

Lou walked down the causeway a few steps then dropped his jacket. As he reached down to pick it up he quickly glanced toward the suspicious man just as a woman and little girl ran up to him smiling and giving him a big hug. Lou smiled and thought to himself that he was getting a bit too paranoid. Not surprising after the events of the past couple of years. On the plane he will get his bearings and work on his professionalism.

18

The older, very attractive, flight attendant handed Lou a double J&B with an impressive United Airlines smile, then continued down the aisle of the first-class section of the Dreamliner 777 that was already cruising at thirty-eight thousand feet eastbound.

Over the intercom the captain greeted the passengers, "Good afternoon and welcome to United Airlines flight 368, destination, our great capital Washington DC with connections to the world. I am the captain of this flight, Jonathan Harris. We should be arriving slightly ahead of schedule this afternoon at approximately 2:45 p.m. Eastern time. I'd like to especially welcome Mrs. Niece and the seniors from the Prescott High school on their senior trip to the historic city of St. Petersburg, Russia, I hope you have a wonderful experience and may all of the passengers of flight 368 enjoy the flight."

Lou turned in his spacious seat toward the flight attendant, he wanted to ask her if there would be a snack, or anything to eat on this flight. He hadn't eaten a thing since he left Las Vegas in his motorhome yesterday afternoon. The attendant was handing a drink to a man two seats down on the other side of the aisle that looked vaguely familiar; *the man at the airport,* Lou remembered, *across from the bar, with the wife and daughter.* He sat back in his seat, the flight attendant would be back soon enough. He closed his eyes.

"Mr. Bennett, Mr. Bennett," the flight attendant gently touched Lou on the shoulder. He opened his eyes and looked at her in a slight haze. "Mr. Bennett,

139

Please fasten your seatbelt, we will be hitting some rough air over the Rockies, sorry for the interruption, it's necessary." Lou fastened his seatbelt and closed his eyes again, forgetting that he was hungry and wanted to ask her about a snack.

"I think you must have been a little busy over the past few days," a voice quietly came from the seat beside him.

He turned, "You haven't thought of me." There, next to him was Lynne, looking radiant. No, glowing in a sort of spiritual glow that you think an angel would look like. *Well, that would make sense, Lynne is dead and he is dreaming,* he thought.

"You know me when I'm working," he smiled, "all work, strictly business. But you are always with me, my life is you, my darling." He leaned over to put his arms around her in a needed embrace, but only caught air. He pulled back perplexed.

"I'm alright, Lou, you need to move on in your life. Everything will be good. When you are finished doing what you are doing you will be able to move on, you will find happiness. There is much more to your life, you can only imagine my sweet." The dream vanished as there was a tremendous crash and Lou woke up. It seems that is how his dreams about Lynne seem to end.

The voice of the captain came, once again, over the speaker. "Sorry about that, we have encountered a bit of turbulence. Some of it could be a bit rough." Just as the plane seemed to drop then suddenly hit hard in space. "That will be about how it'll be for the next fifteen minutes or so. Nothing to worry about, we go through this routinely in this area of the continent. Hold on and stay calm, we're not in any danger, just a bit rough. Make sure you have your seatbelts on and follow the directions of your flight attendants, Thank you."

Lou unbuckled his safety belt and began to stand up, but then he remembered about the turbulence and decided to wait to go to the restroom. The attendant, who was sitting in her seat buckled up, smiled in acknowledgement of Lou's wise decision. Flying through such a turbulent area can cause a body to fly up against the ceiling of the plane in extreme cases.

As Lou sat back into his seat he caught the profile of another passenger. This one was a woman sitting two seats in front of him. It was the woman in the airport terminal that was hugging the man outside the bar. But where was the girl? Was that just a ruse to throw off his obvious suspicion? Now Lou was seriously getting paranoid, or at least suspicious. He had no thought that the events that took place in Vegas ended the attempts on his, and his comrade's lives. *The game is on, Mr. Medvedev, I am going to turn this thing around and you will be the one living in fear now*. He thought.

The captain made another announcement ending the turbulence and saying that they caught a nice tailwind and it should be smooth sailing from here. Lou decided to take this time to go to the restroom and while he was at it scan the rest of the passengers. He thought that Medvedev, might just be a little more determined to get him out of the picture, after what happened in Las Vegas. As he turned toward the back of the plane the man from the bar looked away. Lou could have gone forward to the first-class restroom, but he wanted to get a picture of the coach in his mind. His warrior instincts were clicking in and he knew he should know his surroundings, Ranger 101.

As he came out of the restroom he glanced one

more time into the coach section of the plane. He could see that the plane was packed. The Prescott High seniors filled the last half of the plane. There must be over fifty of them, including chaperons. He was glad he was in first class, much quieter.

The flight attendant was serving a woman in aisle five a soft drink in a plastic cup, pouring it out of a can of coke. The gentleman that was sitting in front of her turned and asked the attendant, with a strong Russian accent, if he could have another "wadka." A red flag immediately flew up in Lou's mind. He made a quick analysis of the man. He was maybe about five nine and, as far as he could tell in his seat, built like he was in the military, or Medvedev's security, maybe. He looked to be about in his mid-thirties, clean shaven with short cropped light brown hair. Just as Lou finished sizing him up, as he turned to his seat, the Russian's cold gray eyes met Lou's. They hung there for an instant, an instant that told Lou all he needed to know about this man and his purpose. He was going to try something, maybe not on the plane, too risky, but after they disembarked. He could see it in the man's cold heartless stare.

Lou turned and vanished behind the curtain separating the coach from first class. His defenses were up now. He was going to spend the rest of the flight surveying his options and developing his plan. This might be a one-way mission but if it ended with the death of Grigori Medvedev it would be accomplished successfully. That was all that was important. His life, not so important. He thought that even as a picture of Soyala crossed his mind like a gentle reminder that life might be worth living. He shook that off, no distractions!

A gentle vibration in his shirt pocket indicated that he had a call on his cell phone. Lou looked at the screen, he didn't want to talk to anyone right now but it was Paul Wells. "Hello Paul," he said into the device.

"Lou, I know what you're up to. I want to help. When you land I will have a couple of my people meet you." Lou just listened, "They will bring you to Langley. We have the same goals here, we need to work together," the CIA Chief said. Lou didn't respond right away, thinking about what Paul said. "LOU!"

"OK, Paul, I'm willing to listen to what you have to say. I guess I could use some help, I don't even know what I'm going to do when I get there." Lou said, "but I only have an hour before I have to catch my St. Pete flight."

"Don't worry about that flight, we'll get you there when you're ready. Besides, Greggy isn't in St. Pete, He's on his way to Prague."

19

The rest of the flight was relatively short. Lou mentally reintroduced himself to his warrior Ranger training and his training as a delta operative. There was so much he forgot over time. He could remember the constant training, a redundancy that never got boring thanks to the ever-present pounding of the voice of his instructor; a relentless reminder that his life depended on his ability to perform this training flawlessly when it counts. He realized that his military training was the only thing that would keep him alive. He couldn't help the feeling that there would be a life after Medvedev's death. He had an elusive resurgence of hope.

As the rest of the passengers disembarked the plane, Lou held back. Either he needed to be the first one off, or the last. There was no tactical advantage to being stuck in a long line of anxious tourists. Besides, he wanted to see if the three passengers also held back, or anyone else for that matter. He didn't like the odds, but he had seen worse.

The woman, a cute, slender brunette was conservatively dressed in a business type attire, left at the front of the crowd. The first-class passengers were always let off first. He was sure that she was the same women at the bar in Phoenix. The man, though, hung back. He was on his cell phone. When he was finished he walked over to Lou and said, "Mr. Bennett, I'm Ryan Alexander, Paul Wells sent me. I'm to escort you to the office." Lou never saw the third man get off and never saw him again. He thought he was being followed by agents of Grigori Medvedev, but now it appears that he has , also, drawn the attention of the biggest spy agency in the world.

CIA, Langley Virginia

It's no secret where the CIA has its main offices. Every government bureaucracy has their public side to it, even the super-secret intelligence agency of the most powerful nation on the planet. What happens inside, however, is another story. Lou was about to see some of the darker side of the protection of the United States of America.

Lou entered the building as Ryan held the door. The lobby was cold and hard. Marble floors and walls. To the left was a plain marble wall with a number of stars on it. "Those are in honor of the fallen. There are no names, their lives were clandestine and remain so in death. It is the greatest honor," Ryan said with total conviction.

Lou couldn't help but think that this guy is well indoctrinated. Then so was he when he worked for the agency with Delta. "Good evening Martha." Ryan smiled at the girl at the reception desk. "I need a visitor pass for Mr. Bennett here. Show Martha your ID. You can call Director Wells for conformation." Martha made the call, then handed Lou a visitor pass.

After a few hallways and elevators, all requiring a pass, they came to an office with a sign on the door, Paul JR Wells, Director of European intelligence. The office wasn't much, an outer office with a secretary at her desk; and an inner office for the boss. Quite Spartan compared to other government offices. The Agency had a tight budget and couldn't waste money that could otherwise be used to bribe foreign bureaucrats or pay bounties on wanted terrorists and fund the clandestine operations of the spy network.

"Lou, I'm so glad you decided to come," Paul said, as he stuck out his hand in friendship.

"It didn't seem that I have a choice," Lou replied, happy to see an old friend but a bit uneasy about the circumstances.

"Of course, you have a choice, Lou. You could choose to come in and let us help you, or, you can refuse and we will have to help you without your cooperation." Paul said, half joking but quite serious. "Come with me and we'll show you what we know about 'The Bear'. I think you will find that we know a bit about him, we've been keeping tabs on him ever since he was released in November 2009. Since then he's been rebuilding his criminal empire. During his stay with us his business was run by his assistant, Timur Balaban. He pretty much went legit after the fall of the commies. When Greggy got back he took over and continued his evil ways. We haven't been able to get close to him, he has a seemingly impenetrable security, very loyal to him; he pays them very well," Paul looked at his guest. "If you are so determined to go after him, you will need our help." Paul was talking the whole time they made their way down the hall to the 'Russia' room.

Paul is the director of all matters related to the European theater. "This is where we keep tabs on the Russian intelligence." Paul said, as he opened the door. The room was huge with at least a hundred, or more, cubicles. In the middle of the room, on the south wall, was a number of huge flat screen monitors. Paul walked down an isle to about the third row of cubes. "This is Richard Kerensky, he is assigned to The Bear, he knows everything we need to know about him; including his location at any time."

Richard reached out to shake Lou's hand. "The Bear' as we affectionately call him." He looked up at Paul as if to ask permission to continue; Paul nodded affirmatively.

"Well," continuing, "The Bear has something going on, but we can't figure out what. Our man inside only gives us just enough info to wet our whistle; but anything is better than nothing. So far it has all checked out."

"Wait, you have someone on the inside? Who is he? Will he help me?" Lou asked excitedly.

"Well," Paul looked a little bit uncomfortable. He probably didn't want Lou to know about the informant. "We don't exactly know who he is, it might be Timur Balaban, but we don't know for sure. In any case he is no concern of yours; he might just as well turn you in to save his own skin." He changed the subject, "Go on Rich, where is Grigori now?"

"Yesterday he got on his private jet at Pulkovo. His flight plan was Prague but disappeared from radar about 200 clicks out.

That Falcon 900 LX has a nonstop range of 8000 miles, no telling where he might be going," Richard continued, "My guess is he went East, Far East, back to North Korea. Colonel General Hyon Yong-Chol has been tracked to freedom bridge, I got that from down the hall, NK, Johnny keeps me posted on his movement since he's such pals with The Bear."

"And you think The Bear is headed that way for another meet with Hyon," Paul asked, "but still no intel as to what they're up to?"

Lou added his thoughts to the brief, "Two of the deadliest anti-American criminals on the planet getting together for a little lunch, what could possibly be wrong with that, just 'ole buddies I'd guess," sarcastically.

"Yeah, they're old buddies alright, they've been up to no good for over thirty years. Hyon got his promotions on the back of The Bear's enterprise. We believe that it was Hyon who built the cyanide gas bombs that the Iranians used during the Iraq war; there was a lot of Kurdish families that went to heaven on the family plan in that one. Of course, it was The Bear who brokered that deal with the Iranians." Richard is a walking encyclopedia on The Bear.

The rest of the evening they went over everything that Lou needed to know about The Bear and his operations. The Bear has been very busy since he was released. The START II treaty didn't go as it was supposed to but releasing The Bear has created some evil consequences around the world. The company wanted to eliminate him, but the administration wouldn't go for it. They were a bunch of peaceniks, except when it was in their interests, like Libya Colonel Kaddafi. The new administration seems to be more amiable to keeping the options open.

"Well, Lou," Paul finally concluded, "that's about it for now, you know about his organization and their nefarious dealings. Oh, yes I almost forgot. It seems he has a couple of gimmicks up his sleeve, literally. I'm not saying he's paranoid, but he isn't going to get taken again. He carries a Makarov in a holster strapped to his left leg. He also has a switch blade in his pocket, right, in a custom-tailored pocket. This man is so worried about his enemies he might have any kind of defense embedded in his clothes or, well we can only guess. I've even heard that he has cartridges of some kind of poison gas sewn into the sleeves of his suit jackets, which seems a bit dangerous, unless he has been immunized to the gas."

"That's it huh," Lou said with a smirk on his face. "I guess I'm ready to get this thing done. Your man said you would get me there, first class, I hope, that's what I paid for."

"Bear won't be back for a few days, Lou," Paul put his hand on Lou's shoulder. "We put you up in the Hampton Inn for the night, you'll need a good night's sleep. Tomorrow we'll take you to the closet and get you some gimmicks of your own. We booked you on a first-class flight from Langley Air Force Base at 1300 tomorrow afternoon. We can only throw you a little support, unofficially of course. But we have people over there, we'll have your back."

20

Paul Wells phone started ringing at 6:30 a.m. His cell phone was charging on the night stand next to his bed, at home. He was a light sleeper, part of the training in his line of work. But this morning his wife, Peggie, had to give him a quick shake. "Wells," he said into the phone as he sat up in the bed.

"Sir, Williams here," Bill Williams spoke with some sense of urgency in his voice. "He's gone. I got here at 6:15 and he's already gone. I had to get the desk to give me a key and it doesn't even look like he even got in the bed. I think he took a shower and left."

Paul Wells was fully awake by then, "Shit! Check the airports. I'll call the office, they'll find out what flight he got on. He's on his way to St. Pete."

The flight to Prague would take about 11 hours, non-stop. Lou was settled in his first-class seat sleeping for the first time in days. He wasn't sure where to start when he got there but at least he should be there when The Bear is scheduled to be there. He doesn't speak Czech but most people in the country speak English and there are still some that speak Russian, mostly older, a throwback from the days of the soviets; according to google.

If The Bear is building some kind of super weapon he would be dealing with the darker side of the town. Prague is a big town, though, so Lou took another route to find The Bear. Richard filled Lou in on The Bear's family in Karlovy Vary, a Russian tourist village a few miles out of Prague. A likely place to begin as it is likely The Bear would visit his home and family while in the Czech Republic. Now, however, Lou put on his Bluetooth headphones and booted up the Russian language app on his cell phone. He would need to refresh his Russian, he is a little rusty and there is some slang he needed to catch up on. It wasn't long before he was fast asleep. He will arrive at eleven a.m.

"You'd better know what you're doing, Louis Jerome Bennett. It's one thing to fly into the eye of a hurricane, but you can't fly into a tornado; that just ain't gonna happen." Lynne was sitting in the seat next to him.

"You look as beautiful as the day I met you, standing on that runway holding that sign that said, "Welcome home troops." I thought that was the funniest thing I ever saw. Hell, Granada wasn't much of a war. I fell in love with you right then and there." Lou stood up and took Lynne's hand.

She stood up and slipped gently into his arms. They embraced for an eternity. Lynne looked Lou in the eyes. She had that look she always had when he was going on a mission. She put her hands on the lapels of his jacket and kissed him on the lips. "Remember that Master Sergeant, in Pakistan? Remember Master Sergeant Burmandi, Mr. Bennett."

"Mr. Bennett, Mr. Bennett," the flight attendant gently shook Lou on the shoulder. He opened his eyes. "Please fasten your seatbelt, Mr. Bennett, we'll be starting our approach to Vaclav Havel Airport. You should be in Prague by noon.

Lou didn't have any luggage, just one overnight bag. He wouldn't get too far in the Czech Republic dressed in clothes he bought from JC Penney's. He needed to find a store to buy some clothes that would fit the local look. Never being in Prague before he wasn't sure where to start. He walked out of the terminal, stopped at the curb and took in his surroundings.

A taxi pulled up to the curb, opened his passenger window and said in Czech, "Taxi Mister."

Lou had a blank look on his face, so the driver tried again, this time in English, "Do you need a taxi." Lou opened the rear door and got in. he noted that the cabbie spoke pretty good English, what little he spoke. *He must have spent some time in the states*, Lou thought. "The Hilton Hotel," Lou told the cabbie. He had thrown his bag on the seat as he got in, but there was another bag there, on the floor, behind the driver's seat. "Somebody left a bag in your taxi, driver," Lou said to the cabbie.

"That's for you, Mr. Bennett. You left so suddenly you didn't have a chance to gear up. This is not up to the level the boss had in mind for you, but it will do, somewhat." The driver never took his eyes off the road.

Lou didn't say a word, he grabbed the bag. It was about carryon size, brown leather with a zippered compartment on the side, a large center garment compartment, and a shoulder strap. He thought that it probably was something a local might carry. He opened the side pocket. It contained a Makarov PM semi-auto hand gun and a box of cartridges. *That will come in handy.* He thought. He put the weapon back in the pocket, zipped it up and unzipped the main compartment. It had clothes in it. A hat, he took it out, put it on his head, it fit.

"I hope I got the size right. It should be close." The driver still didn't move his head when he talked, just went about the business of driving.

Lou pulled out a jacket, a pair of slacks, a shirt, a belt, underwear, socks, shoes, and a handkerchief; oh, and a pair of glasses and a watch.

"You should change while we drive. Put your clothes in the plastic bag on the floor, I'll get rid of them. You'll fit in with these clothes. There are more in your room, a suit, and dress shoes." He took his eyes off the road for the first time, looked in the rearview mirror, "You don't have to go Rogue, Lou."

They had plenty of time to talk in the two-hour drive to the Karlovy Vary. Lou had some questions while he changed his clothes. He put his discarded clothes in the bag, then, in a moment of thought, picked his old slacks out of the bag and reached into the watch pocket. He pulled out a red ribbon.

The cab pulled up to the curb at the Hotel Heluan. The cabbie turned and discretely handed Lou a room card covering a cellular phone.

"You are in the rattlesnake's nest, Mr. Volkov. room 205 in the back by the outside fire escape. My number is in the phone. I'll be around. Also, in the phone is an app, 'Czech Today' listen to it, it'll help you assimilate. I'm Piko, that'll be twenty euros." Lou handed him a twenty-dollar bill.

"I put an envelope in the room with Czech 'Crowns' in it, that's the currency to use here. There's also some Euros. Get rid of the dollars." Piko stuffed the bill in his shirt pocket.

Lou handed Piko the rest of the money in his pocket, about eight hundred dollars. And got out. "Spacibo."

21

The Heluan was a nice enough hotel, Lou wondered why the CIA would put him up in this, old, hotel, is it a company asset? He walked past the front desk, bag in hand. As he scanned the lobby he thought that this building has been around for years.

As he walked toward the stairs the Woman behind the desk looked up, "Good afternoon, Mr. Volkov," in Russian. There was no elevator; They didn't have them in 1715 when the building was built. There was only one other person in the lobby, a man sitting next to the window reading a Russian newspaper, presumably not unusual in Karlovy Vary. There was a dining room to the right of the stairs with a few couples taking a late lunch.

The stairs went up to a half flight then circled around to the left up to the second floor. It continued circulating the floors to the 5th floor suites. The hall way was clean, three rooms on each side; Lou's was the first room on the right. He liked being close to the stairs. He slid his card into the lock and the green light lit; he opened the door slowly pushing it in as he stood at the threshold. It was empty, as it should be, no CIA, no bad guys, not that there was a difference.

It was a nice room, and there was a bathroom, they didn't have them in the rooms back in 1715. He walked over to the window. It looked over the back street, and, there was a roof about 8 feet down, presumably the back entrance to the hotel. The fire escape was off the hallway past the next room. *That's why the company uses this room, an easy escape route if needed…The Company, huh, now they got me thinking it,* he thought.

He tossed the bag on the bed and walked over to the closet, opened the double doors and gazed upon a bare armoire with only a suit and a pair of dress shoes in it; *my wardrobe.* He left the doors open and sidestepped to the dresser. The top drawer had two dress shirts and three ties. Moving down to the second drawer he found some underwear, socks and two handkerchiefs; all locally bought, he assumed. The other two drawers were empty.

Walking over to the bed he grabbed the bag. He pulled out the 9mm Makarov. He was familiar with this weapon, it is standard issue for the Russian military, compact, reliable; the magazine was empty. There was a full box of bullets. *They didn't give me a loaded gun? I guess they thought I might whack the cabbie.*

He loaded the automatic, taking care to use a handkerchief to keep his fingerprints off the shell casings. On the slim chance that he might get away with this, he didn't want to leave any amateur evidence that would lead back to him. He then wiped his prints off the pistol and put it in the holster; no prints until he had to use the weapon.

A knock on the door! Lou walked over to the bag, took the Makarov out of the bag, holding it discretely behind his left thigh as he walked over to the door. With his right hand he reached for the door handle, keeping away from the door in case someone rushed the room, he slowly opened the door a crack.

"Mr. Volkov," a man asked in English, he spoke with a deep Russian accent. It was the man from the lobby, the one reading the newspaper. Lou just looked at him without a word. The truth be known he took a few seconds to realize his cover name. "My name is Anton Federoff, I have been sent to assist you while you are in Czechia." *Silence...*

"Uh, may I come in?"

Lou opened the door wider and stepped aside. He closed the door behind the Russian. "Have a seat Mr. Federoff," Lou said in Russian. "What assistance do you have in mind?" He stood there still shielding his pistol behind his left leg.

"You speak good Russian, Please, call me Anton, I am here to help you to understand the Karlovy Vary. It can be a very dangerous place if you do not know it. I will help you understand who you will have to be contacting. You can holster that Makarov, you won't need it."

Lou walked over to the bed and put the pistol in the side pocket of the bag, handle up; then he sat on the edge of the bed next to the bag, without a word.

"Okay, Mr. Volkov, if that is your name," Anton said this time in English. "The Karlovy Vary is a famous tourist attraction, mostly due to the natural hot springs, you should check them out, they are very invigorating." He waited a moment for a reaction, but Lou just looked at him, attentively. "I would suggest that you do your investigations in the guise of a tourist. That way you can freely move around the city with impunity."

Lou thought that this Russian has a good vocabulary even if he has an accent. Maybe he spent time in an American or English embassy, maybe KGB. "I don't have a whole lot of time." Lou was not sure where to go with this, Anton was not CIA, maybe an asset or an informant.

"You have two days before Grigori Medvedev will be in Prague. He has a house in Karlovy Vary but he doesn't stay there much. His daughter Cristina lives there with her mother while she attends a private school, she is nine years of age."

"What is your part in this, Anton, how do you

know why I'm here in Czechia."

"Let me just say that my employer and you have similar objectives, I cannot say more. Now let me tell you some things about the area. Medvedev has been seen in the industrial section of Prague, an area down by the Vitava river. He is up to something, I cannot say, manufacturing something I think. I would expect that on this trip to Prague he will come to the Karlovy Vary to see Cristina, He adores her, his first; at least with Marta, his second wife."

"What happened to his first wife, uh, Cristina also wasn't it? Did she not wait for him when he was taken? And there are two children too?" Lou remembered that from his briefing for the Yazy mission.

"It is well known that his family was killed when the Chechen rebels attacked the compound near Leningrad, ah, St. Petersburg. He did not know until he suddenly reappeared in 2009, he was in a prison, he said, but did not say where. It was very traumatic for him. He was very depressed for months until he met Marta, his wife now. It was then that he regained his old self and took over his old position at Liberty Arms Company. But, you know that I assume."

Lou suddenly had a hollow feeling in his gut. *Did his unit kill Medvedev's family when they blew the station? There were living quarters above the station, but we didn't know his family was with him. We didn't know! Not that it would matter, the mission came first.*

"No, I didn't know. Where is his house in Karlovy Vary, and, the factory, where is it located?

"I do not know where his factory is, but he is working with a well-known figure in the criminal element of the city, Artem Butov, He runs military factories near Moscow. He has connections to the factories in Prague. The factories in Prague are unknown to me. Grigori has many underworld connections around the world, and many legitimate also."

"Where can I find this Artem Butov, Anton?" Lou was getting interested now.

Anton continued almost without delay, "He owns two luxury apartments in Karlovy, one is on the hill on the road to Chomutov, the other is above the Moscovy café, oh, that is what the locals call it, it's true name is Staroslovanska Kuchyne. It looks quite common from the outside but is very nice on the inside. He owns the café and can be found in the back booth at dinner time, when he is in town. Butov also has a house in Prague near the museum, I wrote down the addresses on this paper. Artem Butov is a dangerous man, Mr. Volkov. As are some other residents of the Karlovy."

Anton continued for another half hour, barely giving Lou a chance to ask a question. When he was finished he got up, "I hope this was helpful Mr. Volkov," in Russian this time. "one thing more Mr. Volkov, do not trust anyone, not even me." He closed the door behind him.

Lou locked the door, walked back to the bed, and laid down on his back. This was a lot to think about, he needed a little time to come up with a plan. It was early evening, but he fell fast asleep as soon as his head hit the pillow, jet lag.

22

As the Falcon 900 streaked across the Tatra Mountains of Southern Poland, The Bear slept in his favorite luxury recliner in the cabin just behind the door to the cock pit. He had a bed in the rear of the jet, but he preferred to sleep on the recliner. It settled his back pain better than the bed. Besides, the location just before the wing gave him a more stable ride; and he was close to Lyev in case he had inquiries. A tone over the speaker system, then, "Gospodin (Mr.) Medvedev, we will be making our approach to the Vaclav Havel in fifteen minutes."

The Bear reached down the right side of the recliner and pushed on the button that brought the seat to its upright position. He gathered the papers that he had been studying and put them in his brief case. "Is my car at the gate, Lyev, I am anxious to see Cristina and Marta, Ah, Marta my beautiful wife who saved my life, Did I ever tell you the story…But yes of course, Lyev, many times. But I have so much to be thankful for, my friend."

"You, first, have a meeting, Gospodin Butov is expecting you at his factory." Lyev said with a half-smile on his face. "Soon everything will be in place, and you can fulfill your plans, boss. Gospodin Butov has sent his driver to take you to the factory; I will attend to the other matter you have requested." Lyev Yakoblev is a loyal friend and bodyguard of The Bear. About six feet tall, dark hair, slender muscular build. Lyev has his loyalty from the history of their family ties.

During the Siege of Leningrad Aleksandr Yakoblev, Lyev's father, became friends with Grigori's older brother Anatoly Medvedev, who taught chemical engineering at the Leningrad state institute of technology. Yakoblev was in the Red Army, He would smuggle food rations to his friend in exchange for lessons, they became good friends. Young Grigori Afanasyevich Medvedev looked up to Yakoblev like a hero.

Years later when Aleksandr Yakoblev was arrested for treason to the Soviet state, for his 1972 publication, *Against Antihistoricism,* an article criticizing Russian nationalism. A young KGB upstart was put in charge of the interrogation of the traitor, Grigori Medvedev. No one knew the relationship that existed between the two. Although the interrogation was harsh, or apparently so, it was determined that the long time loyal party member was innocent of the severe charges. The recommendation was to remove comrade Yakoblev from his influential party position. He was made Ambassador to Canada, an exile of sorts for more than a decade.

In 1983 he guided Mikhail Gorbachev, Soviet Agricultural Minister, an old friend, on his tour of Canadian agriculture. It is said that here is where the two sealed a fate that would lead to the fall of the Soviet Union. Young Lyev Yakoblev never forgot how Grigori saved his father from execution for treason and his family from disgrace. His credentials as a fighter pilot in the Russian Air Force and later Spetnaz enabled him to become the bodyguard, and trusted confidant of Grigori Medvedev, The Bear.

23

"Do you think he can be trusted, Mr. Federoff?" Lynne softly stroked Lou's hair away from his eyes. "He seemed to be a little aloof. I don't think he is who he says he is. He knows too much all the while saying he knows nothing."

"You are always so beautiful, my darling. I'm so happy to see you. I feel centered when I'm with you."

"No, my sweet, I'm not here. I'm only in your mind. Your mind uses me to give your thoughts more impact. But I don't mind helping you in that way. You have gotten a little rusty over the years. Think about your training. You will have some troubles ahead. Remember Master Sergeant Burmandi." She was gone.

Lou rolled over onto his back. "Master Sergeant Burmandi," Yes, our old friend from India. Our trainer for the mission in Pakistan, the one where Bill Anderson joined the team. What? Yeah… "Never think that your foe is thinking your thoughts, he has his own vectors to mold his thoughts. That can become an advantage for you. Even the best of them can be thrown off by your actions. You just need to know him better than he thinks you do."

A tone sounded, a single note. Then after a second, another. Lou reached into his bag, the side pocket where he had placed the Makarov, and removed the cell phone that Piko had given him. He touched the red symbol of the old fashion phone receiver and put it to his ear, not saying a word. "Are you settled in, my friend?" It was Paul Wells. "Are you ready for some assistance from the powers to be?"

"It seems that no matter how hard I try, my friend, I can't seem to lose you."

"You need to trust us, Lou. We are after the same thing. I see Piko found you. He will be your contact. Anything you need or want to know he will assist you, as well as be your chauffeur." Paul was very serious now.

"What about the other one, Anton Federoff, how does he fit in?" Lou filled Paul in on that encounter. He told Paul that he didn't trust him, but he seemed to have some potentially valuable information.

"That name doesn't ring a bell. I'll give it to Kerensky. I wonder what his motivation is, and who is his employer? If you see him again, and I'm sure you will, get a pic of him on your phone and send it to me so we can ID him. Be discrete about it, he may not want his picture taken," Paul said. "I'll have Kerensky send you some pictures of people of interest who may have it in for The Bear. Also, some of his associates."

A short moment of silence then Lou said, "Federoff said something about The Bear that has me concerned. He said that Medvedev's first wife and children were killed when the Yazy installation was attacked by the Chechen rebels. They might have been sleeping in the living quarters above the station."

"That would explain why The Bear is seeking revenge on the team. Our intel didn't catch that one, not that it would have mattered." Paul said.

"He didn't even know about it until he was released. He was grieving for months after his return. Didn't come out of it until he met his present wife, Marta. They have a daughter, Cristina, named after his first wife, I guess," Lou continued. "Federoff said his daughter is his life. I don't want to hurt her, but maybe we can put her under protective care for a spell. Use her for leverage."

"You have the makings of a real operator, Lou. I'll get some intel on the whole thing and get back with ya, meanwhile try to call home more often. Get with Piko and let him show you around. We have The Bear back in Prague sometime today."

"Will do, and thanks boss." Lou hung up. It was eight o'clock in the morning. Lou fell asleep in the afternoon of the previous day. So much for jet lag. He sat up on the bed, looked at his reflection in the mirror on the dresser. He thought about all the circumstances that led him here. Not exactly the way he thought it would end. "No, I don't want it to end, I'm only sixty, I have a lotta years ahead of me." Just then he realized, Looking at his watch, "today's my birthday, sixty-one!...Happy birthday to me."

He felt invigorated. The call from Paul Wells gave him confidence that he is on the right track. Soon he would finish this mission and get back to his mundane life RV'ing throughout America like a million other baby boomers. Lou took a shower, it was wonderful. He was gaining his sense of perspective, though he is about to do something that didn't look to end too well, something in the back of his head told him that the odds are getting better. He's not alone in this, he has help, good help. There is a chance that this is will work and he can get back on track, whatever that is. "What is back on track?" He said to himself as he dressed; even as he grabbed the red ribbon that was on his dresser and put it into his watch pocket.

As he left the hotel he is struck at the beauty of this picturesque town. The Karlovy Vary is not a suburb of Prague. It's a small tourist town about 120 km west of Prague on the Ohre River. It is known for its healing hot springs which have been, officially, drawing visitors since the fourteenth century.

The Carlsbad Springs are the reason so many ex-patriots choose to live in Czechia. He stopped just outside the entrance to the hotel. He really felt like a run. When he was running his head cleared and he could think better, he needed to figure out just how he would go about his mission.

Down the steps of the hotel he paused and looked around. Next door to the hotel was a clothing boutique, open. He stepped in. A small men and woman's casual clothing store. Piko did well enough getting him started but he needed a few more items. Running clothes for one, and some running shoes.

The store had what he needed; along with a couple of pairs of slacks and some shirts. He left the store and went back to the hotel with his new clothes. In his room he dressed into his running outfit. He stopped in front of the bathroom mirror for a look. Not bad, he will fit in well. His dark complexion and hair fit the description of most of the men in Czechia.

Before he went back downstairs he had a thought. He picked up his cell phone and brought up Google Earth. The screen showed an image of the planet earth. He tapped the search icon and typed in the Hotel Heluan, Karlovy Vary. The earth on the screen started to rotate. When the continent of Europe showed in the middle of the screen, the screen started to zoom in. The continent adjusted slightly as it targeted the area of eastern Europe then continued centering as the screen pulled the earth closer. Finally, coming to a rest in a city with a red balloon indicating that spot was the Heluan Hotel. The technology is amazing. Using two fingers he could move the screen throughout the city.

The city has a unique layout. Many of the blocks are completely surrounded by beautiful buildings, enclosing a common area within their confines. Not all the blocks were built like this, but many. The Heluan is not on one of these blocks. The front of the hotel leads to a street that descended to the left toward the river. The rear of the building led onto another small street, Lou typed in the Moscovy café, nothing, so he typed Staroslovanska Kuchyne and the screen started to move to the left. It stopped at a building along the river about, maybe, a half mile from the Heluan across the river. *That seems like a good place to start,* he thought.

Lou trotted down the steps to the street. He already knew that he would turn down toward the river walk. The map showed that was the way to get to the Moscovy café, owned by Anton Butov, the associate of The Bear. He just wanted to scope it out, get a bearing on the location, the layout of the streets, and the escape routes. It is the attention to detail that ensured the success of the missions that his teams were on.

Sure, he has been out of play for way too long, but he would now have to rely on the training that had been drilled into his survival genes. In fact, there was a good chance he wouldn't get out of this one alive. That didn't matter, as long as he accomplished his mission. He had to kill The Bear. That was the mission. To end The Bear's path of murder on what was left of his team; Juan and the girls, Paul, Charlie, and Jilani. His life was expendable so that he can save what was left of his team, and their families; it was obvious The Bear was killing whole families.

What a sick twisted mind that man has. I guess being cooped up in solitary confinement for twenty years with no idea of the fate of the ones he loved will do that to ya, he thought. *Then to find out that that American team of murderers killed your whole family, yeah, I can identify with the way he felt.*

He did the same thing to me, and most of the team. Revenge is a terrible bedfellow, now it's my turn. His mind was infuriated.

Lou was getting himself worked up, so it was good that his phone beeped in his pocket. He stopped his jog and leaned against a tree to check the message. It was from Paul. There were a number of photos appearing on the screen. He checked them one by one. 1/6 was a villa in Karlovy Vary. The caption said, 'The Bear's residence'. This is where his family lives, and The Bear, when he is in town. There was also an address. A photo of a white Falcon 900 had the caption, 'The Bear's PJ'.

Then there was four photos of men. The first one was The Bear, dark photo of a short pudgy man, nice suit, getting into a limo. The next one was a photo of our Mr. Federoff, the caption read 'Timur Balaban, personal assistant and right-hand man to Grigori Medvedev'. They looked alike. The other two photos were of Anton Butov, and an Ignatii Karlov, a major competitor to Medvedev in the arms business. Lou sent a message back to Paul. "Got it, it appears that Anton Federoff and Timur Balaban are the same, send more on him, thx." He put his phone back in his pocket and turned down the river walk.

He only took a few steps when his phone buzzed again, "See Piko for the info."

He put the phone back in his pocket, and then, it rang again, this time it was the phone, not a text. He tapped the icon, "You just couldn't make it another minute without hearing my voice I guess."

"Lou, ya know…I've been thinking about your predicament," Paul said with a slight southern slur.

Lou bit, "Well pardner, predicament ain't quite how I've been assessing the situation, but, what's ya thinkin boss."

"It comes to mind what a mutual friend once said to me," Paul changed his accent to Indian, "If you don't have a will to live, your mission will not be successful."

Lou was silent for a moment then he took a long breath, "Are you going to quote that crazy masochistic Hindu Sergeant Major Burmandi too?"

"Too? Who else in your life knows Burmandi, I thought we were in an exclusive club."

Lou was about to tell Paul that his dead wife was coming to him in his sleep and she also referenced Burmandi, but then he thought better of it. "Believe it or not, I was just remembering when Lynne mentioned Burmandi. What a quinki-dink, ha."

Paul just said, "don't make this a one-way trip, my friend," and hung up.

Lou was slightly taken aback. *One-way trip,* he thought. Then he started running again. The city was set up at the convergence of the Tepla and the Ohre rivers. On the surface it is a quiet little tourist town with its history dating back to 1370. Named after the Holy Roman Emperor Charles IV, King of Bohemia, it is 'the' vacation destination place in Eastern Europe.

The hot springs were discovered by Charles IV during a hunting expedition into the woods west of Karlovy Vary in 1350. He recognized their healing qualities and developed the 'Hot Springs of Loket' or Carlsbad, named after himself, according to legend. All this Lou remembered from his Google search on the flight to Prague. Now that he is here he is fascinated by the beauty of the architecture of the buildings that were built in rows, all between five and six floors and each one painted in bright contrasting colors. He rounded the blocks, exploring the unique style in the formation of the blocks. Truly a block system, he thought. Rather than two rows of buildings with an alley between for servicing, the buildings on these blocks surrounded the block forming a common area in the center which was a community into itself. Lou came upon an archway that led into the community of one of the blocks.

He decided to take a look. As he entered the square he felt a bit out of place as everyone looked in his direction. A man standing near the door of a small café, a hole in the wall café at best, walked up to him and as a big smile came to his face he said something in Slavic. Lou recognized the meaning and said "No, no," to the man. But the man was persistent and attempted to pull Lou into the café by his arm. Lou went along and sat on a stool at the counter. "Kofe."

The man made sure Lou was seated at the counter, then returned to his post at the door. The woman behind the counter, his wife presumably, brought Lou a steaming cup of coffee and a pastry. Lou wasn't going to turn it down, he was the only one in the little place. She said something in Slavic that Lou couldn't understand but assumed it was the price, so, he pulled out a five euro note and laid it on the counter. She took it away and returned with a pile of Koruna's. Lou just shook his head and took a sip of his coffee. He tried Russian, "Is this your café, it is quite charming."

She turned and smiled, "Yes! My husband

Johan and I have owned it for three years. Your Russian is good, American?"

"Yes" Lou replied honestly, thinking that as good as his Russian may be, he could not pass for a native. "My parents were diplomats at the Russian embassy in United States. I was educated in United States." a lie but he thought it was a good time to make up a credible cover story to account for his obvious accent. "I am here on holiday from my job in St. Petersburg. I work for company there. I am salesman." Lou thought that was a good start, but he knew the people he would be dealing with here are not stupid.

Johan had accosted another couple passing by and was seating them at the table in the corner, so his wife had to go to get their order. I don't know how anybody makes a living in a hole like this, but, here it is. He tossed one hundred koruna on the counter and left. "Spacibo," Waving one arm.

Lou made his way back to the street and walked uphill toward the street that would take him back to his hotel. A taxi pulled up next to him. Piko hit the button that rolled down the passenger window, "Mr. Voltov, get in, I can show you the town much faster than you can walk."

Lou got in. "Have you seen the restaurant that Mr. Butov owns, I will show you where it is."

"That is a good idea, Piko," Lou smiled.

The cab made a sharp right at the next street, then down the hill, through the intersection on the river road and across the bridge over the Tepla river.

"It is not far now," Piko said as he squealed around the next corner. "Look, Mr. Voltov, there." Just ahead there was an outdoor café on the sidewalk.

Staroslovanska Kuchyne was written on the sign. Piko made a quick U-turn and pulled up along the curb, "Do you want to go in and look around, Mr. Voltov?

"No, take me back to the hotel. I'll change my clothes and properly prepare for... well, Murphy's Law." Piko took off in the same direction that he came. He made the turn onto the bridge and across the intersection on the other side.

The cab was halfway through the intersection when the sound of squealing tires to the left caught Piko's attention. He looked out of his window just as a delivery truck T-boned the driver side of the vehicle. Piko's head smashed against the side window, knocking him cold. Lou also was flung to the left as the cab was forced to the right.

It was surreal, Lou saw everything pass by in slow motion as his body was thrust into Piko's; they both were caught up in the physics of the crash. The truck went into reverse before the crash settled, then took off down the street.

Simultaneously, a Mercedes G11 pulled up to the right side of the cab in a screeching stop. Two men got out and opened Lou's door. One of them grabbed Lou and pulled him out of the wreck while the other put a black hood over his head. Then he was thrown into the back seat of the Mercedes, followed by the thug that pulled him out of the cab.

The other thug pulled out his suppressed Makarov and put a bullet in Piko's head. He turned, got back into the driver's seat of the Mercedes, and squealed away; leaving the cab in the middle of the street with Piko's body slumped over the steering wheel. The whole thing happened in less than two minutes. There were no witnesses as those that were in the street mysteriously disappeared.

The intersection was deserted. In the distance was the sound of a police cruiser getting louder as it approached the scene of the hit and run accident; as the police report would indicate.

24

Butov Ironworks, Prague

"Artem my good friend, it is so good to see you." The Bear passed by a young Russian who was holding the door. As he walked across the room of the small factory office toward the smiling Russian behind the desk, Artem Butov rose to his feet to greet his longtime comrade. Butov was a short stocky Russian who rose to high rank in the People's Army as a logistics officer. He was a delightful man, unless you got on his wrong side, then he had no scruples about his revenge. Grigori Medvedev and Artem Butov were more than comrades in arms, they were cohorts in some of the most lucrative business dealings in the USSR and now the Russian Federation; dealings that were up to no good.

"Grigori, I too am pleased to see you, we have much to discuss," Artem walked over to a cabinet against the north wall and took out a half full bottle of Beluga Vodka. He opened the bottle and poured two glasses. As he walked around his desk he handed The Bear the one in his left hand. He remained standing as he raised his glass, "My friend we have been through much, overcome many obstacles and had the greatest successes of our lives together."

The Bear stood, raised his glass and added "Yes, my brother, and here's to our greatest enterprise of them all."

"Yes, Grigori... have you read Pravda today?

"I have been too busy reading the information that Colonel General Hyon gave me while in Josan Ri. Why, Artem, has something happened?"

"Yes, something has happened," Artem reached for a newspaper on his desk. It was folded to the international section. He handed it to Grigori.

Grigori took the paper and read the article under the headline "North Korean House Cleaning". As he read the paper he settled into his seat, he sighed, "Well Artem, it appears our friend Colonel General Hyon Yong-Chol, Minister of the army of Korea, has been executed. We were so close to achieving our goal." There was a long thoughtful pause. The Bear stood up and blurted, "Well, I guess we will just have to get the Iranians to pick up the baton, they have the facilities and they hate the Americans as much as we do. Now, my glass is empty Artem, what kind of a host are you, my friend?"

Artem snapped to his feet and retrieved the bottle from his desk. He filled both glasses, "We will be delayed, but the Iranians will also be happy to cause much misery to our mutual foe."

The mobile phone in The Bear's pocket vibrated, he looked at the screen, then tapped the icon, "Lyev, you have good news for me?" He listened, "Very good, take him to the hanger, I will meet you there in the morning, I must go home to see my little Cristina." The Bear looked at Artem, "Maybe it is good that we are delayed, something has come up, a matter that I must address. I will be returning to Leningrad tomorrow evening. I will call you in a week."

He stood up and drank the rest of the vodka in his glass and straightened his arm toward Artem, "One more drink and your driver can take me home, yes?" They raised their glasses, "For the Motherland."

"For the Motherland, my great friend." Artem said as he raised his glass and gulped its contents down.

The limo made the 120-kilometer drive to The

Bear's home in Karlovy Vary in an hour and a half, not bad since there are no freeways. The Bear called to tell Marta that he was on his way, and he talked to his little Cristina, he loved them so much.

When the limo approached the villa, Grigori handed the driver a hundred-euro bill and thanked him for getting him there so fast. As the limo came to a stop in the drive way the front door of the villa opened. Cristina and Marta came out onto the front step. Marta waited but Cristina ran to the limo yelling "Papa, Papa." She was so happy to see her Papa after so long a time apart.

She jumped into his arms almost before Grigori could get to his feet. He lifted her over his head, then pulled her into his arms "Malen'koye solnyshko (little Sun) you are getting so big, I can barely lift you anymore. Soon you will be a woman. You make me so proud.

"I missed you so much Papa. Are you going to stay long? I have a violin recital tomorrow at my school, can you come? We can go to the park. Oh, Papa, I missed you so much."

"Yes, yes, kotyonok (kitten) I will stay and attend your recital, nothing will keep me from your beautiful music." Delaying his plans in an instant, he will text Lyev later.

"Oh, Papa, you make me so happy."

When they reached the top step, he put Cristina down and embraced Marta, the love of his life. "Marta, moye serdtse i dusha tvoya (my heart and soul are yours). Come let us go inside and you can tell me about my beautiful family." They turned and, arm and arm between his loved ones, Grigori led them into the villa.

Marta had dinner ready for them. Grigori and Cristina sat at the table and talked while Marta went into the kitchen to instruct the housekeeper, Galina, that it was okay to serve obyed (dinner) as Gospodin Medvedev was at the table. Then she went back into the dining room to be with her husband. "Papa, you always make me laugh, where do you learn those silly jokes."

"Cristina, your Papa knows many people and he has many stories to tell you about distant lands and customs," Marta said as she entered the room.

"Oh, Papa can you tell me about all the distant places you have been, tell me about America. You have been to America haven't you? I hear it is a wonderful place, much different than here, or St. Petersburg. The people are so friendly in America."

Just then Galina came through the door carrying a tray with a big pot of schi. She served the family each a ladle of the cabbage soup in bowls she had pre-set at the table that morning in anticipation of the homecoming. She filled the glasses, also in the table set, with kompot, a fruit juice.

"Da lyubov' moya (Yes my love), I will tell you stories about my many travels, but first eat your soup, I have not been able to enjoy my family for too long. Galina, this schi is delicious." When they were finished with their soup, Galina took away their soup bowls and replaced them with plates of kotlety (meatballs) and mashed potatoes.

"Ah, all my favorites, I have been eating out of restaurants too long. It is good to enjoy this homed cooked meal, Galina you are as good as the best chefs in all of the Soviet, uh, Federation." Galina smiled, did a slight curtsy, and off she went to the kitchen.

Their dining was more formal than a typical Russian family where they would place all the food on the table to be passed around; but the Medvedev home was not a typical Russian family. Grigori, in the years since his release from the American prison, has amassed a fortune to make him one of the richest businessmen in the Russian Federation, a billionaire. He did not live as lavishly as you might expect of one of his stature. He lived a modest life relatively speaking. He had homes in the Karlovy Vary and St. Petersburg; but he also had apartments in Moscow, London, the Emirates and a villa on the Black Sea. Galina would travel wherever the women would go. Lyev was The Bear's personal valet, as well as his many other duties.

Galina reentered the dining room carrying a tray, she set it down on the credenza. Then she placed a dish of strawberry kisel at each setting, and poured hot Zavarka tea into the cups of the adults and filled Cristina's cup with Oolong green tea. She then took away the dishes, only Grigori was finished but Marta and Cristina had Galina remove their dishes too.

The jellied strawberry kompot was a favorite in the family, especially Cristina who did not hesitate to begin devouring the delightful treat.

When the dessert was served Galina went to the credenza opened a hot dish holding warm towels and placed one at each family setting.

"Well lapochka (sweetie pie) you have practiced and practiced and practiced and now you are ready to show the world that you are a violinist."

"Papa, Papa," Cristina laughed "the world will not be at my recital. My teacher Gospodin Vasiliev says I am ready but there will only be parents there watching. I will play my best because you will be there for me, Otets (father). You miss so many of my school activities. I am so happy that you will be there for me tomorrow night."

Marta interrupted, "If you two don't mind I think I will go to help Galina in the kitchen. It will give you two a moment to talk." She left the room.

"What else have you been learning in your school, Cristina?" The loving father asked his precious daughter. "I can tell that you have learned so much in the weeks that I have been away."

"Well Papa, I have learned the entire dictionary and have skipped all my years so that I will graduate in the spring at the top of my class."

Grigori had a sudden chill in the realization that his precious daughter is growing so quickly and soon will marry and be out of the house before he even had a chance to know her childhood. Cristina has been the reason for his life, and Marta. Without his family he would still be depressed in St. Petersburg. *Marta saved my life and Cristina gave my life meaning*, he thought.

"Cristina moya lybov' (my love) you are only seven years old. You try to have fun with me, but I am not so dumb as I look." They both broke into laughter.

"Otets" the conversation took a serious note, "We have been studying about world history. Why is there so much hate in the world? Why has there been so many wars and so many people died because countries cannot live together? What makes this happen, Papa?" I cannot find answers, I ask questions but my teachers do not have answers."

Grigori was struck by this question. Cristina did not know that her Papa was one of the people in the middle of many of the conflicts that sprung up around the world. The Bear, a term that was unknown in the family, was responsible for the arms that many of the warring factions used to kill their adversaries. A week ago, he sold arms to rebels in Mali who were fighting the radical Muslim government, to whom he sold weapons three months earlier.

Did he detect a small bit of guilt, considering his beautiful daughter was so passionate about her questions? "Malysh (baby), lyubov moya, the world is a complicated place, there are things that cause countries to go to war. It is the way it has been since the beginning of man. I wish it could be different," Grigori's voice did not show any sign of guilt.

"Yes, Papa, I wish it could be different too. That is why I will be taking classes in politics. I want to be a diplomat when I grow up. I want to try to change this thing. I want peace to come to the world when I grow up!"

25

The Mercedes G11 drove the distance from Karlovy to Vaclav Havel Airport. Entering a private gate, the automobile turned left toward the private executive hangers. The driver opened the storage compartment on the arm rest and pulled out a remote control. Pushing the top button on the device, the hanger doors began to open slowly. When there was enough room for the Mercedes to get through he pulled into the hanger and pushed the second button on the remote to close the doors. He drove past the Falcon 900 to the office in the corner. Lou and his abductor, Lyev, were in the back seat, Lou was unconscious. Lyev had injected him with ketamine, the black hole drug; he was out-out.

Lyev got out at the office, ordering the driver, Joseph, to drive the unconscious Mr. Bennett to the Falcon. "Carry him inside the jet and put him in the first seat on the opposite isle, fasten his seat belt and strap his arms to the seat." Lyev handed Joseph three velcro straps. "Secure his legs and sit with him until I get there."

Lyev went into the office and booted up the computer. Logging into the airport website, he filed a flight plan for the Falcon, Vaclav Havel Airport to Karlovy Vary. He will pick up Gospodin Medvedev at Karlovy Vary in the morning.

Grigori tucked Cristina in, gave her a sweet kiss, "Spokoynoy nochi moya milaya printsessa (good night my sweet princess).

As he slowly closed the door he heard a sleepy voice, "Spokoynoy nochi moy dorogoy Papa."

Grigori quietly walked down the stairs and went into the sitting room where Marta was waiting for him. "Now, moya lyubov', I will have my time with the love of my life. Do you have time to love an old man?

Marta put the book down that she was reading, it missed the end table and fell to the floor, she looked at Grigori, then slowly raised herself off the lounge and slipped into his arms kissing him all over his face. "I have missed you so much my old tiger. Now I will be your pray."

Grigori embraced her then put his right arm down around her thigh and picked her up into his arms. He kissed her in the nap of her neck, "Poydem so mnoy, moy malen'kiy golub' (come with me my little dove). He carried her up the stairs and briskly into the master bedroom.

It was early when Grigori text Lyev to let him know about the delay. They would instead be leaving tonight, he texted, at ten, after Cristina's recital and the little time he could have with his beautiful family. After he made love to his young beautiful wife, Marta; he didn't text that part.

It was late, Grigori slowly opened the door of Cristina's room, "I love you my kitten," he whispered and closed the door.

"Ya tozhe lyublyu tebya, Papa"

Lyev was waiting, engine running as The Bear came out of his villa. Grigori leaped down the steps and got into the front seat of the limo, something he did only when they would be alone for the trip. "Lyev, I love my family. I always rest from the stresses that our business produces. This afternoon Cristina played the most beautiful violin that even David Oistrakh would be amazed.

"Esperanto (boss), I am so happy that you have had some time with your family. Everything is ready for our departure; our package is ready for the transport. We leave in one half hour for St. Petersburg." The Bear did not say a word during the trip to the airport. Instead he was deeply contemplating his enjoyment of the past two days.

26

Alexandria, VA.

It was 4 a.m. The phone to Paul Wells bedroom rang one time, he picked it up, "Sir, they took him!

"I'll be there in 30."

"Mmmm, Paul you have to go? I love you, be careful," Mrs. Wells sleepily said as she fell back asleep. She was used to these early calls.

CIA headquarters, Langley, VA

Paul J.R. Wells walked briskly up the hall of the east side of the CIA building. Before he got to the Russian room Kerensky came out of the door, "Director, I am so glad you got here. Piko has been shot and Louis has been abducted and is missing." They both went back into the Russian room.

The Russian room was alive with activity. "Director," said young Marlena Vasiliev. "We have word from the police in Karlovy Vary that a cab driver named Pyotr Dvorak has been found dead in his cab in Karlovy Vary, he was alone."

"Piko," Paul whispered barely heard.

"Yes, Director, Piko; and Mr. Bennett is missing."

"Okay Richard, get Vlad over to Karlovy Vary to check it all out. I'm thinking that they will transport him somewhere in the Falcon, find out where it is and where it will be going. Get all our assets on alert and keep me informed."

"Sir, SIR!" a female voice came from the back of the room. "Director Wells. I have linked into a camera near the intersection that the abduction occurred. You

187

need to see this, sir."

The Director walked over to the young woman. He immediately recognized the face. "Let me see that video." The intern pushed a button on her console. The video showed a gruesome depiction of the events of the morning of the abduction. Everyone looked with amazement as they witnessed the abduction of Lou Bennett and the execution of Piko. "We have to put every asset in the Federation from St. Pete to Siberia on this. I want to know where Lou Bennett has been taken. Put everyone on it. And you," he looked at the intern, "I'll see you in my office in ten."

Paul walked out of the Russian room took a hard right to his office down the hall. He went in and sat at his desk. He took a deep breath, "Shit!" He picked up his phone and said, Pennie, get me the President." He sat there for a moment in silence, the buzzer on his phone rang, he pressed down on the lever, "Pennie?"

"The President on line one, sir."

"Mr. President, our man is in trouble. I think we should initiate 'Operation Bear Trap'." Paul Wells listened as the President of the United States of America talked with intent. Five minutes later they hung up. The director was working on a plan, a plan in which the President had some important input. This was suddenly elevated to a top priority directive.

There was a knock on the door. "Come in." The door slowly opened, and a head appeared around the edge of the door.

"Director Wells?" a meek voice came from the talking head.

"Jessica Vega."

"Uncle Pauo," with a warm smile on her face. She entered the room and sat in the chair that Director Wells motioned to in front of his desk. She was not sure why she was summoned.

"That was good work in there, Miss Vega. You have shown promise during your internship. Off the record, you're a natural. I am particularly impressed that you took the initiative to search the area for video evidence of the abduction. While everyone was reacting to the news, you kept your wits about you, even as you have an emotional tie to Lou that would have broken most people. That was impressive." The director paused, giving her a chance to comment.

"It was just that emotional tie that made me search for that camera at the bank across the intersection. It was obvious that this was an abduction, not an execution. I know every second counts, maybe it's just part of my DNA. Pop has been training me since I told him I wanted to be a spy at five. At first it was just fun, but I took to it like a fly on sh.. well you know all that."

"Yes, Jess. I'm aware. Your father has done well with you. He told me that, if you were to go into the services, he wanted you to be as prepared as possible. You're fluent in Russian, and you even learned Farsi at the university. You're a black belt in karate and jiu jitsu. You're an expert in weaponry and a sniper rated marksman. And your computer skills are impressive to say the least. I'd say you are determined to be a spy, as you said at five. That's why I've enrolled you the next class at Camp Perry, in one week. You can take some time off before you start."

Jessica was smiling widely. She stood up and walked around the desk to give the Director a kiss on the cheek. "This is the last time I'll do that, and the last time I'll call you Uncle Pauo, Mr. Director. Thank you, thank you." She turned to leave but suddenly turned back and said to the Director, "As for time off, I'd rather spend the time here. I have some ideas that I want to explore. The Bear has a plan for Uncle Lou. He doesn't intend to kill him, or he'd would have already done that. I think he wants to imprison him, like he was imprisoned for twenty years. That is his revenge, I'm sure of it. I have been studying as much as I can find out about Grigori Afanasyevich Medvedev."

She almost turned to leave once more, but stopped one more time, she wasn't finished, "I know his business dealings, his family life, how he spends his leisure time, I think I know how he thinks. So, with your permission, I'll get back to work."

Jessica turned, once again, and left an impressed Director Wells alone in his office. She jogged down the hall, anxious to get back to her cubicle. She was concerned that too much time had passed for her to get access to other cameras near the incident; most closed-circuit cameras were on a twenty-four-hour loop at which time they would record over the previous twenty-four-hour taping. Some of them may have been updated to digital, which would allow many more hours of recording, depending on the gigabytes of memory in the system. It has been twenty-two hours since Lou's abduction plenty of time to retrieve information; but these queries take time. Time that flies by when she needs time to stop.

Jessica marched directly to her cubicle, not taking a second to Look into any of the other cubicles, they were all engulfed in their own tasks and, she was deep in thought.

As Jessica came to her cubicle a young Johnathan Amoroso, in the cubicle before Jessica's, looked up and spouted out, "Jessica!" he stood up to cut her off before she passed his cubicle. "Jessica, I have something you might like to see." Johnathan escorted Jessica into his cubicle and sat in his chair. Then he grabbed a side chair, "Sit down Jessica. This is a view of the crash taken from a dash cam, I found it uploaded on YouTube using our advanced recognition software."

"This is amazing, Johnathan, it shows more detail than any of the other pic's that we've found." Zooming in on the Mercedes, Johnathan pointed at the plate, "2D74257."

"How 'bout the truck that T-boned the taxi, run that film beginning to end to get as much detail as you can." Jessica gave instructions to Johnathan like she was his superior, not an intern, and Johnathan followed her directions.

They were onto something and there wasn't enough time to question. "It's too bad the light changed and the car with the camera had to move on before the men got out of the Mercedes. I'll follow up on my computer," Johnathan, good work."

When Jessica got to her cubicle she immediately sent Johnathan a text, "I wonder if there were any cell videos of the crash, please see if you can find out. And let me know who the registered owner of the Mercedes is, thx." Then she downloaded the dash cam recording on her PC and put it on her dashboard for future reference. She then sought out other security cameras in close proximity. Time was against her.

There was a bank across the street from the other security camera she found. It would have been a great angle, but the twenty-four-hour loop had already taped over the time slot. The next closest security cameras were at least a block away. Suddenly she heard a dull tone sound and a text message icon appears on her dashboard. She clicked on it, "Eureka, I got it!" It was Johnathan. She stood up and hurried over to the next cubicle.

"You can count on millennials uploading everything to the net," Johnathan said with excitement. Using his pointer, he rewound the video to the beginning. It didn't show the actual crash, probably just after the crash, as soon as the video app could be turned on. He ran the video. The audio was useless; the sounds of amazement, disbelief and shock. The video, however, was perfect. It starts just after the crash; the truck against the taxi. The whole thing happened fast. The truck started backing out of the crash just as a black Mercedes pulled up alongside the taxi. The truck continued backing out, turned forward and left the scene.

Two men got out of the Mercedes and ran to the passenger side of the taxi. In an instant they opened the door of the taxi, pulled out the passenger, put a black hood over his head, and shoved him into the back seat of the Mercedes. One of them got in the back seat with the hooded man while the other pulled out a pistol and shot the taxi-driver once, then got into the driver's seat of the Mercedes. In an instant the Mercedes disappeared so fast that most of the witnesses didn't have time to process exactly what just happened. The person taking the video made some expletives in shock, then it looked like they ran away, for good reason.

Jessica and Johnathan looked at each other.

"Call your supervisor Johnathan, this is too hot! And share this video to me."

Jessica then had a thought, *if the plan was to wisp Uncle Lou out of the country on the Falcon then the airport!* Jessica started typing on her keyboard. The picture on the monitor instantly changed to a number of search sites for the airport in Prague. She started scrolling down to find the one that would get her into the airport security…"Wait!" She said out loud. "They wouldn't waste their time driving to Prague. They would fly out of the airport at Karlovy Vary, but, is it capable of handling the Falcon 900? Yes!" She remembered the research she did on The Bear. *He bought that particular jet for two distinct reasons, the distance it was able to fly, and, its ability to land on short landing strips.*

Her mind was working at light speed. She already had the cameras booted up at the Karlovy Vary Airport. To her surprise the airport is the forth busiest airport in the Czech Republic, plenty big enough to handle larger jets than the Falcon. The software, that only the CIA and maybe the NSA had, was capable of hacking into any camera system connected to the world wide web. Soon she had a video of the Falcon departing the airport, at…10:20 p.m. last night? *Wow, why did they wait, uh, thirty hours and twenty minutes to fly out? What was the reason for their delay?* "You'd think they would get the hell out of there as fast as they could," she said softly, out loud.

"Jessica," the voice of Carmela Medina, her supervisor, suddenly broke the train of thought that Jessica had going.

"Yes, Ms. Medina?"

"I've been watching you follow your instincts in your search, Jessica, I'm very impressed. Where are you going with this?" She had a look of great interest on her face.

"Ms. Medina, I think I know where they took unc, uh, Mr. Bennett. The Falcon left the airport at Karlovy Vary at 10:20 last night, Czech time, bound for," she tapped a key on her keyboard, "St. Petersburg, Russian Federation. They should have landed about an hour ago."

"That's good work, Jessica." Ms. Medina then turned to Jonathan, in the next cubicle, "Jonathan, follow up on Jessica's research, find out where they went after they left the airport, check the offices of Liberty Arms. Don't leave any stone unturned! Jessica, come with me."

But, Ms. Medina, I'd like to finish this one, I have…"

"Jessica, Jonathan is very highly trained and will follow up on your good work. I have something more important for you to do." She turned, Jessica followed her out of the Russian room. As they walked down the hall Medina began to give Jessica some instructions, "The Director called me and instructed me to send you to the farm for some preliminary instruction prior to your officially entering training. You have impressed someone up there, Jessica, and I agree."

"Thank you, Ms. Medina, but I'd like to finish…"

"You can gather your belongings and report to Mr. Polomar in room 155 in twenty. Don't be late. This is important, Jessica. You're in!"

They stopped walking in front of Ms. Medina's office. Medina opened the door, walked in, and shut it behind her; leaving a stunned Jessica standing in the hall. She didn't take any time to think about all that just happened, except to wonder why she walked her all the way to her office, only to tell her to go back to get her stuff and report to Palomar in twenty.

Jessica turned instantly and jogged back to her cubicle. She gathered what little stuff she had into her bag, then sat down to her computer. *I have about fifteen minutes to go,* she sat down and began typing.

Jonathan popped his head over the divider, "What was that all about?"

"I've been reassigned," Jessica said without

looking up, "I still have a few minutes before I have to go."

Jonathan said, "I don't seem to be able to find out when the Falcon landed at Pulkovo."

"That's because they diverted from their plan," Jessica impatiently retorted, "Like they did on the way to Prague." She was typing a mile a minute on her Keyboard. "Jonathan, I have to go, you need to check every airport from Lake Lagoda to Siberia, we need to find that Falcon." She showed her frustration as she got up from her computer and turned to leave.

She stopped and turned to Jonathan, put her hand on his, "I have faith in you Jon, keep looking we have to find him." She turned again and left the Russian room.

27

Falcon 900, somewhere over Northern Siberia.

Lou's eyes fluttered and then opened into little slits. He was groggy, but he remembered his training from…hell, he couldn't remember. Everything was blurry. *Where the hell am I,* he thought. He stayed still, trying to figure out just what happened to him. One thing he was sure of, it wasn't good.

"You are coming back to the world, Mr. Bennett," The Bear said with a seemingly comforting voice. "You had a very bad crash, it was a good thing that my men were there to get you out before the police got to the scene. I'm sure you would not want to have to answer their questions. Carrying a gun in Czech Republic is terrible thing, you could go to prison for years, unless you have diplomatic immunity, Mr. Bennett. You don't have diplomatic immunity, do you, Mr. Bennett?"

Lou remained still, listening to *The Bear*, he assumed.

"Louis, open your eyes, I know you are awake."

Lou was still trying to get his bearings. He couldn't seem to move his arms, he must be strapped to the chair. He opened his eyes.

"That's better, Mr. Bennett. We have much to talk about. It will not be too long before we reach our destination."

"What destination?" Lou replied sarcastically, "Why am I tied to this seat Mr. Medvedev?"

"You know the answer to all those questions, Louis, think about it, it should be very obvious." The Bear leaned back in his seat and took a drink of the glass of U'luvka Vodka he had in his cup holder.

Lou looked out the window of the Falcon, "That's a lot of white out there, where are we, Siberia?"

"It doesn't matter, my friend, you could be in Fiji for that matter, look out the window, and enjoy the sun. get into that beautiful view, soon you will pray for that view, and the fresh air to go with it."

The Dassault Falcon 900LX streaked across the white-out landscape of northern Siberia. "By the way, Mr. Bennett, the cabbie, Piko, I'm sorry to say he did not make it, he is dead. I'm sure Director Wells will feel his loss as he places another star on the 'Wall'. Maybe he is the lucky one."

Lou began to speak when he felt the sting of a needle piercing his left arm, everything went dark.

28

The Falcon 900LX, Southbound

Revenge is an addiction in a mind that only had the hope of revenge to keep it's sanity, or lose it. The Bear never thought he would escape the hell hole that had him entrapped for what seemed like an eternity. And then, after finally being released, to find that his family, "My beautiful Cristina, and my young son Vladimir…and little kotyonok Katarina. Dead! DEAD!" Grigori lamented quietly, wiping a tear from his cheek.

"Lyev" he spoke over his shoulder. The Falcon streaked Southwest bound. There would be a slight change in plans, again; the Falcon would be going elsewhere. The Bear has his most important deal of his career. "Lyev, what time will we arrive in Tehran, I would like to get a quick nap before we get there. Lyev!" he put on his com unit and spoke again, "Lyev…"

"We have a strong tail wind, boss, that will get us there in four hours, you have plenty of time to rest, sir," Lyev replied. The Falcon banked twenty degrees bearing south at 32,000 ft. for Tehran. The Bear settled in for the flight, his thought turned to the deal he must secure with the permission of the Minister of Defense, Hossein Dehghan. The political atmosphere in Iran requires a special touch. A talent that The Bear has honed throughout his career as the most sought-after arms dealer in the world, by those who want his services, and those wanting to stop him. The Bear is known for his ability to get the most sophisticated weaponry to anyone able to pay the cost. He has no credo, no conscience…no loyalty.

The Iranians are the one customer that must

be dealt with in full disclosure. Their actions are dictated by their Holy Qur'an, or the interpretation of the book by the Ayatollah Ali Khamenei. The Bear would tell them exactly what he wanted to do. He needed their help. He could only hope that the Iranian supreme leader would approve his plan to cripple the American Eagle, their mutual enemy. There can be nothing done unknown to the Supreme Leader.

"Boss," Lyev spoke over his shoulder. The noise of the Falcon's engines much quieter than when they were climbing, earlier.

"We will be arriving at Mehrabad Airport in approximately twenty minutes. We have clearance to land straight in on runway two. You'd better get your things together and buckle your seat belt for the descent."

Get your things together. A memory crossed The Bear's mind, a stark reminder of why he must get his revenge. He gathered his presentation together and put the papers neatly in his brief. Now, it was time to go to work!

As the Falcon taxied toward the executive terminal, as it had in the past, a caravan of four GAZ-2975 "Tigr" (Tiger) four door all terrain combat vehicles, the best Russian made multipurpose vehicle that The Bear could get them, escorted the Falcon to a large military hanger. As the Falcon approached the hanger the large doors opened so they could quickly get sheltered from the American spy satellites. Once the Falcon was secured the crew wheeled out a Russian made Sikorsky UH-60M Black Hawk tactical transport helicopter.

As the Bear and Lyev descended the Falcon steps, a platoon of Iranian Republican Guard infantry surrounded the Falcon. The commander of the group ordered Lyev to stay with the Falcon and wait for further orders.

The Bear was escorted to the Sikorski, which was now warming up for the impending flight. Grigori turned to Lyev, "I will be safe in the company of my friends Lyev. Keep ready for a quick departure." General Mostafa Najjar escorted him to the helicopter. When they completed the hundred meter walk a soldier opened the sliding door on the Sikorski and motioned to The Bear to get in. The general followed, sitting in the seat next to The Bear. He motioned The Bear to put on his safety belt and headset.

The Bear said, almost yelling before realizing it, "Mostafa, it is so good to see you after all these years."

General Najjar did not answer him but looked to the open door as two more passengers appeared, Hossein Dehghan, Minister of Defense and Armed Forces Logistics (MODAFL); and his aid. The Minister and his aid secured their safety belts and headsets, "Comrade Medvedev, my old friend, it is good to see you, I understand you have some new weapon for me to consider," The Minister said in Farsi. Then he signaled to the pilot to proceed.

"Yes, my old friend," The Bear replied in flawless Farsi, "but I was hoping to meet in your nice quiet office, this is of some importance, and quite technical."

"Patience Grigori, I have to inspect one of our new technical facilities. It won't be so long, and we will have our quiet meeting. Oh, I have no manners, Grigori, let me introduce General Najjar, our new commander of Irregular Warfare." He did not mention the aid.

The Bear did not acknowledge that that he knew the general. He reached out to shake the general's hand. "It is so good to make your acquaintance, General Najjar." The two have a long, though very discrete, history; so, it is not unusual that the Minister is unaware of their history.

General Najjar is an Iranian politician and retired IRGC General. He was Interior Minister of Iran from 2009 to 2013 and Minister of Defense in the first cabinet of Mahmoud Ahmadinejad from 2005 to 2009. That he is now the head of the super-secret 'Irregular Warfare' unit is somewhat surprising to The Bear, he is qualified, to be sure. It is just a surprise to hear that the infamous unit has been resurrected; it was thought to have been dissolved in 1982 after the Iranian war with Iraq. The world was shocked by the use of weapons of mass destruction, in the war, by both the Iranians and the Iraqi's. Thousands of Kurdish civilians killed, and the entire village of Halabja nearly wiped out in 1988. The technology used to produce the cyanide gas bombs and artillery was provided to the Iranians by the young KGB arms dealer, Grigori Medvedev; as was the technology to produce the mustard gas used by the Iraqi's. Now, years later The Bear is about to give the Iranians the ultimate weapon to be used against the Americans, their mutual enemy.

Minister Dehghan, also had an impressive past. He was the commander of the Iranian contingent in Lebanon during the bombing of the American and French military barracks in 1983. It is widely believed that the orders and the training for the bombings was coordinated through the Minister. The emergence of Hezbollah as the predominant anti-Israeli terrorist group can be directly linked to the Minister's presence as the commander of the Iranian presence in the region. Hezbollah is an arm of the Iranian anti-Israeli insurgency. If the Iranians pulled their support for Hezbollah, the lack of funds would starve the movement.

The Sikorsky landed about an hour later. The cabin the four occupied had no windows so The Bear did not know his location. It did not matter where he was, only if he would be able to get back. The Bear was well aware that the Iranians could change his plans in an instant. There was no friendship in the end. The fact is, the Iranians were only concerned with their own future. If the world ended tomorrow their only concern is whether they were on the side of Allah.

The helicopter came to rest, and the sliding door opened immediately. The Minister was the first to get out, followed by his aid, The Bear was next, and General Najjar last to get out. Grigori had a slight feeling of claustrophobia as he filed out snugly between the others.

"You will have to please excuse me Grigori," the Minister said as he waited for his guest to catch up. They were beyond the blades of the chopper. "Come my friend and we will find a place to talk. I have brought you with us on this trip for a very good reason. We need to come to a…a, let's just say we could use your special talents."

The Bear was intrigued, "You know, my friend, I have the resources to get you whatever you may need for your defense. Also, Defense Minister, I have a proposal that you should, I am sure, find will align with your future plans." He left it at that for the moment hoping that the Minister would take the bite.

"Come, my friend, you will have to stay in my suite until I finish my inspection, for security reasons uh, about a couple hours at the most, then we talk." He escorted Grigori into his private suite, "I may not be able to drink the spirits, but, my friend, I have brought in a bottle of Your favorite, U'luvka, to comfort you while you wait." Then he graciously left, the door lock clicked.

The Bear was just a bit apprehensive, this is very unusual. He felt that there was no reason to worry, but, still... He used the time to second guess the 'special talents' the Minister may have need of. The Iranians have become very resourceful in the procurement of their military needs. They have a capable defense industry and have bought much of the equipment that was left by the Americans as they deserted Iraq. The insurgency was more than glad to trade the American equipment for the arms they needed.

The Americans made a big mistake, underestimating the cowardice of the Iraqi regular army. At the first sight of resistance the Iraqi fighters abandoned their positions, dressed in civilian clothes and melted into the population. The light armored insurgents did not need the tanks, trucks and other abandoned equipment. They sold it to ISIS, Iran, and all takers; it was very profitable. The deals worked well for Iran but put a slump in The Bear's business.

The Bear wondered where he was. The chopper had no windows, for very good reason. And, they were keeping him in seclusion. His best guess would be Natanz, the secret underground nuclear base. The Americans knew about the base. They also knew that it was a nuclear hardened facility, deep underground. What they didn't know was that attached to the facility was Iran's nuclear laboratory. If The Bear was to make an educated guess he would think he was in Natanz. If this was true, he could likely help the Minister; and, the Minister could help him.

29

Karlovy Vary

Vladimir Drugov arrived in Karlovy Vary Mid-afternoon. He went directly to the corner where the accident happened, so he could interview any witnesses before they, conveniently, forgot what they saw. Inspector Drugov of the NLC (National Law Enforcement Agency of the Czech Republic) is well known in Karlovy Vary. He is the son of a Russian KGB interrogator and a Czech mother. His parents disappeared a few years after the fall of the USSR; but not until they sent their two sons Pyotr the younger by eight years, and Vlad to stay with the Dvorak family in Karlovy Vary. The boys took the name of the family who took them in, Anna and Karl Dvorak, when the boys grew up Vlad changed his name back to Drugov; while Piko, as the family called him, kept the name of the only parents he really knew.

Vlad walked the intersection where the accident occurred. He knew that the accident could not have gone unnoticed. All he had to do was to find some of the people who saw it take place. He walked into the bank on the southeast corner. Inspector Drugov walked directly to the bank manager's office. "Mr. Coufal, it has been years since we last had the pleasure to meet," inspector Drugov said with his hand outstretched, "how is your family, your beautiful wife Katrina, and Sophia, she must be a lovely young woman my friend?"

"Yes, my good friend she is my pride and joy,

what brings you into my bank Vladimir?"

I am investigating the accident that happened in the intersection the day before yesterday. Your bank has, perhaps, the best vantage point."

"Did any of your people see the accident? I must know everything, this is a matter of international concern, Stepan."

Vlad spent about a half hour interviewing the three employees of the bank. One young man, a teller trainee, had taken a video with his smart phone. The video was uploaded to YouTube. It went viral, about three hundred thousand subscribers saw Lou Bennett get abducted and Piko murdered. Vlad downloaded the video from YouTube and confiscated the banks outside camera feed and headed to the morgue to identify Petro's body. *Piko you are too young, I will find who did this to you, my little brother*, Vlad lamented.

Inspector Drugov opened the door to room 205 at the Heluan Hotel. He didn't check in to the hotel, CIA field agents never do. He had been chasing leads all day. He was tired, but he still had some business to take care of. He threw his brief case on the bed. "Now Mr. Bennett, let's see what you left behind." Vlad was a veteran investigator, if there was a clue in this room he would find it.

There was a chair sitting in the room, kind of out of place, it was away from the table awkwardly as if someone pushed it away as they got up. The other chair was also at an angle from the table, but it was in a position that would be expected when someone casually gets up. He first looked at the guest chair.

"This person was not comfortable in this room,

he was Federoff, why was he anxious to be here?"

Federoff's chair was clean, he noted as he turned it in his hands to check every surface. Then he went to the table, *this is where he would put a bug,* he thought. As he gripped the table to turn it over he felt something under the lip. "Amateurs," he said to himself as he turned the table over. "Our Mr. Federoff put this here in a hurry. He knew that Bennett was a trained police officer and he put this here when he had a small opportunity.

"I am surprised Mr. Bennett let his guard down to allow this to be put here, maybe it was there when he checked in." Vlad stood the table upright and put the bug on the table and placed a glass over the top of it, "If it is live that will muffle it." He would send it to the lab for analysis. They can tell its origins, and maybe give a clue to the owner.

Vlad combed the rest of the room, it was clean. "Strange, Wells said he had a bag with a change of clothes and a Makarov. Maybe it was in the cab, but it wasn't logged with the evidence. I'll be checking in with the locals again. Corrupt bastards."

There are other things Vlad has to do, but they will wait until tomorrow. Now, he has to send the information he accumulated throughout the day to his handler, Director Wells at Langley. There's likely not much that the analysts don't already know, "These guys are good...but not as good as me."

30

Secret Military Base, Natanz, Iran

There was a click as the lock on the door was turned. A man, tall with an obvious military build, walked into the room. He was dressed in the kind of suit that was typical of the Iranian secret service. "Have you been comfortable, Mr. Medvedev," the man said as he walked across the room. "General Najjar Has sent me escort you to his office, please come with me." He turned and extended his arm toward the door.

The Bear left the room, there was another man, dressed in military fatigues, outside the door who started walking as The Bear turned down the hall. The man in the suit followed, locking the door behind them. No one said a word as the three men made their way out of the building, it was dark. The place was busy with activity but looked much like any other Iranian base that he had been. He, still, was not completely sure where he was. The men crossed the street, dodging an armored vehicle, and entered an office building.

There was a sign across the top of the doorway, written in Persian, 'National Police Headquarters.' Grigori didn't have a good feeling about this unusual situation as it was unfolding. He followed his escort down the hall into the elevator, third floor, room 317. He was being very observant at this time, a trait he picked up over the years. The two escorts stayed outside as Grigori entered the room alone.

"Okay, Grigori," General Najjar said with a subdued smile on his face, "now we talk."

"I am so glad you came to Iran," the general continued, "you know you are practically a national hero, at least to the few who know you. Tell me my friend, is it true, what I have heard about the dealings you have had with the nation of Jordan? Did you arrange for them to buy the schematic for our anti-missile system? Is that true, my friend? I am so very disappointed with you."

The Bear looked the general in the eye and confidently said, "General Najjar, you understand I have many clients that I deal with. Yes, I have recently sold the Jordanians the schematic of your Iranian A5 system, the one that your scientists scrapped last year. It was a fool's play, my friend. They paid well."

"Yes, Grigori, that is your main concern, I see. But, you see the scientist that gave you the information was a spy for the Americans, and the plans, that you arranged for the Americans to get through their ally, Jordan? Well, let's just say that Scientist is now facing the judgement of the most holy one. He did wish to be martyred."

Suddenly this meeting did not feel as welcoming as he had hoped. The Bear stood up, knowing what was to happen next. General Najjar got up and walked to the door, opened it and the two men waiting outside walked in to take The Bear away. They returned to the helicopter that brought them to the base. Then returned to Mehrabad.

Much to the surprise of The Bear and Lyev they were allowed to fly the Falcon out; but, they both had the same thought. "They will shoot us down at the border, Lyev, never trust the Iranians. General Najjar was as corrupt as they get. Do we have the defenses armed and ready?"

"Yes, boss, but you should fasten your five-point harness." Lyev would arm the defenses when needed, or it would be detectable.

The Falcon 900 streaked across the Northern Iranian desert at 500 miles per hour. not fast enough to outrun the two MiG-29's that escorted them as they departed Iranian air space, over the Caspian Sea. Lyev put the Falcon in overdrive, that's what he called it. The custom fitted Falcon was not the ordinary corporate Falcon. The Bear would spare no expense to fit this super Falcon 900 with the most advanced air combat system available. "My kind of business sometimes requires a smart get-away."

Lyev keyed his mic, "Thank you for the escort, my friends, I will no longer be needing you." He then lifted open a red switch guard on his control panel and flicked the switch up, the writing under the switch, LMA, meant 'Left Missile Armed'. He repeated the same procedure for the RMA; armed and locked. An alarm on his radar screen signaled that the MiG's were seeking 'Lock' on the Falcon.

Lyev pushed the red button on his control stick, firing the two guided missiles from their hidden rear fuselage tubes, then he pushed his stick forward into a critical dive. At 20 thousand feet he had some room to maneuver. The Falcon was heading directly at the Caspian Sea. He then banked to the left and leveled off at five hundred feet. One more bank to the right put the Falcon back on coarse below radar detection.

The wreckage of the two MiG-29's fell to the sea. Never firing their missiles; The power of surprise saved the day, a ten-million-dollar upgrade worth every penny. "You okay boss?" Lyev said over the intercom.

"Holy Shit! Lyev "My stomach is on the ceiling and my breakfast is in my pants, HOW THE HELL DO YOU FLY THIS THING LIKE THAT?" He knew why he paid Lyev one million a year, also worth every penny.

The rest of the flight over the Caspian Sea was at Mach 1 at five hundred feet. A fishing boat rocked and the fisherman dropped their nets, ducking down, as the jet blasted a sonic boom just over their heads.

The Falcon used a lot of fuel for the next 23 minutes until they approached land. At that point Lyev ascended to thirty-eight thousand feet and slowed to a normal 400 mph and flew to Moscow to re-fuel for the flight to St. Petersburg. The Bear would never do business with Iran again; and, Iran would pay.

31

Prague

The Strakonická along the Vitara river was quiet this afternoon. Vlad didn't put his signal on as he abruptly took a left turn into the Butov Ironworks. It was Friday, so he didn't know if Artem would be there, but it was a good bet. He walked past the guard at the front door, the guard didn't make an effort to stop him, but after he passed out of sight the guard picked up his phone and dialed 2212. The line was picked up, "Da…"

The guard spoke two words, "Inspector Drugov," Vlad knew where he was going, he had been to see Artem Butov before. He walked through a large warehouse to the office in the corner. He wondered, *why does Artem Butov work out of this crappy office in the warehouse? He is one of the richest men in Eastern Europe; certainly, he could afford a plush office*. Vlad walked past the two men playing cards at a picnic table outside the office, they did not even look at him, he opened the door and walked in.

Butov was sitting behind his desk shuffling a stack of papers. "Inspector Drugov, what is the pleasure of a visit from the NLC this afternoon?" He spoke Russian.

"Artem, my friend, it is always a pleasure to visit a fellow expatriate of the Soviet. You are not pleased to see me?"

"Yes, yes, Vladimir, of course you are always welcome to my place of business, but, I am thinking this is also business that brings you to see me?"

Vlad did not waste time, He got right to the point. "Gospodin Butov, there was an accident in Karlovy a few days ago, a delivery truck collided with a taxi. The passenger, an American, was abducted and the taxi driver was shot, one time in the head."

Butov looked up, expressionless, "Why, Vladimir, are you coming all the way to Prague to tell me of this thing that happened in Karlovy Vary. Inspector, is there a connection to me, you think?"

"I looked at security tape from bank on corner where accident happened. The truck was clearly identifiable, it was one of yours. So, I am here." Vlad did not beat around the bush, he knew that Butov would have an explanation, he just wanted to hear it. Butov could not be implicated, he is too powerful, but Vlad has to follow the leads anyway.

"Yes, inspector, it was one of my trucks that hit the cab. The driver is new working for me. He panicked and fled the scene. Would you like to talk to the boy, inspector? I can give you his address. Young Viktor Bezak is at his home here in Prague, he is afraid." Butov handed Vlad a piece of paper with the name and address of the driver on it; as if he expected this visit.

Vlad took the paper, "Thank you Gospodin Butov, you have been very helpful." He got up from his chair and left Artem Butov shuffling his papers. He knew that there was no sense pushing the issue, besides, what he needs to know is the occupants of the Mercedes.

The neighborhood is working-class. Viktor Bezak must be new to the Butov organization, his apartment building appears a bit rundown. You might expect a seasoned employee in such an organization to live better. Likely he was hired simply as a delivery driver. It was unclear whether he truly just had an unfortunate accident that ushered in an opportunity for the guys in the Mercedes to take advantage, or was he setting up that opportunity. This might have been his first hit job for the Russian mob.

Vlad entered the apartment building and walked up one flight of stairs to apartment 205. There were four apartments on each floor of the six-story building. He knocked. A baby cried, then whispers. The door opened as far as the security chain would allow. A very young woman stuck her face into the crack, "Yes can I help you?" she said in Czech.

Vlad showed her his badge, "I need to talk to Viktor," he said with authority. She closed the door slightly and slid the chain loose. The NLC did not need a reason to break down a door, there was no constitutional rights in Czechia. He walked in. A young man was standing in the room holding a newborn child, a boy judging by the blue pajamas.

The three room apartment had a small sitting room, bedroom, and a cove that was the kitchen. There were dirty dishes in the sink. Only two windows, one in the kitchen and another in the bedroom that opened to the fire escape. The bathroom was down the hall, cozy. No wonder he joined the Butov, he needed to support his new family, whatever it took.

Viktor gave the child to his young wife, who then went into the bedroom and closed the door. "Mr. Butov told me you are on the way. I have nothing to hide."

"Sit, Viktor. You left the scene of an accident, that can get you into a lot of trouble; do you understand?" Viktor nodded his head. Vlad continued to put pressure on the nervous boy. "Tell me what happened to cause the accident."

Viktor blurted out, "I was coming up to the light when it changed to green. The taxi ran through the light late, and I hit him; it was bad, I panicked, so I took off…that's it, I swear."

"You know, these days there are always video cameras that see everything, Viktor, are you sure that's exactly the way it happened, Viktor."

"Yes, yes!" Viktor shouted, then looking to the door of the bedroom, he lowered his voice. "I don't know for sure, it happened so fast and I was in a hurry. That is what I remember."

Vlad did not let that go, "did you talk to anyone about what happened, go over what you would say to me?"

"No, well yes, a little, I was scared, and they just tried to help me arrange my thoughts; I needed that." "Tell me about the Mercedes, Viktor."

"When the accident happened, I panicked, I didn't stick around long enough to notice anything about the SUV."

"You know more than you think, Viktor, think. Tell me what you noticed about the two men, what did they look like? Have you ever seen them before, Viktor?"

"No, sir, I did not look at them, the windows in the SUV were dark, I could not see them. I just backed up and left, just as the SUV pulled up."

Vlad knew from the video tape that part was

probably true, but Viktor knew more, that was for sure. "Viktor, I could take you right downtown now and charge you with murder, or accessory to murder at the very least, do you want that? Think of your family in that bedroom. Think about it, do you want them to go through that?" Vlad leaned over and whispered, "if you tell me everything you know, Viktor, I will forget the whole thing, I'm not after you, I want to know who those men were, and I want to know who owns that SUV! I must know who killed my br...the taxi driver, and I must know where they took the American. You tell me that, Viktor, and I will not take you off to prison. Do you understand?"

Viktor was almost crying. "I don't want to go to prison, inspector. But I do not know. I was just told to drive the truck into the taxi." He slumped in his chair, "They gave me a radio and told me when the taxi was approaching the intersection. They told me that if I did not get it done right I would be on the street and never get a job. I had no choice!" Viktor was crying now, like a baby.

Vlad understood his plight. That was how they recruited their people. They get them to do something, then they hold that against them for the rest of their life. Vlad had seen it too many times, they could make him do anything; and, now so can Vlad. He had more to tell the inspector, though. "Viktor, I know. You have a wife and child and you can not risk them. I don't want you to do that. I will not tell anyone what you tell me, Viktor, but I need to know one more thing from you. "Who, Viktor, who told you to do it. Who were the two men, Viktor, that is what I need to know. Tell me their names, Viktor."

Viktor was gaining his composure, but, very nervous. "One of them was Joseph Popov, he works for Mr. Butov, he was the driver. I don't know the other one. I never saw him before. Joey called him Lyev, that's all I know, inspector, I swear it is true."

"Thank you, Viktor, that will do. I will not tell Mr. Butov that we had this long conversation. You can tell him you told me exactly what he instructed you to say. Tell him I was tough, threatened to send you to prison, tell him I believed you that you were afraid and drove away before the SUV stopped at the scene. Tell him that I said I was not after little fish like you, thanked you, and left. And Viktor, this is the most important thing. Do not ever tell anyone, not your friends, not your wife, or they will find out. They will kill you and sell your pretty little wife into prostitution. You understand, Viktor?" He nodded his sunken head.

"One more thing, Viktor Bezak, I know everything. Now you have to help me further. If you hear anything, at any time, you will call me." Vlad handed Viktor his card. "Remember this number to contact me, memorize it Viktor, then give it to Butov and tell him I gave it to you if you think of anything else. Viktor, do you understand me?"

"Yes, inspector, yes. I will memorize the number."

"Viktor, if you ever hear the name Lyev, or if Lyev should ever come to see Mr. Butov, You must call me. I need to know everything about him, Viktor, do you understand, Viktor?"

A nod. "If you cooperate with me, Viktor, I will protect you from Mr. Butov; if you do not, Viktor, I will tell Mr. Butov and you know what will happen."

32

Alexandra, Virginia

Ms. Penny Money, no not really but Director Wells called her that as a joke. Her name was actually Pennie Mooney. It was too good to pass up. Anyway, they have been together a long time. Pennie came up the ladder with him from when he was first made a handler. She did all the work, he got all the glory. She pushed the lever on the intercom, "Director Wells, inspector Drugov on line two."

Director Wells picked up the phone and hit the second button. "Inspector Drugov, to what do I owe the pleasure of this call." They always kept protocol when speaking in public; in this business everything is public. Vlad and Paul have been friends for a long time. They first met after the breakup of the Soviet Union. Vlad and Piko were being smuggled out of Russia; Agent Wells was their handler then. A seventeen-year-old and a nine-year-old being smuggled out of post-Soviet turmoil. That was a great adventure; they were hooked. Vlad's connections in the CIA helped him into the police force, and eventually the NLC.

"I have some critical information that's too important to follow the usual diplomatic channels." Vlad was being very diplomatic, one agency to another. "I have found the names of the men that were involved in the accident. One was an American, the one you asked for information about. There were three others, the taxi driver was shot. One of the perps, as you guys call 'em, was a local guy, a Joseph Popov, I'll take care of him myself. The other is unknown to me, a man by the name Lyev. I have sent all I know about Lyev, some pictures; he is allusive, but he has some connection to Butov."

"You think Lyev is the link to the American, Inspector? We will find out who he is, Thank you Inspector Drugov, you have been very helpful. And Vladimir…We will all miss Piko." The call ended.

The Director hit the intercom, "Pennie, get me Kerensky."

A minute later the intercom came back to life, "Kerensky on one."

"Thank you, Pennie." He pushed the first button,

"Kerensky, I will be forwarding some information from Prague about Bennett and the guy who took him; his name is Lyev, ring a bell?"

"No, boss, but we'll look at it from every angle. I'm missing Vega, she had an instinct about this stuff, she's a natural. It's seems like she's always one step ahead of everybody else.

"Keep on it, Rich, I think this guy is key. Find out who he is and let me know as soon as you have something."

33

Harvey point Defense training activity center,
Herford, NC. (Spy School)

It was dusk, the sun was low to the west. A blinding sunset behind four heavily armed agents helped give cover as they worked their way east on Jefferson St. A voice came into the ear of the four, "movement in the window." The four took defensive positions. Just then the door to the house opened, a hand came out and tossed a grenade into the street between the agents. Three took cover.

One of the four bolted for the apartment door and entered. The terrorists in the house never knew what hit them as the agent unloaded a hail of fire on them. One of the terrorists ran for the back door, opened it and was gone. By the time he reached the end of the ally the agent was hot on his heels. The next thing the terrorist was being tackled to the ground and hand cuffed.

"That's it, all home," the voice came into the ears of all the participants. The dead terrorists got up and walked out of the apartment, turned right, along with the agents that were covered in red paint from the grenade, if this was an actual operation they would have been blown to bits. "In the briefing room, on the double," they all picked up their step.

Once in the briefing room they took their seats. A man, dressed in black fatigues, stood in the front of the room. "That's just what we are trained to do, getting blown up is part of the plan. Except you, Vega, you took care of the whole terrorist cell single handedly. That's the kind of instinct the rest of you will need to develop if you want to stay alive. This is just your first shot at it, so you'll get better, or cut. Vega come with me."

Jessica followed the colonel into the office on the far end of the briefing room. "Close the door, Vega, have a seat. What's up with you, Vega, you are worlds ahead of everybody in the class. Are you a plant?"

"No, sir, I just have been getting ready for this job all my life. My father…"

"I wasn't asking you for your life's story. Before new recruits get into this facility we know more about their lives than they do. For instance, I know your father was in Delta, he had quite a career, classified of course. I'm sure he was the reason you wanted to join the service."

"With all due respect, Sir, is this about me, or my father?"

"I knew your father, Vega, He and I worked together once, I can't talk about that, classified too. He's a good man Vega; but, this is about you. I have, on my desk, a request for you to return to Langley. This is unusual, but not unheard of. You will be a good agent, Vega. It always concerns me when a recruit gets taken out of training. I'm sure they know what they're doing, but, when you get into the field you become an asset, like this desk, you are expendable. The job is more important than the tools, you can be replaced, that's why we have this school.

"I guess what I'm trying to say Vega, we train for every general scenario, but, you can never know what twists and turns a situation will take. You're smart, Use your instincts, know what is happening around you at all times, situational awareness. A wise Indian sergeant I worked with gave me some of the best advice I ever needed, "Your adversaries cannot know what is on your mind, use that to your advantage," or something like that. Oh, and more importantly, "If you don't have a will to live…"

"Your mission will not be successful, Master Sergeant Burmandi" Jessica finished.

"I shoulda known, your father was on that mission." Colonel Gooding said, nearly smiling, "Get your things and report to Ms. Parker ASAP. And Vega, good luck!"

34

Prague

Joseph Popov was a second-tier enforcer in the Butov organization. He handled some of the intimidation that was often needed on the shady side of the business. At five foot eleven he looked more like an accountant than an ex-KGB interrogator. He had no conscience, He liked it when his 'clients' objected.

Popov was working tonight. A little pressure needed to be put on a local business. Sometimes that's the way it was done. When the Russian mob wanted something they usually got their way, one way or the other.

Letov Kbely aircraft company, a company founded in 1918, was the oldest aircraft company in the region. In the wars that followed the company mostly manufactured parts for various aircraft of the conquering nations. During the Soviet era they made parts for the Russian MiG's. In the year 2000 the company, having fallen on tough times, was acquired by a French company for the manufacture of parts for large passenger aircraft.

Now the Russian mob was getting into the picture. Butov, by request of Grigori Medvedev, had his lawyers contract the Letov Kbely aircraft company for the installation of a very unique modification, manufactured by the Butov Iron Works, to a fleet of ten commercial jetliners. The CEO, Demetri Koval, declined the contract. He thought the 'Tanks' were suspicious especially coming from Butov. It all was just too clouded in secrecy. Letov Kbely is a respectable company and he was not about to get mixed up with something he thought might be used for criminal purposes.

It is precisely the reputation of the French owned company that made The Bear want to contract this company for his needs. The fittings were similar to the tanks that were used to make chemtrails; but this one had all the earmarks of a smuggling operation. His company could easily install the holding tanks, it was no big deal, and the payoff was huge; but, the French were not so quick to take such contracts as were the previous owners of Letov Kbely.

Popov drove the five kilometers from the Butov factories to Letov Kbely factories with the radio blaring. He had four incendiary bombs in the passenger seat. He wasn't worried about getting stopped by the police, they were taken care of. There was an incident on the other side of town. He saw the car behind him, keeping a good distance. Probably nobody, but…

As he turned on Aviation way, so did the other car. He thought it was nothing, but he pulled his car over and put his Makarov under his right leg. He turned off his lights.

The Czech made Skoda Octavia drove on by, took a right turn at the next street. Not suspicious, but Popov had a feeling. It was these feelings that have kept him alive over the years. He started his car and pulled out onto the deserted street. He took the next left onto the street along the factory, and parked.

He just sat there for a minute, everything was quiet. With all four grenades in his hands he got out of his car and walked up the street, turning into a short alley about half way up the block. The Octavia parked across Aviation Way did not go unnoticed.

Drugov pulled across the street slowly. He knew Popov was up to something but didn't know what. He pulled his car up to Popov's car and turned it off, leaving the key in the ignition. As he got out of the car he touched his right belt where he holstered his revolver.

Then he touched his left belt to see if his garrote was in its pouch. Drugov stood waiting along-side his car when there was the sound of glass breaking, Popov casually walked back to his car tossing the grenades into the windows of the factory as he walked.

The grenades were set on 15minute timers, he had plenty of time. He noticed Drugov standing next to the same Skoda Octavia that passed him a while back.

"Popov, I have been wanting to talk to you," Drugov said in Czech as Popov approached the vehicles.

"Why do you follow me on these dark streets, Drugov, what are you thinking, I could kill you right now and nobody here to witness."

"I was thinking the same thing, Popov, nobody would care if a degenerate like you got killed. They would probably throw a parade right down the Strakonická if you ended up dead, Popov."

Popov picked up his pace as he got closer to Drugov. "I thought you would be looking for me,"

Popov lunged at Drugov, throwing a punch as he got close enough.

Drugov stepped aside putting his left arm up to deflect the punch. Popov lost his balance as he swung around, but he caught himself. He reached for his Makarov, but Drugov had his pistol already in his hand. Drugov fired a shot into Popov's right forearm. He could have killed him right then but that would be too easy to a guy who made a career torturing his enemies. No, Drugov was going to make Popov pay for every one of those insidious crimes; especially Piko. He shot Popov in the knee.

"You are going to kill me slow, Drugov," Popov said, leaning against Drugov's car. "You think that will make you feel better? Your brother was a punk, sticking his nose in places that gets him in trouble. Piko was too easy to kill, I didn't even get a thrill at that one."

Drugov shot Popov in the other knee and he fell to the curb. Popov tried to reach for the pistol he dropped. Drugov shot him in the left shoulder.

"You are so evil you don't even die easy, you bastard."

"It seems that now you are the evil one, Drugov."

Drugov reached down and grabbed Popov by his bleeding knee and pulled it up, swinging Popov around with a subdued scream.

Popov tried to sit up but felt the sting of the wire as Drugov wrapped his garrote around his neck and choked the life out of Popov's body. "Go to hell!"

The first explosion was like fireworks of satisfaction as Drugov tightened his garrote. Then another explosion, then another, and another. Drugov stood there looking at the body of Popov for a long minute. Revenge is the heart of a tortured soul.

35

Langley, VA

"Director Wells, Ms. Vega is here."

"Thank you, Pennie, send her in." The director closed the file on his desk and looked up as the door opened. "Come in Vega, have a seat."

"Yes sir," she said. Holding back the urge to call Director Wells Uncle Pauo.

"Jessica, I've been keeping track of your progress at the ranch, You're a stand out."

"All that playing spy with my dad and Uncle Lou is paying off. They showed me everything they knew. I thought it was a game, but, before I knew it I was sure I'd be a spy when I grew up; and speaking Russian too!"

"Well, that's just it, Jessica, you've aced every test they gave you. You may not quite be ready, but I think we can do a little OJT to make up for your missed training. The fact is you'll get better training this way, from the best in the business. I think you're ready." The Director moved forward in this seat a bit, leaning forward, "Do you think you are ready, Vega?"

Jessica didn't bite, "Director Wells. If you think I'm ready to join the ranks, I'll trust your judgement. I know I may be ahead of the class, but I have a lot to learn in developing my tradecraft. I am looking forward to my new instructors, if that is what you want for me, Director."

"That is exactly what I have in mind, but not yet. First, I have a little unfinished business, Kerensky needs you in Russia for a while. We're still following the abduction of Uncle Bennett. Report to Kerensky, he'll fill you in on the details."

Jessica sat there for a moment, then, realizing they were done, got up, turned to the Director, "Thank you, sir." The director didn't look up, she didn't look back.

Rich Kerensky was waiting to greet Jessica when she opened the door to the Russian room, likely tipped off by Pennie. "Vega, I'm so glad you're here, come with me please."

Kerensky led her to her old cubicle, next to Jonathan. Jon jumped up when he saw her, "Jessica, Jessica, your back! Now we can get to the bottom of this mystery."

"Jonathan will fill you in on our progress," Kerensky told Jessica, "we seem to have come to a block in the hunt. These guys are pros, for sure."

"Jon, whatcha got so far?" Jessica got right to business.

"The truck belonged to the Butov corporation. A Russian mob front organization. Our man in Prague did some investigating and came up with the name of the driver of the truck, who gave him the name of the two men in the Mercedes. A Joseph Popov and another man, Lyev; that's all he knew about him. Lyev is the man who abducted Mr. Bennett. We're stuck there. Lyev is a common name in those parts."

"Lyev just happens to be the name of The Bear's personal bodyguard. I don't think that is a coincidence, Do you Jonathan?" Jessica sat down at her computer and started typing. "Jon, do you have any idea when The Bear took off from Karlovy Vary airport? Was it about the time of the abduction?"

"No, his jet left Vaclav the afternoon after the accident for Karlovy Vary. Then the Falcon departed Karlovy Vary the next night for Moscow, at least that was his flight plan; he has a habit of going out of his plan."

"I think they were delayed getting out of Karlovy, for some reason," Vega said, "but, I'm convinced Lou Bennett was on that plane. Lyev, The Bear's pilot, is the same Lyev in the abduction, I'd bet on it." Vega continued, "Not only that, The Bear paid a visit the day before to Butov at his factory. And in a possible related incident, last night Joseph Popov, a Butov henchman, was found dead outside the Letov Kbely aircraft company. His body was found next to his car when the first responders answered a call to a fire at the factory. Residue of incendiary grenades were found on the passenger seat of Popov's car. He apparently did the bombing. His body had multiple gunshot wounds, not enough to kill him, that was done with a garrote. I got this from the investigating officer, Vladimir Drugov. Drugov is also the investigator on the abduction of Bennett.," Vega had been doing her homework in her spare time.

"How did you know about Vladimir Drugov, Jessica?" Jonathan's very curious about Jessica's knowledge of the case.

"I read that Uncle Vlad was on the case in Karlovy, so I called him. He told me everything I just told you. I didn't tell him about Lyev and The Bear, I thought that would be outside my responsibilities." Jessica was typing as she spoke. "Jonathan, wherever the Falcon went is where they have Uncle

Lou. That's what we are investigating, as well as the reason The Bear paid that visit to Butov, just days before one of Butov's men firebombed the Letov Kbely aircraft company. We have work to do Jon."

36

Siberia

"This is another fine mess you've gotten us into."

"Ha, Ha, ha hahaha, Lynne, you keep making me laugh. The guards must think I'm going nuts." Lou looked into emptiness, but he saw Lynne just as clear as if she was there, "It's just as well, let them think it. I would be going crazy if I didn't have you to get me through."

He didn't know where he was. A cell someplace neatly tucked away in obscurity. He could imagine that The Bear felt just as isolated in his cell for all those years. Lou suddenly had empathy for the revenge that crazed Medvedev over the years. He, though, wasn't planning to spend the rest of his life in this 8x10 cell. What has it been, three, four weeks now; he wasn't sure.

Assessing the situation, he knew two things about this operation, first, this is not a prison; well a legitimate prison anyway. Second, he didn't think it should be too difficult to break out, given a chance; which so far hasn't happened. So far, he hasn't even been allowed out of the cell. He has no idea what's behind the door. His two meals a day are shoved through the slot in the door. Good Russian food, home cooking he guessed. He only needed to get a break, find out what is outside the door and plan his escape. Sooner or later he thought they would have to let him out, to take a shower at least, he really needed a shower.

"Keep it together, Louie, you'll get your chance sooner or later. We'll get out of here, we'll bust our way out. There ain't a prison built that can hold us, see." Lynne still found something to make fun of, even though this whole thing was anything but fun.

37

Langley, VA

Following every lead that could possibly be associated to The Bear, Jessica was getting some strange thoughts running through her head. Logic told her that if she simply followed the Falcon, it would lead her to Lou. That was easier said than done; the Falcon seldom follows their flight plans.

She was tapped in to the Keyhole Satellite System. A network of classified satellites around the world that enabled the DIA (Defense Intelligence Agency), to track, in real time, the activities of objects the size of a tennis ball. Russia had the tightest web of surveillance. Jessica had been tracking the Falcon since she got back to her cubicle two weeks ago. The Bear was a busy man. He had visited St. Petersburg, where she picked up the Falcon, to Prague, to Moscow, back to Prague, then to visit his family in Karlovy Vary.

Something was going on, she thought. The times he landed in Prague he would visit his longtime associate Artem Butov, according to Vlad, the CIA asset on the ground in Prague. The information that Vlad had supplied to the team at the Russian room was very valuable indeed, but only led to speculation as to what he was up to. Maybe his normal arms deals with the enemies of the US; but, Jessica was thinking that something more diabolical was afoot.

The Bear is a demented, determined terrorist, and he is up to something. He showed his lunacy in

Las Vegas and he will not stop there, she thought as she tapped on the keyboard.

An icon of a jet appeared on the top right corner of her screen; *Bear is on the move. The Falcon is departing St. Pete.* She tapped some more at a frantic pace.

The flight plan appeared on the screen. *He is heading to Moscow. At least that is the plan submitted.* "I've got you this time you bastard, you won't go anywhere without me." She said under her breath. "This is going to be a long night."

Jessica has her computer set to an auto tracking mode. She didn't have to be there. The computer would track the target, the Falcon, wherever it went; as long as it wasn't to one of the 'dead zones' that the satellite network wasn't positioned to cover. She would have to reposition one of the satellites to cover an area not in the network. But that would be in parts of Siberia; places that even the Russians didn't go to. To reposition a satellite took an act of God, Geo-Synchronized-Diversion. Which can only be authorized with the proper codes, which changed randomly on the micro-second.

Jessica picked up her cell phone and hit the speed dial, Jilani answered. "Jessica, they let you make calls now from spy school?"

"No, idiot, I'm not in school, I'm at the office. This is a personal call. I'm just calling to see how you are doing?"

"Not too bad for your usual run of the mill idiot, and you?" He was being sarcastic now.

"When will you be at the job? I need a favor." She got serious.

"I will be at my desk at 3:00 p.m."

"I'll call you then, SL (secure link), I have a request. 'Till then, my love, I'm on to something, bye." She looked at the tracking screen, as she thought, *the Falcon was out of plan, flying north toward the Arctic.* It was 5:30 p.m. eastern time, making it 2:30 in Vegas. She got up, "I better see the Director."

The intercom buzzed, "Yes Ms. Money Penny."

"Ms. Vega would like a minute of your time, sir."

"That's about how much time I have, send her in." The office door opened slowly, "Come on in, Jess. What is it?"

"Sir, I've been following that little Falcon 900 all over Europe…"

"Jessica, I'm on my way to a meeting with the President's security advisor, so make it quick."

"The Falcon has taken an unusual detour, it's heading north. There is a secluded air strip in a little town, Tiksi, that is long enough for the Falcon. I have a hunch…"

"You think he is going to see his prisoner? You think he is somewhere near Tiksi?"

"I have a hunch, this is off his usual routines."

The Director looked curiously, "What do you want from me, Jess?"

"Our stationary satellite has a hole in that part of Siberia. I need KH6245 repositioned 12 degrees northeast. I need to find the Falcon, I think it will be sitting on that runway, but only for a short time."

"Okay, I'll make the call after I get back from this meeting." He started for the door.

"Sir, time is critical, every second…"

Paul knew that before she said it, "Okay, your

right," He took his cell out of his pocket and hit speed dial, "I'll get on it. It'll take a few minutes, but you have to be on your monitor when it opens, we don't know how long The Bear will be there." He walked out of Mooney's office as the phone connected, "John, I need a favor…"

38

Somewhere in Siberia

The Falcon glided onto the north runway of an obscure airport off the southern coast of the Laptev Sea, a Siberian gateway to the Arctic Ocean. The airport, in disrepair since the breakup of the USSR, is the regional airport serving the Sakha Republic of the Russian Federation and the port city of Tiksi, an isolated oil hub, seasonal shipping, and fishing port. The airport also had a more infamous use in the Soviet years as the port of entry for the Gulag, 'Konets Sveta'. Its name translates to 'End of World', in Russian. Once a prisoner was exiled to 'Konets Sveta' he was never seen again. The facility was one of Stalin's most secret prisons, where his most dangerous political enemies were exiled. Stalin could have just shot these adversaries, and he did kill many thousands; but, this gulag was where he sent the ones he wanted to suffer.

Joseph Stalin died of a brain hemorrhage in 1953; at least that was the official cause of death. Gulag 'End of World' however remained a destination for the enemies of state for a succession of Soviet premiers. After the fall of the Soviet empire, the Gulag, 'End of World', continued to operate, but in obscurity and disrepair. The new government just didn't know what to do with the prisoners that were being held, some for decades; and they didn't want the world to know the true nature of this hell on Earth facility. Today there has been a quiet revival of the facility. Vladimir Putin, once a guard at the Prison in his very early days, realized the usefulness of the facilities to dispose of his political enemies.

Grigori Medvedev, who also had an intimate knowledge of the 'End of World', used his political connections to imprison his most hated enemy; the man he saw most responsible for his imprisonment in another highly secretive American prison, the hole, that held him for twenty years.

Coming to a stop at the west end of the runway, in take-off position for a quick departure, the Falcon was met by a vintage M14 Chaika, Soviet built staff car. Lyev would escort The Bear this time to the prison, it was somewhat disconcerting for The Bear to revisit the 'End of World'; so many terrible memories. There were ghosts roaming the halls of this evil place. Lyev gave a certain security to the memories that The Bear had of the many people he had seen tortured in the dungeons of the facilities darkest corners.

If you were to view the facility from Google Earth, the buildings simply look like a rundown Soviet communal factory. Many of the buildings are in total ruin, and the ones still in use looked like they were abandoned long ago. There would be no satellite evidence of the true nature of their historic uses. American intelligence does not have the 'End of World' in any of its classified files. As far as the CIA knows, the facility was once used to process the iron ore that was abundant throughout the coastal region of the Laptev Sea.

The driver pulled up to the main entrance and parked his auto in the middle of the street, he was not worried about blocking traffic, he was the only visitor today. He hurried up the four steps and opened the door, holding it as his two visitors walked into the dilapidated entrance to the prison.

One could only notice that the inside was not in much better condition than the outside. A lone guard at the security desk just inside the entrance was the only sign of life in the building. The guard made a call to the west cell block guard, who came out of a squeaky door down the hall to the left. "Visitors for 28."

There were only seventeen prisoners being held in this low budget prison. Most of the detainees were political adversaries of the current regime of the Russian Federation; but seven were holdovers from the USSR. Men who just, simply, disappeared from political opposition. There were questions, but they were ignored; a typical method of Russian diversionary politics.

One prisoner, Lou Bennett, was celebrating his second month at the facility; well, The Bear celebrated, while Lou was isolated in solitary confinement. Lou was meditating on the floor, to keep his sanity, in his hand he held a red ribbon. The sound of the lock on the iron door suddenly pierced his mental euphoria. His eyes opened slowly, trying to adjust to the sudden light that had been missing for, seemly forever.

A man dressed in the uniform of the National Guard of the Russian Federation, entered the room carrying a chair, he set it down in front of the door. As he left, the silhouette of a short stocky man came in and sat in the chair. "Mr. Bennett, You are comfortable in your new home?" He spoke in English.

Lou knew his visitor, even though he could not make out the face that was darkened by the bright light coming through the doorway. "It is not exactly the five-star accommodations that I requested, but the food is excellent. I can't complain, Grigori. May I call you Grigori?" Lou replied sarcastically.

"Yes, please. We now have so much in common, you and I, like good friends should. You are not kidding me; your food is good?" The Bear seemed compassionate. "I think you should know what I had to go through for the years you had me in your prison. Now, I get my revenge on you, my friend."

Lou thought of jumping up and strangling the life out of The Bear, but what good would that do, he probably wouldn't get near him before the guards would come in and beat him for his arrogance. There would be a better time, he hoped he would be let out sooner or later; for exercise or for medical attention.

The truth be known, he didn't have a plan, other than just fighting his way out, and he knew how that would end. For some reason he wanted to live; a feeling that there was a ray of hope. "You knew that I was just doing my job, I didn't even know who you were when we took you. Why do you blame me for doing the job that I was given?"

"Louis, may I call you Louis?"

"Yes, of course you may, call me Lou." The Bear was toying with Lou; and Lou was playing.

"Good," The Bear smiled. He was having fun in his revenge. "I had so many more years to develop the hate that drives me with you, Lou." He shifted restlessly in his seat. "I knew that if I ever got out I would take my revenge on everyone that was connected in my atrocity. You should have just killed me, but to do what was done was a big mistake. I lived for the revenge that I knew I would, someday, be able to take on you. I planned so meticulously that you didn't even know that I was responsible for the demise of your families, and then your team. I wanted you all to cry, as I did when I found out, an eternity after you abducted me, that your team killed my family. My hate took me over."

Lou thought about telling The Bear that he didn't know about his family, that his mission was simply to destroy the station, that even he, was a secondary objective. What good would that do. His mind was infected with hate and nothing would change his plans. "So, you will keep me here until I die, Grigori."

"No, I don't think so, Lou, that would be very cruel. I don't really know what to do with you, my friend." Grigori leaned forward on his chair, "To Tell the truth, Lou, I have been getting weary of this revenge. It is taking too much time from the important plans that I have, my true revenge. Not, as you say against your team for just doing their job; but, I will have my revenge against your arrogant country. I intend to make your country pay horribly." His smile tormented, "And you will be in here, unable to stop what you know will happen. Helpless."

Lou was caught, "So you intend to attack the United States, you cannot get even close, what are you talking about. Your nuts."

Now Grigori was caught, "No, my friend, it is all planned, and I will succeed. No one will suspect until it is too late. Many will die. Your fellow Americans will suffer tremendously for what 'you' have done."

Lou thought The Bear would spill the whole plan if he could attack his ego. "You're bullshitting me, I see through your game. You are an evil man, Grigori. But you know that you are helpless in America. The authorities have men investigating your connections to the Russian mob. They will dump you to protect their interests. They know you are crazy in this revenge of yours."

"I don't need any 'people' in America to do what I have planned. My plan can never be detected. Many thousands of your American citizens will be infected, indiscriminately."

The Bear took on a dark aurora, "No one will be protected when I release my contagious biological weapon into the air of your cities. It will infect many Americans before your CDC even knows what happens. And no one will trace it back to me. I am telling you this because you will never get out of here to tell anyone, and who would believe such a fanciful story anyway. It sounds like an Ian Fleming plot. The guards have orders to shoot you if you give them any trouble. I just want you to suffer with the knowledge of the future."

The Bear stood up and turned toward the door. The guard took the chair away. The Bear started to leave when he turned one last time, "Enjoy your conscience, Lou." He left.

39

Sat-KH6245 Hissed as a small amount of hydrazine passed across a catalyst, Shell 405, causing it to ignite. The ignition caused a burst of jet propulsion to send the spy satellite toward a new geosynchronized position. When it gets to its desired position, another spontaneous combustion of hydrazine will bring the satellite to a stop. The maneuver would take about thirteen minutes.

"Jilani, do you have the feed?"

"Yes'm it's just about on spot. I've sent you the link. Do you see what I see?"

"I knew it, it's the Falcon, Jilani, I think we found Uncle Lou. Now we just need to verify the exact location. What is there? Where do they have the facilities to imprison someone?"

"Notice the Falcon is in take-off position, it won't be there long." Jilani moved his focal point. He had an idea. The Bear was not at the airport.

"Jilani, do you see the staff car between the buildings south of the airport? The place is in ruins, but there are a couple of buildings still standing."

"I got it. This could be an old Soviet military base. It could have a detainment center, that's where they got Lou. Jessica, keep on it, I need to talk to my supervisor."

Jessica zoomed in on the staff car. This top-secret military satellite view was real time. She was looking at the scene as it was taking place.

"Movement." Three men came out of the building. One was dressed in a military uniform, he held the door for the other two. The details were unbelievable. Thousands of miles away and she was watching The Bear getting into this staff car outside a dilapidated building, in Siberia. The shorter stocky man was The Bear, for sure. She didn't know who the other man was. His body-guard maybe, the pilot, "Lyev, yes...Jonathan!" Jessica stood up and leaned over the cubicle.

"Jonathan, I need you."

Jonathan, who has been working on the Prague connection with Vlad, looked up. "Jessica, I've got something happening on my end."

Jessica wanted to just order Jonathan to watch the Tiksi feed while they have it, but she knew that whatever Jon was working on is connected to the whole picture. They can review the recording later. The whole thing is a mess and was adding up to something even messier. "What have you got?"

"Well, last month there was a bombing at the Letov Kbely aircraft company in Prague. When the first responders got there, they found a body on the street near the bombing. The body was Joseph Popov, also, if you remember, the driver of the Mercedes that abducted Mr. Bennett. He is the one who shot the cabbie, our man Piko. The whole thing ties in too much. Anyway, since the bombing there seems to be some cooperation between Artem Butov, The Bear's associate, and the Letov Kbely aircraft company. At the airport, the Letov Kbely hangers, there have been, so far, seven Aeroflot Airbus A380 super jets in the hangers being fitted for something that the Butov company manufactured. It is all very secretive and too coincidental not to be connected."

Jessica could see that Jon's work was too important to take him away, "Thanks Jon, I think you are correct, something is in the works and we have to find out what it is. It's all connected."

She had to fill the Director in on what was happening, but she also had to monitor the Tiksi feed. She dialed Pennie, "Pennie, Jessica," she was well known to Pennie, the first time they met was when Jessica came to visit Paul with her dad, she was nine.

I need to see the director, we found him!"

"He's not back from his meeting, but he told me to call him if you found anything. I'll call him right now and get back to you, Jessica."

"Thanks…SHIT!" Jessica sat back down at her monitor. She thought for a moment…then began typing on the keyboard. "Letov Kbely aircraft company," she said softly to herself.

A head suddenly popped up over the cubicle. "Letov Kbely aircraft company, founded in 1918. It had a vicarious history, pretty much working for whatever country occupied the Czechs at the time. They produced parts for everything from the first German bi-planes to the Russian MiG's. A few years ago, the company was taken over by a French company. They've been contracted to make certain parts for Airbus." Jonathan said with a know-it-all sarcasm, "You know, that is what I have been doing for the past two weeks, well, that and the connection to the Butov organization."

"Jon, I don't want to burst your bubble but there is something big going on. There is a connection to Letov Kbely, Butov, and The Bear. That's what we need to connect!"

"Well, let me continue, if you can pull your hair off the ceiling. The Butov guy that was found dead outside the Letov Kbely factory, Popov, likely was the bomber. Our man in Prague has an informant in the Butov who said that the bombing was to change the mind of the CEO, Demetri Koval, who previously refused to work with Butov. Apparently the Butov Iron works manufactured some storage tanks that they want the Kbley to install into some Airbuses. What for? I don't know, Yet."

"Well..." Jessica sat down. "It seems that you've been doing quite a job, I'm impressed Jonathan." She turned to her Monitor. There was a spread sheet on the screen. "Now, let's move on. I hacked into the company server at Kbely." She scrolled. "Here, an entry for Butov. It's a requisition for work to be done on ten Airbus A380's, the newest airbus luxury jets."

She scrolled down again, "The tanks you were talking about. Seven done with an estimated completion date of, two weeks! The work is being done while the jets are in for routine servicing. That way the work can be done discreetly."

"You think The Bear is behind the contract between Butov and Kbely?" Jonathan was very serious now.

Jessica's phone rang, she picked up, and listened. "Thank you Pennie, will he see me now? Thanks, I'll be there in three. Jon, Can you spare a minute to go to fill Director Wells in on our work? We are at a critical point." They left.

The door opened to Pennie's office and a head popped in. "Come in Jessica, and Jonathan, he's waiting, go right on in."

"Thanks," Jessica said softly. She popped her head into the Directors office.

"Come in, have a seat. Tell me everything."

Jessica sat down, took a deep breath and filled Paul in on the details of the Tiksi satellite scan. She told her analysis and even told the Director where Lou was being held, which building. "I am 90% sure that is where they are holding Uncle Lou, 100%!"

Jon then filled him in on the latest revelations about the Kbely Butov connection, "We think there is a connection there to The Bear."

"I think they will use those tanks to transport something, possibly drugs, to the U.S.A., maybe."

Jessica cut in, "I've studied Medvedev, He is a true psychopath bent on revenge..." When she was done she sat back and waited for a response from the Director.

Director Wells looked at her for at least a half a minute. "Very good work." He pushed the button on the intercom, "Pennie, send him in." While they waited, he asked Jessica, do you think Jonathan can follow your leads?" Before she could answer the door opened. "Colonel Pettis, this is Vega, I think you will find she is everything I told you about her."

Jessica was stunned but she dared not say anything. "Sir?"

"I'm reassigning you to Colonel Pettis' unit. It is part of your ongoing training. As much as we will miss you here, you will be more valuable with the colonel's Delta team. Your team has been assigned to extract Mr. Bennett."

40

Sankuru, Democratic Republic of the Congo,
Deep in the African jungle

The airstrip was short, but long enough. Lyev had landed the Falcon under worse conditions. At least they ran a blade over the runway to level it off, they were well paid for the inconvenience.

"Lyev, we will stick to our procedures for these third world countries. Stage the Falcon in take-off position. I have the beeper, one time for ready, two times for emergency take-off, and continuous for rescue. I don't expect any problems, this poor community will do well with the money that we are paying them, do you think they have seen fifty thousand dollars before, what a bargain for us." Grigori fastened his seat belt and prepared for the short, bumpy, landing.

Lyev made his final turn toward the east runway, Flaps down, reduce thrust to minimum, and just miss the jungle canopy; and…touchdown. Reverse thrusters, it will take all the runway to stop; but, he will need to take-off on three quarters to clear the canopy. No problem.

The Falcon came to a stop at the end of the runway, turned and slowly made its way back up the runway to the shack that the village called the terminal. After letting Grigori out under the protective custody of the local militia, they were well paid and should be trustworthy, Lyev retrieved the steps and closed the door.

Lyev taxied the Falcon down to the East end of the runway. He needed to fly out into the wind, hoping to have a strong head wind; and hoping that the wind did not die, or change direction. They needed to have a smooth take-off; nothing could go wrong. The risk was too great if the precious cargo was unleashed in the African jungle. No, The Bear needed to release the deadly virus over the United States, where the criminal nation would be punished for its criminal acts against him, and the rest of the world. Justice will be done.

The drive to the jungle laboratory took about ten minutes. The Bear had time to talk to Dr. Mubutu. "Dr. Mubutu, I trust that you have been successful in our contract?"

"Yes, isolating the Ebola virus was not a problem. It grows very fast. If you put one ounce into the container you described to me, it will take about eight hours to reach its optimal capacity. You will need to discharge it within twelve hours or it will begin to overpopulate and die out. If you release the virus at high altitude it will freeze until the particulates get to a warm enough altitude to thaw; then it will fall like rain to the ground. The virus has a ten-day incubation period, which will make it very difficult to discover the source" Dr. Mubutu seemed very proud of his accomplishment.

"That will work out very well Dr. twelve hours should do fine. What is the risk when we put the virus in the tanks and what is the liquid will we use?"

I have had the virus put in bio-degradable bags that contain the virus but will dissolve when put in the Liquid. The liquid is simply sugar water, one cup per one hundred liters. You will not be exposed if you take minor care. I have made eleven units of the virus, enough to fill all of the tanks you have. But don't drop the bags, if they open it will be devastating.

They arrived at the lab, a wooden building that looked like it might have been a school at one time. Grigori wondered if there was a new school somewhere in the village.

Dr. Mubutu led the way up the steps and unlocked the door. "Here we go Mr. Medvedev, I have put the packages in the bag on the table, all ready to go. You can check it out, they are safe. And, here my friend," he pulled out a small satchel, "enough antidote for you and your close associates, twenty-five doses. We will immunize you and your pilot before you leave, just to be safe."

"That will be fine Doctor, I believe you. You dare not betray me."

"No, my friend, I have done everything you asked of me, you will be happy with the results."

"Okay, put the bag in the trunk, I will leave immediately." He reached in his pocket and pressed the button once. Lyev will be ready.

The trip back was somber, the reality of his revenge was heavy on his shoulders. He thought of his darling Cristina, "Papa, I want to be a diplomat when I grow up. I want to try to change this thing. I want peace to come to the world when I grow up!"

Grigori sat there staring at his hands, *I will have my revenge, then I will be free of this heavy weight on my back.* When he looked up he saw several fresh graves off in the jungle. *Was that why there was no one else at the laboratory, no technicians, no scientists, only Dr. Mubutu. The good Dr. must have used the antidote for himself but not for his people. No witnesses, except Mubutu.*

41

Tiksi, Siberia, on the Arctic Ocean

"Natasha, there are strangers at that table, hurry to them, they look like they can eat, push the Borscht."

Natasha finished the table she was serving and went straight to the long table in the corner. "Gentleman, can I interest you in the specialty of the day, and every day, the Borscht."

The four men didn't bite, "I'll have a big T-bone steak and, Vega, wadka for the table." Captain Bullis, formerly of the Airborne Rangers, said in English.

"Well if you don't have the Borscht you'll have to starve, that's all we got," Jessica Vega said in Russian.

The boss was walking toward them now. "Are you men from the oil fields?"

"Yes, we will be glad to be making good rubles for the next year. We'll all have some of that Borscht, your pretty waitress says it is the best around." Bullis said in Russian.

"Ah, good, Natasha you can get the food and I will get these boys some drinks. You are not from here, your accent, Ukraine?" the old man was being friendly.

"Yes, I was from Ukraine but after serving with Army I settle in Moscow, for the work. Now I work here for one year." His Russian was good. "Why don't you tell that girl to sit with us, we will pay for her time," he handed the owner a thousand ruble note.

His eyes widened, "Yes, yes, anything you want, she is yours until you leave, longer if you want."

Natasha, Vega, came back to the table carrying four big plates with something on them that looked like it was already eaten. "Natasha, these men have requested your company, stay here with them, and give them anything they want. They will leave you a big tip." He didn't wait for a reply, he walked away.

She sat down next to Sergeant Pierce, former Ranger, tall, blond good looking. He was smoking a hammer & sickle cigar, "You look like a good place to start," She leaned over and gave him a peck on the cheek. "Is he gone?"

"Now I know how you get all your information. I was almost ready to give up the words to 'A Yellow Bird." Pierce said in Russian with a swoon and laughter from the group.

Captain Bullis said, "Good, let's keep up the frivolity in between business, we have to give the old man a little spin."

Vega stood up and wiggled her torso at the men, they all broke into riotous laughter, then she sat down next to the captain and snuggled his arm.

"I have been entertaining the national guardsmen that guard the prisoners at the airport facility. It's amazing what a little female company will do to loosen lips. Everybody wants to talk about their jobs, and these men have been silent too long. They talk as if I'm not even here." Jessica smiled proudly. She had a knack for making men feel comfortable around her.

Gunny Sergeant Josh Decker, recruited to Delta from the Marines Advanced Recon, broke in,

"Get lively, he's coming back." Everybody laughed again riotously.

The old barman approached with another bottle of Vodka, "You boys need more drinks, don't worry, it's on the house."

The forth man grabbed the bottle that he brought earlier and poured it into a plant behind him, then returned the near empty bottle to the table before the old fish noticed. Rodney Littleton, the CIA man on the team, former Navy Seal, said with a boisterous slur, "Good Vodka and good company, we will be coming here plenty while we are here, you will see." His Russian was also flawless, but obviously not local.

"Ah, you have a southern drawl to your accent, Georgia?"

"Yes' Georgia is right," but not the Georgia he was thinking, Albany Georgia, USA. "Batumi, on the Black Sea."

"Yes, that's it, I knew Georgia," he was proud of his ability to get accents.

"Go away, old goat," Decker said, "We are having too much fun with Natasha, you are no fun. Leave the bottle and go away."

Natasha jumped up and hugged the old man, "Oh, don't you listen to them, we are having so much fun, go. I will take care of these good customers for you."

He left smiling and mumbling to himself, "She knows how to get the guys to spend money, I am so lucky to have her here, business has been very good since she has come to me." The men laughed loudly as the old man went back to his business.

Vega got up once more and danced around a bit before she grabbed a chair from another table and put it between Captain Bullis and Littleton, whom she knew from Langley and 'The Farm'. "How does a girl get a little attention around here," she got serious.

"There are only four guards in the night shift. Not too much going on at night. In the day time there are more, they have to feed them and, you know. Anyway, the boys on the night shift don't have much to do, they make their rounds on the half hour and play cards and nap in between."

"What about the doors and the locks on the cells." Captain Bullis asked.

Vega reached into her apron and pulled out a ring of keys, "I borrowed these from one of my friends, he is off for two days and I left him pretty drunk, we'll have to act tonight. I'm sure he will miss them in the morning." She jingled them then handed them to the captain.

He fiddled with the keys in his hand. Some had numbers on them, "These must be the cell keys, the numbers go from one to seventeen, and twenty-eight, are there eighteen prisoners in this prison?"

"Yes, the prison, a well-kept secret, has been around for a long time, since Stalin. They still use it for political prisoners they want to disappear. They call the prison the Gulag Konets Sveta, 'End of World'. I don't think even our guys know about it."

"Well, everybody will know about it when we are done. Since we don't know which cell Lou is in, we'll have to open them all until we find Lou. That's gonna make a big stink. We'll go in tonight at midnight. Full gear, Chechnyan rebel. Our escape will be by sea. The Navy has a stealth sub off shore, on the bottom of the Laptev, waiting for my sig. If all goes to plan we will have Lou and be crossing the Pole before they know what really happened."

They all laughed loudly. Then the boys got up and left the bar, leaving Natasha with a big tip, more money than she may have seen at one time if she was a native of Tiksi. She will leave it under the register where the old man will find it tomorrow, a parting gift.

Later that night a commandeered UAZ-452 Russian 4x4 minibus made its way down the airport road, lights off once they neared their turn. There was still enough ambient light for the rest of the trip. They would stop short of the target and make the last quarter mile on foot.

No light could be seen coming from any windows, or doors, everything looked lifeless and deserted. Vega had done her homework, there were cameras on the buildings opposite the doors. They knocked them out with a single silenced shot to each one. Three keys did not have numbers on them, one should open the front door, logic said it would be the big one, it was. The door opened and the sweet young waitress from the pub entered, whispering "Nikolay, Nikolay, where are you my igrushka. I am here, you can have me."

The young soldier looked up from his monitors, "Natasha, what are you doing here, how did you get in here." Vega pulled a silenced Makarov from behind her back and put one bullet between the eyes of the startled guard. The others entered the building behind her. There were three other guards somewhere.

Decker used the keys to open the main door to

the cell blocks, while the other three entered followed by Vega, who was still dressed in her waitress garb. Decker then took a defensive position at the monitors, pushing the body of Nikolay off the stool where he was face down on the panel of monitors.

There were three corridors approximately ten meters in from the main door. Each having their own locked entrances which fanned out in the directions of the compass. They gave the keys to Vega who opened the corridors one at a time from the right. Captain Bullis entered the east corridor, no one there. He hit his earpiece "No guards, Decker, be aware they gotta be somewhere." One click meant he got it.

Vega followed the men in, keys in hand and started opening the cells one by one. When the doors were opened the prisoners covered their eyes at the sudden burst of light to their, otherwise, dark cells; most having been there for many years. They just stayed on their beds, not sure what was happening. Bullis shined his light in their faces, "The American, Lou Bennett, where is he?" Captain Bullis yelled as he checked each of the opened doors. No one said anything. Lou wasn't in this block. "You are free, courtesy of the Chechnya, Special Purpose Islamic Regiment. We are not Russian!"

Pierce joined Decker at the front, they needed to locate the other three guards. There was another hallway past the reception desk. That corridor had more doors, two to the left and one to the right. The men made their way down the hallway. Pierce put his hand on the handle of the first door, looked at Decker who gave a nod. The door opened, and Decker entered ready to take out anyone that might be in the room. Pierce stayed out to cover his back. No one, the room was a rec-room of sorts, for the guards. There were cards on the table like someone was playing a game, but no players. The one door in the room led to a commode, No one there either.

"Cell block two, clear, no sight of Lou," came a voice in their ear piece. "The American, where is the American, Lou Bennett?"

Pierce and Decker continued to the other two doors at the end of the hall, one to the left, the other to the right. The door to the right had a small window in the upper middle. Pierce moved along the wall to get a peek, it led to the outside, an exercise yard, presumably. No one in sight.

Decker was at the other door on the other-side of the hall, hand on the handle; Pierce gave him a nod, and the door opened. It led to an office, an infirmary, empty and no place to hide. That left only one place that the three other guards could be, outside in the yard. "The building is clear, no sight of the three guards," Decker informed the others. All the cells were opened, no sign of Lou.

"He isn't here," came the voice of Captain Bullis.

Vega and Littleton double-checked the cells in all the blocks in case they missed him, he may have been bed bound. "Not here," Littleton informed the rest.

"Okay, let's check the yard. Be ready," said Cap.

They gathered on either side of the door to the yard. Decker got the nod from the captain, he opened the door. Pierce was first, he stepped in and took the defensive position. Decker followed and took the position of the other side, followed by Cap.

The yard was deserted. It was dirt with some benches along the building. There was a chain link fence stretched between the wings of the building; the fence was only about fifteen feet long with barbed wire along the top. Nobody here. There was a door on the other side of the yard.

The two CIA agents stayed in the hall way and maintained a defensive position. They didn't want anyone coming in the front door while they were following ghosts in the yard. Vega remembered that there was another key, number twenty-eight. "Rodney, there is another cell, twenty-eight," she looked at Rod.

He put his hand out, "Let me see those keys." He took them from Vega and counted them. "Your right, but where is the cell for key twenty-eight. There is another cell block somewhere, not in here. Come-on." Rodney started walking toward the door, "That is where our guards are."

Vega followed, but turned toward the yard door, "The others, shouldn't we tell them?"

"No time, we can handle this," Rodney said as the two CIA agents left the building and looked around the front of the building. No sign of life outside.

Vega noticed the door, in the same building, but down towards the other end, "There." They quietly rushed the door, thinking that this was the other cell block. When they got to the door Vega used the same key that opened the main door to the first cell block, looked at Rodney, he nodded.

Rodney rushed in and took his position on the left, Vega followed, her silenced Makarov in the ready. There was no one at the monitors in this wing.

They moved, each taking an opposite side of the hallway. First Rod moved to the guard station. Then Vega moved up and took her position at the cell block door. She started to insert the keys into the lock, "Wait," Rodney whispered. She looked at him. He pointed to his ear then down the hall. She heard it, Men were talking, and laughing.

The two made their way to the first door on the right. Rod took the opening side of the door, Vega took the handle. They assumed the door was open if they were in there. Rod nodded, Jessica slowly turned the handle, it was unlocked. She pulled the door open and Rod entered, she followed.

The three guards were hovering over a prisoner that was strapped to a chair. When they heard the door open they all looked up. The agents couldn't see the face of the prisoner. Vega shot first hitting the closest guard in the chest. One of the guards reached for the pistol in his holster but Rod put a bullet between his eyes before he could get his hand on the handle of the sidearm. The other guard, one Vega knew as Dimitri, from the bar, put his hands up, "Don't shoot me."

Prisoner 16 was slumped in his chair, head down to his knees. Rodney put his hands on either side of his head and gently raised it. He was dead. "Not Lou," Vega sighed somewhat relieved that there may be hope that Uncle Lou was still alive.

"The American, where is he" she said to Dimitri. Dimitri pointed. "In his cell."

"Take us," Rodney said shoving his weapon into Dimitri's ribs. First the guard left the room, followed by the two agents, pistols pointed at his back. He led them out of the 'interrogation room', back down the hall to the door of the cell block. He then pulled his keys from the clip on his belt and unlocked the door.

Dimitri went in first, followed by Rod, then Vega, who scanned their flank to be sure nothing was stirring. When inside it was identical to the block on the other side of the building. Dimitri walked to the door on the left, and fumbled his keys, he opened that door and went in. the place was as quiet as a church, except for the footsteps and the jingling of the keys. They walked down to the second cell on the left and Dimitri fumbled his keys and then put the key into the lock and opened the door.

Lou covered his eyes with his hands, squinting as the silhouette of what looked like a woman in a fluffy dress came into view. The woman ran to him and, sitting next to him on the bed, put her arm around his shoulder. "Uncle Lou are you hurt?"

Nothing made sense to Lou, who was disoriented anyway. He thought that this was as good a time as any to make a stand, come what may. But, he recognized her voice, "Jessica?"

"Yes, we are here to take you home, you are safe now."

Lou was in shock. Here is the daughter of his best friend, in a frilly dress, sitting next to him in the cell that he has been in for, ever, hugging him with tears in her eyes, telling him he is safe. "This is a dream, right? This is not really happening."

"No...YES! it is happening, you are safe. Come, let's get out of here. Uncle Lou, I thought you were lost, but I never gave up." She helped him up and led him out of the cell.

266

As they left the main cell block door into the hallway there was a gunshot and the plaster in the wall next to Rodney's head exploded into dust. Rodney backed into the room, as the sound of an AK74 automatic exploded from the direction of the main entrance. The guard that Vega shot in the chest earlier, gyrated from the bullets hitting his body, forcing him back to the wall. He fell to the ground.

"All clear, came the voice of Captain Bullis from the source of the fire storm. They locked Dimitri in Lou's cell and cautiously made their way out, stepping over the dead guard, not knowing if the unsilenced AK may have triggered an alarm and response from another, unknown guard detachment. They were on the alert.

As the six Americans left the building and made their way to their minibus. Littleton held back long enough to take out a can of Montana spray paint, popular in Russian urban art, and sprayed 'SPIR' on the door.

The prisoners that were freed, during the search for Lou, slowly made their way out behind their liberators, they were without direction. As the commandos drove away, Captain Bullis pulled out a cell phone and called the extraction team just off shore in the darkness of the Laptev Sea. After he hung up he dialed the local police to report gunshots at the prison. They will tend to the prisoners, who will verify that they were rescued by a group of rebels.

42

Multiple Airports in Europe

London, Dublin, Paris, Berlin, Prague, and Moscow International airports. Flights destined to Los Angeles, San Francisco, Portland, Seattle; all destinations that take the ten specially equipped Airbuses across the contiguous United States. The plan, to slowly release a mist of the deadly Ebola virus from the special tanks that Artem Butov, and The Bear, forced the Letov Kbely aircraft company to install, secretly, on ten Aeroflot A350-900's in Prague. The jetliners were grounded for regular maintenance before the jets were dispatched to scheduled service. The jumbo-jets are the newest, state-of-the-art additions to Russia's biggest commercial airline.

The ground prep crew had last minute, unusual, orders to add a special liquid to the tanks before take-off; and then before sealing the containers dropping in the special packets, that looked like dishwasher packets, into the tanks. They were told that the tanks were something new, containing a detergent that reduces air pollution emitted from the huge jet engines. Similar to the DEF (Diesel Exhaust Fluid) used on diesel trucks, they understood that concept. In any event they were just doing their job; following the directions of their supervisors, who also followed the directions given to them by their superiors. Somewhere in the line of command there was a bribe that may never be discovered in a subsequent investigation.

Paris, France, Charles de Gaulle Airport

Mr. and Mrs. Boisclair had planned their trip to see their daughter in Los Angeles for months. "She is a big star in Hollywood," she told the young girl at the airport check-in. "Do you know how long it will take to fly to L-A, mademoiselle?"

"Madame," said the girl as she lifted her left hand and massaged her wedding ring. "It will take about twelve hours, if there is a good tail wind."

"Oh, excusez-moi, you are so young, you must be a bride." Suddenly the departure boards for all US flights flashed 'CANCELLED' in bright red. "Oh, what is this, I am so sorry Mr. and Mrs. Boisclair, your flight has been cancelled. I do not know why, but it is no longer!" Then the board started to go crazy as all the other flight status changed to 'DELAYED,' one by one from the top to the bottom of the screen.

Aeroflot Flights 3976 and 4207 were backed out of their gates and taxied to a secluded area of Charles-de-Gaulle Airport. Two black assault anti-terrorist armored vans followed by a caravan of black Renault Koleos SUV's moved across the east runway and out to the segregated jet-liners. In the terminals, all gated flights were thoroughly checked for retrofitted tanks before they were released for departure. They were not taking any chances.

Similar precautions were being taken for every Aeroflot flight to America from all European International Airports; with the focus on ten Aeroflot A350 Super-jets, departing from five major airports: Two departing Václav Havel Airport, Prague – Two departing Charles-de-Gaulle, Paris - Two departing London's Heathrow - Two departing North Dublin International Airport - One from Domodedovo, Moscow - One from Tegel, Berlin. All the targeted A350-900's had undergone routine maintenance by the Letov Kbely aircraft company in the past month. Once they have all the jetliners secure they will have to remove the virus and decontaminate the areas.   At the counter-terrorist wing of Interpol in Lyon France, the logistics of this complicated plan is unfolding. There has been no publicity, no press releases, total secrecy has held as the agents clean up the bio-elements as well as the capture of those involved in the conspiracy.

Prague

A military anti-terrorist team entered the Butov Ironworks factory and arrested everyone there, Artem Butov was not on the premises. Luckily, they had the fore site to jam the cell tower servicing the factory and cut the land lines. Vladimir Drugov entered the factory with the trained Interpol commando's. As they led the terrorists out of the building, Vlad pulled Viktor Bezak out of the line. "This one is one of mine," he said to the captain. "He will testify for the prosecution," looking reassuringly at Viktor, "he will, then, enter witness protection. Viktor your wife and young son are safe."

It took longer to convince the Russians that there was a real terrorist threat at their airport. When they got to the airport, flight 242 to New York and San Francisco. Had already taken off. Russian MiG fighters were scrambled. The mission, get the jet to land, safely, so it could be decontaminated. Interpol had determined that the release of the virus was triggered through GPS, but that there was manual cell phone activation system that could trigger the bio-agent at any time. The Jet needed to be neutralized ASAP.

43

St. Petersburg

Traffic on the Galemyy PR-d was usually heavy at ten in the morning. This morning, however, the streets were barricaded surrounding the block where the building, that is home to the Liberty Arms Company, is located. A flat screen TV in The Bear's office was on the BBC. The reporter on the television was telling of the unusual closing of a number of European airports, for no given reason.

The Bear also had six surveillance monitors that he is watching. He watched as the police moved into position outside the building. He has, maybe, ten minutes before the police crashed through the front door.

The reporter on the BBC was quite thorough. He named all the airports where nine Aeroflot jetliners were being searched, the fear was of a terrorist attack. No word was mentioned of Domodedovo Airport, Moscow.

"I still have one" Grigori said to himself. "I will have to discharge the virus now, I will have the last laugh." He typed on his keypad and the flight plans for Domodedovo came up on the monitor. Flight 242 was listed as OFP, off flight plan. There was a nationwide search for the jetliner. Terrorism was suspected. This turn of events was certainly not part of the plan. He decided not to release the virus, not wanting to reap such destruction on his mother Russia. The Bear closed down the PC and rushed through a door.

Minutes later the door busted open and six city anti-terror swat police entered, followed by two CIA agents. The Bear was sitting at his desk, he didn't make a move. Director Wells and Vega secured The Bear while the Russian police secured the transmitter. He did not fight the restraints.

Vega and the Director pulled up chairs in front of the secured criminal and began asking him questions. "Mr. Medvedev, You have been up to no good for too long, now we got you."

A trickle of white foam started showing in the corner of The Bear's lips. Then he went into convulsions and collapsed in his seat. "Shit, get a medic over here," Vega yelled.

Director put his hand on her shoulder, "it's too late, cyanide, he's gone."

"That scumbag coward! He had to pay!" Vega got up and quickly jogged over to the computer on the desk. "Let's see what he was up to, this thing is too crazy, that idiot wasn't gonna fail." She typed on the keyboard,

"Here…here! This is the site I want. The Falcon, the Falcon is his insurance policy. Where are you? You dirt-bag!"

44

Flight 242

"Shut up!" The young man told the flight attendant, in Russian, he held a Makarov at her face.

"Just do as I say, and no one will get hurt!" The terrorist did not care if any of the passengers lived or died, he was on a mission. Chechnya will be independent and the 'Special Purpose Islamic Regiment,' SPIR, will achieve it; in the name of the most glorious, almighty, most wise, ever merciful, Allah!

The jetliner flew straight south-south-east toward the Russian province of Chechnya, where the terrorists are fighting the government to achieve their independence from Moscow; as they have for decades. This hijacking will force the Russian Federation to finally recognize the independent Islamic Republic of Chechnya, they hoped.

"Get on the speaker and tell the passengers to fasten their seatbelts, I don't want anybody out of their seat!" He walked forward to the cockpit, where his friend Muhammed was instructing the pilot.

"Muhammed how are we doing? Will we reach our homeland soon?"

Muhammed turned to look at his friend, "Abukhan, this pilot understands our cause, he..."

The pilot reached for the gun of the terrorist and tried to disarm him, but just as he made his move there was turbulence that threw his timing off and he missed Muhammed's arm. The three lost their balance momentarily. Abukhan gained his footing and pointed his Makarov at the pilot and pulled the trigger.

"NO! Abukhan, it is Okay!" but it was too late. The pilot was bleeding in his chest. "I had him under control! Abukhan!"

"He was trying to get the gun! Muhammed, I had to shoot him!"

"You idiot! Abukhan, he is the pilot! Do you know how to fly this plane? Go back, Abukhan, go back to the passengers before they get out of control!"

Abukhan began to turn to leave when his face suddenly changed, "Muhammed, LOOK!" a MiG 29 was flying just off the right side. "They found us! LOOK!" Another one on the other side. "Oh, Praise Allah!"

"Get back to the passengers! Abukhan." Muhammed turned to the pilot, who was looking like he could pass out at any moment,

The pilot said, "Give me the radio mic, quick!

"Flight 242, this is Major Korchevsky of the air force of Russian Federation, there is an airport ten kilometers ahead You are ordered to land."

The pilot pushed the button on his mic, "This is Captain Viktor Sokolov, I am pilot, I am badly wounded."

Muhammed grabbed the mic from Captain Sokolov before he could finish. "This is Muhammed Mustafa, I am in charge of this plane and WE will not land until we arrive in Chechnya, or all 254 of the passengers will DIE! Do you understand!"

Major Korchevsky radioed on the secure channel and apprised his superiors of the situation. "Major Korchevsky, it is imperative that you get flight 242 to land before it gets over populated area. If they refuse you have orders to shoot the jetliner down in a desolate area, or over the Caspian. Do you understand?"

"Yes sir, I understand." Not knowing why but believing that there must be a good reason they would order the death of 264 souls. "Captain Sokolov, are you able to fly this jet? Are you able to land it?"

The reply was not what he had hoped. "The captain is dead!" Muhammed informed the pilot of the MiG, "I am in charge of this jet now. You will listen to my demands or I will crash into the middle of Volgograd."

Major Korchevsky knew that the city of Volgograd is in the present flight path about forty minutes away. He also knew that there is a stretch of sparsely populated farm land for the next hundred kilometers. If there is a good place to end this, time was running out. There was no doubt in the mind of Korchevsky that the terrorist was not trained to fly the big jetliner. He could, Korchevsky was sure, crash the jet in the middle of the biggest city in the province. That is something that must be prevented. Korchevsky radioed his command for orders.

"Major Korchevsky, flight 242 is one of ten jets that have been fitted with a special tank of a very lethal biological weapon that can kill thousands, that jetliner must be stopped here and now, shoot it down. We have dispatched a team of bio-hazard specialists to contain the crash site."

Korchevsky decided that here would not be the best place to shoot it down. The Volga river was meandering it's way south below their position. That major waterway is too valuable to the local economy to risk contamination. He will have to divert the jet to the east, where the terrain gets mostly desolate. Best place, near the Ozero Buluknta, a lake twenty kilometers to the east.

"Alexei, shoot out the port side engine, we need to turn her to the east, we'll put her down after the turn." Alexei Popovich, the pilot of the other MiG, fired his fifty-millimeter cannon into the left side engine, which exploded and fell toward the farmland below. The jetliner veered to the left immediately and began to dip as it turned. The passengers started screaming with panic.

Korchevsky then took out the right side engine, effectively causing the jet to begin its decent to the earth. Korchevsky could now see the Lake in the distance. The farmlands were giving way to a semi-arid desolate landscape. "let's take this thing down, may God forgive us."

They both fired a burst into the tail as Flight 242 glided east, descending quickly as the passengers were instructed to put their heads on their knees and wrap their arms around and under their legs. The jetliner splashed in the middle of the beautiful natural lake Buluknta. Shortly after the crash six MI-17 rescue helicopters and their HazMat teams landed for the recovery and clean-up.

45

The offices of the "Liberty Arms Corporation"

Jessica Vega was not one to give up. She was going to find the Falcon. The Bear was determined to get his revenge; but, on whom? She stared at the lifeless body of this mass murderer. Here he is, free from all the consequences of his actions. "It's just not right, no, no, it isn't right." She sighed a deep breath while she dealt with a feeling that something was wrong. "Sir, have you ever seen The Bear? How do we know this is him?"

The Director looked at the body. He walked over for a closer look. He tapped on his cell phone and pulled up the photos that Kerensky sent to Lou when they were identifying Federoff. "Jessica, you never seize to amaze me, your instincts are dead on. This is not The Bear...This is Timur Balaban. It's been so long since I've seen him, years. He is my man on the inside. The Bear must have made him, probably feeding him false information for, who knows how long. Jessica, find the Falcon and we find The Bear!"

The Falcon streaked southwest out of St. Petersburg on a heading along the southern coast of the Baltic Sea. Present location, just off the coast of Latvia. Lyev was following the instructions of his employer, The Bear. He was instructed to fly along the coastline of the Baltic Sea. He had registered a flight plan that took him over the former Soviet nations then crossed northern Germany and the Netherlands.

After the Falcon passed over the Hague it would cross over the North Sea, final-destination, London, England. Lyev was instructed to set the release of the chem-trail once the Falcon crossed into Polish airspace. The mist would slowly dissipate over the land mass from Gdansk to the city of London. The Bear would have his final revenge. Lyev had no family and had devoted his life to the exploits of his employer. He would be with The Bear until the end.

The Falcon was detected by radar as it passed across the national boundaries of each country in its flight path, there was no reason to question its legally logged flight plan.

As the jet crossed into the airspace of Lithuania, Lyev heard a familiar voice from the cabin of the jet, "Lyev all is ready here, how long before we reach Kaliningrad Oblast? We will need to be ready to eject when we are over Kumachyovo, where we meet my good friend Artem for our escape."

"Yes Boss, I have been in contact with Gospodin Butov and he is ready for us. We will bail out in twenty minutes. Just as we pass over the village of Kumachyovo, I will slow down to 200 knots for our escape. I have set the auto-pilot to take the Falcon to 10 thousand meters and 400 knots cruising speed keeping to its logged flight plan."

"I got it," Jessica Vega turned to the Director who was searching the files of The Bear. He immediately stood up and walked over to Jessica's desk. The monitor had a list of flight plans that were submitted at Pulkovo Airport. Jessica swiped her finger along the line that documented the flight plan for the Falcon, tail number RA-4994.

"We got trouble." The Director reached into the pocket of his jacket and pulled out his cell phone. He called to the captain of the Russian police that were in the offices searching for evidence and filled him in as he looked up the number of the NATO air command.

The two F-16 fighters dispatched out of the 31st air base in Krzesiny, Poland, caught up with the Falcon as it passed over the western coast of Kaliningrad Oblast.

The Falcon did not answer the calls of the F-16s and maintained its trajectory despite the calls to follow them and land at Lech Walesa Airport in Gdansk, Poland. There was no pilot in the cockpit.

Orders were then given to shoot the Falcon down in the Gulf of Danzig, before it reached the coast of Poland.

Karlovy Vary

Inspector Drugov drove his Skoda Octavia up the circular driveway of the villa owned by Grigori Medvedev. In the seat beside him sat Police officer Adina Alesova. The two officials walked up the stairs and rang the doorbell to the villa.

The door opened and Galina opened the door, "Ano?"(Yes) Inspector Drugov, showing Galina his badge, asked for the lady of the house.

"I will take this, Galina, please go back to your work," Marta said as she approached the door, "is there a problem?"

"I am sorry to interrupt your afternoon, it's your husband. You will need to come with me."

46

Walter Reed National Military Medical Center, Bethesda, MD

Room 315 was alive with activity. Laughter so loud that the nurse came in to tell the four men in the room to hold it down to a light roar. "It's okay nurse Wilson, I'm a Doctor." Juan Vega said as the laughter broke out even louder!

"Come on nurse, this man is a national hero. He singlehandedly saved the world…" shrieked Charley Woolsey.

Lou cut in, "No, No! I couldn't have saved the world without this little lady," he reached over to grab the hand of Jessica Vega, who just smiled.

"I suggest we wrap this up," said Paul Wells, "Lou probably would like to get out of this five-star hotel."

"I'm sure he would," said Dr. Pierce, as he entered the room. "You're in perfect health for a man that has been through all that you have, Lou."

"We'll meet you at my office, Lou, then we can see you on your way." Director wells gave Lou a wink as he left the room with the other men, Jessica stayed behind to escort Lou to CIA Headquarters.

"It seems like forever since I first came through these doors, "What…Three months ago?" Lou reminisced to Jessica.

"Actually, closer to four." Jessica stopped Lou and turned him to look at the marble wall, "You see that last star, Uncle Lou, that one is for Piko."

Jessica opened the door to the Russian room and put her hand around Lou's back to lead him in. Everyone in the room stood up and the sound of clapping was almost deafening.

As she led Lou down the main isle he was patted on the back by at least fifty hands, and the smiles were overwhelming as Lou's eyes teared up. The moment was fitting for a man who dedicated his life to the service of his country.

Director Wells took Lou by the hand in a shake that showed his true friendship and gratitude. He pulled Lou's hand up in the air and spoke, "I have known this man for many years, and he has always been the best there is. So, now WE can give a cheer to the man who broke up the greatest threat to our country by the terrorist Grigori Medvedev, "The Bear.""

The room rumbled into a cheer that likely could have registered on the national seismic monitors. Director Wells then put up his hand for silence, "Lou we want to thank you, and honor you with this simple medallion. It is the highest honor given to our agents, and it is given with your oath of silence in the tradition of the agency. This Agency works in the shadows to protect the people of this great country from the many threats that would seek to destroy our freedom. It is rare that we can bask in the knowledge that our work has directly and almost singlehandedly made a deciding impact. And still, we do it in the shadows, taking no notice, or credit, so that our citizens can live their lives in quiet Liberty."

Lou raised his right hand, "My oath is given, and I wish to take this time to thank you all for not giving up on me, despite my efforts to elude your help.

I would be dead now if not for the heroes in this room."

This caused the room to erupt into yet another round of cheers. Director wells raised his hand to quell the crowd once more.

"As we take the time to recognize the efforts of all of the 'Russians' in this mission, I will remind you all that we still have not brought The Bear to his rightful justice. The Falcon did not contain the body of The Bear when it was retrieved from the sea. Let's get on his tail and find him before he has a chance to get back to his bad acting. We do have an ace-in-the-hole as we have taken his wife, Marta, and his daughter Cristina into protective custody. I am sure he will tip his hand in his efforts to find his family; and we will get him! Now, back to your stations, we have work to do."

47

Phoenix, Arizona

The Department of Public Service equipment services yard on 22nd Avenue in Phoenix opened at seven o'clock in the morning. Lou was there as Sergeant Rick Patterson opened the gate.

"Where's Bruce this morning?" Lou said to him as he followed the trooper to the shack.

"You'll have to wait 'till I get the computer booted up. Do you have your paperwork in order, Sir?"

"No, I'm here to pick up my motorhome, that one back there with the jeep attached to it." Lou said as he pointed to the back of the yard.

"Oh, I'm sorry, I didn't recognize you Lou. We met one time back when you got the Medal of Valor in '05. Bruce retired last month, he told me that you were storing your motorhome in the yard. Almost got auctioned off last week when I was on vacation, I come back from my cruise and find it on the list for the yearly Auction. I had to do some quick talking to get them to leave it. Everybody knows your name, it didn't take long to change their mind. I sure was wondering if you were coming back or not." Patterson went on while he searched the key box.

"You won't find the key in there, I didn't leave one here. Just for the reason you just mentioned, a Murphy's Law thing, you know." Twenty minutes later Lou was heading North on I-17.

Lou clicked the button in his Bluetooth device in his ear, it beeped once, "Call Doc."

The phone rang twice, "You scoundrel, what's your excuse now?"

"I'm on my way, Doc. ETA, oh…about four. Just in time for happy hour."

"I'll believe that when you are sitting at the bar at Casa De Benedevidez with a beer in your hand." Juan was just a little skeptical.

As the motorhome turned onto the transition ramp from I-17 to the I-40 eastbound, memories began floating around in Lou's head. He passed the Butler street exit passing Blackbart's RV park on his right. Lou thought he should have stopped in to say hello, but it was better that he left it all behind. "Time to get back on the new beginning thing. Onward to Albuquerque, and beyond."

Another hour down the road, a few miles past Holbrook, Lou remembered that old Indian, Tim, walking along this stretch of the freeway. No one was walking on the highway now. Maybe that was a dream. The whole thing seemed kind of far-fetched after all that he's been through lately. Lou reached into his shirt pocket and felt the red ribbon that had been with him through it all.

Before he knew it, he crossed into New Mexico. He was so deep in thought the highway passed by like time stood still. Gallup ten miles, a sign read. He thought about his mother and what Soyala told him. *Soyala,* he thought. The sign ahead read, Zuni reservation NM 602. He exited I-40 and headed south. *A quick side trip*, he thought.

Lou wasn't sure what made him take this little side trip. His mom was Zuni. His native heritage is centered right here, and he never took the time to learn anything about it. Truthfully, he never gave it much thought until he took that ride on the Hopi Nation, with Soyala. *Did that really happen?*

NM 53 West, Zuni 17 miles, Lou turned his rig west. The desolate New Mexico countryside glided by as the hilly landscape changed from dry desert terrain to little green puffs of shaggy bark juniper. Black Rock, a small village, passed on the north. There were more houses as he got closer to Zuni, little farms and ranches.

'Zuni Town Limits', the sign read. As he moved into the small city, his interest was intrigued. A sign ahead read, 'Zuni Visitor Center'. *I'll stop there on my way back*, he thought as he continued west through town. Another sign read 'A:shiwi A:wan Museum & Heritage Center'. He turned south, "Let's see what that's about." The motorhome passed houses, with a few stares from local residents working in their yards, making Lou wonder if this was the right turn.

He saw a complex of buildings on the right. Not what he might expect, coming from the big city. The parking lot was dirt, the buildings weathered with rusty tin roofs. He pulled his rig off the road and parked alongside a yellow school bus. He got out, locked up, and headed towards a sign that read, 'Entrance'. He walked up the step and opened the door. He was greeted by a Native woman in a deerskin dress adorned with beads and gems. She wore a beautiful turquois necklace, she was beautiful.

"Good afternoon, welcome to the Zuni Nation, please sign our register. Feel free to look around, I am here to answer all your questions." She pointed to a doorway, "We have a school tour from the Hopi nation in the next room, you are welcome to listen in. It is very educational, if you don't mind thirty curious fifth graders."

Lou smiled, "Thank you, I think that will be a good place to start." He walked through the door, stopping to take in the room. The children were playful and a bit noisy, not a problem for Lou.

Lou's survey of the room paused. The tour guide, a tall native woman with three white braids of hair, long and glowing, turned to him and smiled.

"It's about time you came home." She said as she stepped over to Lou, they embraced.

"Children," Soyala said, they all turned their attention to her. "I would like to introduce you to Mr. Louis Jerome Bennett, part Hopi, part Zuni, and All-American."

The children clapped and surrounded Lou, smiling and asking questions. Soyala asked the receptionist if she could take over for the rest of the tour.

"You have come back to me in one piece, I knew you would." She took his hands in hers and put them on her belly. "Meet your son."

Lou looked down at her belly, then into her eyes, "You are real, you were not a dream." He was happy. He put his hand into his shirt pocket. Pulling out the red ribbon that had been of such comfort to him, Lou reached around her shoulders, he tied the red ribbon at the nap of her three pure white braids. they embraced for a long moment. Lou has found himself again, his life has a future. To love and be loved again is the greatest joy of life.

KONETS

(THE END)

Plan B

Made in the USA
Middletown, DE
25 October 2023

41335051R00177